Our Kept Hearts

Tennille Marie

Although many of the lovely cities portrayed in this novel are very real and you can get in your vehicle and visit them. They would love to have you. The novel itself and the characters, organizations, and events portrayed are completely made-up and fictional. The author let her imagination run wild and if someone or something in this story seems real, then that is just a testament of how wild her imagination has run.

Our Kept Hearts

Published by: Purple Iris Printing, LLC

P.O. Box 861

Benton, Louisiana 71006

ISBN 978-1-962329-02-6 (hardback)

ISBN 978-1-962329-01-9 (trade paperback)

ISBN 978-1-962329-00-2 (ebook)

To all the small-town girls,
who grow up to be big-hearted women.

Waldron
Pop: 1,292

Prologue

Ears still ringing from the report of the rifle, he stared at his shaking hands. He balled them into fists then opened them, but they still trembled uncontrollably. There was blood covering them, smeared on his fingers. The blood came from Hazel's father. It seeped into the crevices and lines of his palms. *How did this happen*? *How could I have let it get to this point?* He wanted his hands clean. Needed them clean. He obsessively rubbed his palms down the sides of his old jeans. The blood smeared across the legs of his pants, leaving faint red fingerprints. He looked at his hands, still tinted pink. His mind whirled and his thoughts were a blurred mess. *What have I done?* He had pulled the trigger—there was no doubt about that. He looked at the rifle on the ground. It lay on the grass next to Hazel's father. His eyes flickered when the man raised a red palm toward him, pleading. Blood ran from underneath his body, snaking its way across the dirt. The forest grew darker as the sun began to set behind the trees. Somewhere far away, someone called his name. His life was over.

Chapter 1

Hazel, October 1953

"Mama!" Hazel screamed. Her face was hot as tears blurred her eyes. She couldn't see and blinking didn't help. *Why was this happening?* Her nose dripped and Hazel tasted snot. She rubbed her forearm across her face. A stream of clear snot stretched across her arm. She wiped it on the skirt of her yellow dress.

Mama didn't even look in her direction as she pulled the heavy tan suitcase out the front door. It bulged at the sides, full of her things. The screen door squeaked open. Mama used her body to hold the door open while she maneuvered the suitcase over the threshold and onto the porch. The door slammed shut with a sharp *smack* against the wood, making Hazel jump. Hazel spun around in the living room not sure what to do. The suitcase thumped across the weathered porch boards as Mama dragged it behind her by the handle.

Hazel ran to the screen door and threw it open like it weighed nothing. She wanted it to make a pop just like it did for Mama, so maybe just maybe, Mama would stop walking and scold her one more time. Then things would go back to how they were, back before she started packing the suitcase. When the familiar smack of wood on wood never came, Hazel turned around and saw Daddy holding the door open.

"Do something!" she yelled. Her blood boiled inside her, and she rushed at him. The soles of her saddle shoes scratched across the porch boards. She shoved him so hard it jarred her body to her teeth, but he didn't budge.

He reached up and set the screen door, so it held wide open. Then he folded his arms and leaned against the doorframe. His huge body filled the doorway. His mouth tight. His soft dark eyes like deep pools of coffee. He looked past Hazel, over her head, at Mama.

The porch steps began to creak, and Hazel turned to see Mama was almost at the bottom. The suitcase made a *clunk-clunk* on each step until it hit the dirt. Mama's heels wobbled underneath her. Her white-gloved hands clutched the suitcase handle. As she pulled it, the suitcase made a tiny dirt path through the gravel to the rusted sky-blue Ford sedan. Mama panted softly while she worked the suitcase through the gravel. The sedan's tiny, circular red break lights stared like evil eyes—an accomplice in her mama's departure. Hazel hated that car.

The forest surrounding their small house was eerily silent. Hazel ran down the steps and looked up at the sky. The sun reflected off the roof. Some shingles hung cockeyed like they were fixing to fall. Hazel squinted against the sun and wished for rain. If it was raining, Mama wouldn't leave because she wouldn't want to get her hair wet. Hazel looked back at Daddy. He was the only one who could stop Mama. He could make everything alright, but he stood there doing nothing. He turned his head and yelled inside the house. "Ruthie, you better come on out now and tell your mama good-bye."

Hazel's stomach fell as Mama hefted the suitcase into the air to put it into the sedan's trunk, which was wide open waiting to receive it. She had to think of something to stop this madness. Her heart popped in her ears. She took off running toward Mama and, without caring about the consequences, she grabbed at the suitcase in Mama's hands. Hazel tried to dig her fingernails into its slick side. She had to keep it out of the trunk's open mouth, but her hands were wet from her dumb tears. They slipped down the side to the edge. Mama tried to push Hazel away, but Hazel planted her feet in the gravel and locked her knees tight. Mama scowled and grabbed Hazel's fingers, stretching them back until they cracked. Hazel gritted her teeth as tears seeped from the corners of her eyes. She tugged harder on the suitcase.

"Hazel! Stop it right now," Mama snapped.

She slapped Hazel's hands until they burned.

"Please Mama, please," her cries coming out more like a whimper.

Mama narrowed her eyes until they were thin lines, but Hazel could still see the fire behind them. Beads of sweat speckled Mama's forehead near her perfect hairline. Loose blonde strands began to work their way out of her perfect French twist. Hazel almost lifted her hand to smooth them back into place, but Mama didn't like it when she touched her hair. Hazel had clumsy hands. Mama slapped her fingers harder. Her skin burned with pink and red marks.

"Hazel, I said stop this. Stop this instant!" she screamed. Spit droplets escaped from her lips and landed on Hazel's face.

Hazel wanted to be bad this one time. She felt a scream building up inside of her chest. She wanted to let her loud words fly in her mama's face. Mothers weren't supposed to leave their daughters. A girl wasn't supposed to be without a mama. How could everyone in the world know that except her mama?

"If you don't move your hands, Hazel, I'll shut this trunk lid on you."

"Hazel."

Daddy said her name so softly, but it still sent chills down her spine, and even Mama froze.

"Move your hands, child."

A sob escaped her throat. Hazel's hands obeyed her daddy's command even though her brain shouted for her to keep holding on tight to the suitcase. Her fingers throbbed. Hazel rubbed them, but it didn't help. Mama looked at Daddy. Her mouth pulled tight in a smirk as if she was taunting him. She placed the suitcase in the trunk and slammed the lid closed. Hazel's chest burned. Her mama's clothing and things shouldn't be sitting in the darkness of the trunk. They were supposed to be hanging in the closet or folded in the drawers of the house they shared.

Mama started to walk to the car's door. Hazel squeezed her arms across her chest. Her mind spun as if she was on a Tilt-A-Whirl. She had to do something. A sick feeling rose in the back of her throat. Then, like sunlight splitting open a dark sky, it hit her. She shook her head. Why didn't she think of it sooner? She'd written a special story for her mama. She'd spent hours writing and rewriting it. Ripping the pages out and wadding them up when they weren't perfect. It had to be perfect for Mama.

Hazel took off for the car. Her legs wobbled and her feet slipped on the gravel. She sucked in a breath, making her body thin, so she could quickly slink around Mama's outstretched hand before she reached the door handle. She threw her whole body against the door. The metal handle dug into her back. It hurt like all get-out, but she didn't care.

"Mama, I wrote a story for you. You're a pretty princess in it."

Hazel's fingers trembled, but she reached into her dress pocket for the folded piece of paper. It was covered with dirt smudges, but she held the paper out, hoping with her whole heart that her mama would take it, read it, and see she could be a princess here, in this house with her.

Mama stared at the dirty crumpled paper in Hazel's hand and frowned. "How could I ever be anything here? Let alone a princess," she said gesturing to the small house.

Mama pushed Hazel's hand away. She didn't take the story. Instead, she grabbed Hazel's chin, tilting her face upward, so Mama could look her daughter in the eyes. Mama's fingernails pinched her skin. The pain brought tears to Hazel's eyes. Mama reached up and moved a piece of Hazel's dark brown hair off her forehead. Horsehair, Mama always called it.

Hazel tried to smile at her mama like a good girl would, but her chin burned under Mama's fingers. Hazel couldn't help it, but she began to cry like a baby. Mama squeezed her chin tighter.

"You're old enough to hear this, Hazel. Fairy-tale stories are for people with opportunities and prospects. Those people find their happiness one day. Not people like us – people with nothing. You need to stop living in a dream world. Writing made-up stories is a waste. Now dry your face and quit crying. You look ugly."

A tiny squeak got caught in Hazel's throat. When Ruthie stomped onto the porch, Mama let go of Hazel's chin with a small shove. Hazel stumbled backward but caught herself before she fell. She touched her chin with her fingertips and winced. The skin felt raw and scratched.

Ruthie stood on the porch. Her arms folded like Daddy's. Her old pink dress was short and came a little too far above her knees. Ruthie's blonde hair was a tangled mess around her head. It glowed in the sunlight like a golden halo of fire.

"I hate you!" Ruthie screamed.

The words were as sharp as hornet stings. "Ruthie!" Hazel snapped. *What a silly ankle biter! What's she trying to do, drive Mama away?*

Ruthie stamped down the porch steps. Her eyes bore down on Mama as the red-hot anger spread from the back of Ruthie's neck to her cheeks. "I don't care," she said. "I do hate her. I hope she dies."

Hazel's mouth flew open. Ruthie was going to be in trouble now. There was no taking those words back. Mama was going to get her good. Maybe even with the belt this time.

But all Mama did was laugh. A loud laugh that rocked through her body. Hazel felt dizzy. She could hardly believe it. She watched Mama walk over to Ruthie and squat down until they were eye to eye. Mama had a huge wide smile across her face.

Dazed, Hazel drifted over toward them mesmerized like a little bug to a porch light. She stood there watching Ruthie's nose flare with each one of her angry breaths. Mama didn't scold her; she gently took Ruthie's hand. She reached up and lightly caressed Ruthie's cheek, but Ruthie jerked her face away.

"You are so much like me," Mama said.

"No, I'm not!" Ruthie huffed.

Hazel's heart twisted. Mama's voice was soft when she spoke to Ruthie. It didn't ever sound that way when she spoke to her.

Mama smiled. "Ruthie, you don't understand now, but you will one day. Sometimes...," She paused and looked up to the porch where Daddy stood inertly. "Well, sometimes you just want more."

Mama stood straight and dusted off her skirt. Her shadow fell over Ruthie and Hazel. She patted the top of Ruthie's tangled blonde head, but Ruthie pushed her hand away. Hazel wished she'd pat her head too.

"I will never want you. Not ever again," Ruthie sneered.

Mama sighed before she turned her back. She walked away without glancing once in Hazel's direction. She opened the sedan's door and began to get inside.

Hazel's feet ran towards Mama before she realized what they were doing. Hazel grabbed Mama's skirt fabric so tight her knuckles turned white.

"Mama, Ruthie's wrong. We do want you. I want you. Please don't go," she pleaded.

Mama jerked her skirt away. It snapped from Hazel's fingers, and Hazel slipped and fell on the gravel. She yelped as she skidded across the tiny rocks. The gravel tore her knees and the palms of her hands. She groaned as she looked at her burning hands, bits of gravel were stuck in the tiny red marks.

When Mama slammed the car door shut, Hazel jumped. The tires rolled and the car began to make its way down the winding dirt road to the highway. Hazel pushed herself up from the ground and ran after the old car. Her throat burned and her ears rang with her screams. But Mama never looked back. Never even turned her head. Hazel ran until her side felt like it had been sliced open, but she couldn't catch her mama. Hazel lifted her hand and cried out when the sedan's round, red eyes disappeared around a curve and was gone.

Hazel's chest heaved and her heart pounded like a drum. Tears clogged her throat and she felt like she was drowning. She crumpled in the middle of the road. Tears ran down her cheeks as she left huge circular droplets in the dirt. When her tears had gone dry, Hazel pulled herself up, her knees wobbling underneath her. She looked down at her dress. It was dirt stained and wrinkled. Mama would be so mad if she saw it. Hazel let out a breath. Her mama was gone. Hazel forced herself to walk down the road back to the house even though her feet felt like they were trapped in thick mud.

The house door was closed when she made it home. Daddy no longer stood in the doorway. The song "Heart and Soul" by the Four Aces drifted from his open bedroom window. The radio was turned up loud, but the melody couldn't mask the harmony of his soft sobs. Hazel's stomach knotted. She'd pushed and yelled at him.

"Is Daddy crying?" Ruthie whispered.

"Go away. This is all your fault." Hazel shoved Ruthie away and headed for the porch. She tried to swallow back more tears, but it felt like she'd eaten glass. Before Hazel could run up the steps, something white caught her eye. It sat on top of the gravel. The wind made the ends of the page rise and fall.

"It's not my fault! She's a bad mama." Ruthie stamped her foot.

"Be quiet!" Hazel snapped, heading to the piece of paper. She stared down at it. *I must have dropped it.* The paper was crumpled, and a tire mark stained the corner.

"Oh! Your story," Ruthie said, running close to her. She bent down and picked up the paper, dusting it off. She held it out for Hazel to take.

Hazel reached for it. The paper felt so heavy in her aching fingers. She looked at her story. It weighed almost nothing, but it felt like a sack of bricks. A clump rose in her throat. Hazel shook her head. It wasn't enough. *I wasn't enough.* Hazel let her story go. It floated down, returning to the gravel. She didn't want to look at it anymore. She took off running. She needed the quiet of the forest. She needed her secret place.

Chapter 2

RUTHIE

Ruthie ran after Hazel. Thorned vines grabbed and scratched at her ankles, but she pressed through them. One caught her bare leg and tore through the skin. She winced. Ruthie looked down at the little beads of blood dappling the red line on her calf. She touched it and looked at her blood-stained fingertips. She wiped her hand on her skirt and kept pushing on. She listened for Hazel. She heard nothing except the faint caw of a crow and the wind through the trees, the rustle of the orange and crimson leaves. But Ruthie didn't have to hear Hazel to know where she'd gone. It was where they always went when they hid from their mother when things got bad. *Gee, oh man*, Ruthie thought, *Hazel's upset big time now.*

She found Hazel sitting under their special tree. Her knees pulled to her chest. Her skirt draped over them like they were trapped in a circus tent. The sycamore's branches arched and curved toward the ground. The base of the tree was surrounded by crinkly brown bark. Ruthie loved to pull the bark off with her fingers. Sometimes her fingers got sticky, and she'd lick them even though Hazel told her not to.

Ruthie loved how the tree's branches were like thick arms. Just like their daddy's arms. The branches hung low to the ground. Cradled in their strength, she'd sat on them many times, swinging, and bobbing up and down. The leaves would swish over Hazel. Hazel wasn't much for branch sitting like Ruthie. She'd spend all her time sitting underneath their shadows with a pad of paper and a pencil in her hands furiously writing her make-believe stories.

Hazel's stories were one thing Ruthie loved even more than the tree—and that was a whole lot. It didn't even bother her when Hazel ignored her or wouldn't play with her, so she could finish the story. All that mattered was that Hazel read it to her. Hazel had even written a story about their tree. In it, the tree was a magical giant frozen in time by a wicked witch.

"Can you believe that mean ol' witch turned him into a tree just because he didn't love her?" Hazel had asked her with wide eyes.

It seemed like a silly reason to turn someone into a tree to Ruthie. "If he didn't love her, she should just find someone else." Ruthie had said.

Hazel laughed. "I don't think it's that easy to find love. You can't just go traipsing around in the forest and it appear out of nowhere."

Ruthie had shrugged. She didn't care about finding love. She just wanted Hazel to tell her stories every night before they fell asleep in their shared bed. Her favorite story was the one about the deer roaming in the forest. Hazel said the deer were a long-lost tribe of forest protectors. They guarded all things in the forest. Sometimes, Ruthie silently asked them to protect her and Hazel too. But she'd never tell Hazel she did that. Hazel would just roll her eyes and call her a silly ankle biter.

She only really hated one of Hazel's stories. It was the new one she'd written. The one Mama didn't even look at. In the story, their mother appeared to be a kind, loving princess.

"That story is the biggest crock of bull I've ever heard," she'd said to Hazel after Hazel read it to her.

Hazel had gotten mad then, so Ruthie didn't say anything else about it after that.

Ruthie plopped down on the ground beside Hazel. The cool dirt made goose pimples run across her bare legs. She hated wearing dresses. *Why can't I wear pants like Daddy?* Ruthie tried to be silent as a mouse as she sat beside Hazel. She gently ran her hand down her sister's long dark hair.

Hazel jerked her body away and clutched her knees tighter to her chest. She burrowed her face in her circus tent skirt. "Don't touch me. I'm mad at you." Her voice was muffled in the material.

Ruthie flinched at Hazel's harsh words. She pulled her hand away like she'd been burned by a hot stove. Her body began to tremble, and she couldn't stop it. Daddy always said, even though she was the littlest in the family, she was the strongest. And she'd always thought she was stronger than Hazel, even though Hazel was the oldest. But Ruthie didn't feel strong now. *Oh man*, she rocked in place. *This is worse than I thought*. Daddy was crying. Hazel was crying. She wanted to be happy Mama was gone, but everyone else was so darn sad and now Hazel was mad at her. Ruthie's feelings felt mixed up inside like cake batter stirring around in their cracked mixing bowl. Of course, Mama would be the cause of all this trouble. Ruthie hated her. Anger began to boil in the pit of her stomach until she couldn't take it anymore. She pointed her chin to the sky and let out a scream that echoed through the stillness of the forest. Hazel's body jolted beside her. Hot tears rushed down Ruthie's cheeks.

Hazel wrapped her arm around Ruthie. She pulled her close to her side. "Shh, don't cry. It's okay."

Ruthie rubbed her face, *why am I crying*? She leaned her head onto Hazel's shoulder and stayed there until her tears ran dry. When she couldn't cry anymore, she lifted her head and looked at Hazel.

Hazel's face was red and blotchy. Dirt smudged her cheeks, but her tears had made little clean trails in the middle of the grime.

"I'm sorry I'm a bad sister," Ruthie whispered.

Hazel's mouth pulled down at the corners. "I know it wasn't your fault. Not really. You're not a bad sister. I'm sorry too."

Ruthie sat back. She pulled her knees to her chest matching Hazel. Her skirt didn't cover her knees, so she wrapped her arms around her bare legs. They sat silently, listening to the sounds of the forest. A click, a tweet, a rustle in the brush. The sounds gave Ruthie peace. This was their special place. Not scary like the girls at school thought. It was a safe spot, a hiding place, a place their mother would never go.

Ruthie blinked her eyes, breaking the forest's trance. "Do you think she'll ever come back?" she asked.

Hazel's head lobbed to the side. "I don't know. I hope so."

"I don't."

Hazel's eyes flamed. "Why do you say things like that? It's not nice."

Ruthie's bottom lip began to quiver. "Well, I don't. She was mean. Mean to you and Daddy. I don't like her."

A tear escaped from the corner of Hazel's eye. It ran down the bridge of her nose to the tip then dripped off onto the ground. "She said I was ugly. She said I had horsehair," Hazel said.

"You do not! She's ugly."

"But I don't look like you."

Ruthie frowned, narrowing her eyes. She stared at her sister giving her a long scrutinizing look. Hazel's long dark hair stood out against her pale skin and dirty pink cheeks. Hazel's big brown eyes watched her.

Ruthie tugged at a wild blonde curl and pushed it behind her ears. "I like your looks."

Hazel shook her head. She stared at the ground and pulled at a patch of yellowed grass. "She didn't like the story I wrote her."

Ruthie pulled her knees tighter to her chest. Her anger started to burn in the back of her throat again. She spouted the only thing she could think of—the word her school friends used when they made fun of people. "That's cause she's so squaresville."

Hazel turned to look at her with raised eyebrows. "What's that?"

Ruthie shrugged, "I heard Margarette Ann say it at school. It's really bad."

Hazel's mouth twitched into a half smile.

Ruthie pressed against Hazel's side. She felt Hazel's boney hip poking into her. The old hateful comments Mama yelled at Hazel rang in her head.

"What a lazy girl you are."

"I hate your horsehair. You might as well go live in a barn."

"Can't you look at all presentable?"

Ruthie squeezed her eyes shut to make the memories disappear. Their mama never treated her the same way she treated Hazel and that made Ruthie hate Mama even more. She squeezed her knees tighter and stared into the forest. The trees seemed endless, growing bigger and thicker the farther into the forest they were, until they reached the hill where the haunted house sat. The house Daddy told them never to go near.

Ruthie raised her chin and looked into the sky. The sunlight through the branches was starting to fade. A bird fluttered to a branch on their tree. In its beak it held a tiny twig with a single brown leaf, curled at the edges.

"Look," Ruthie whispered, pointing to it. "Do you think it's building a nest for the winter?"

"Maybe," Hazel said, looking at the bird.

It was small and tawny brown with a tinge of red on its crest and wings.

Hazel smiled. "It's a girl cardinal. The boys are bright red."

"I love the bright red ones best," Ruthie said. "I heard Daddy say they are good luck."

"That's just an old story silly."

"I don't care. Daddy said red birds love the ones they love for their whole life."

Through the branches of the trees, a whistling song called. The female bird wiggled its tail feathers and flapped its wings before flying off through the trees.

"We better get back," Hazel said. She stood. "Daddy doesn't like us being out at dark." She dusted the back of her dress, but the back of the skirt was already stained with faint dirt spots.

"Can we stay out, please. Just a little longer?" Ruthie asked, not wanting to go back to the house. But her words fell on deaf ears because Hazel had already started walking. Ruthie released a huff of air and leaped from the ground before running to catch up.

Their house was dark except for a small yellow glow coming from the old, rusted sconce. It hung cockeyed beside the screen door. Bugs buzzed and darted around it. Hazel stomped up the porch steps. She reached for the screen door and took the long metal handle in her hand, but she didn't open the door. She stood frozen in place. Ruthie blinked.

"You okay?" she asked, wondering if maybe Hazel had forgotten something.

Hazel lowered her head. "I," she sucked in a breath. "I can't go in there. Not yet."

Ruthie's head dropped. She reached out and touched her sister's arm. Her skin felt cool. "We can sit, if you want."

Hazel nodded.

They walked to the edge of the porch. Ruthie flattened her skirt with her hands and sat on the worn porch boards. The cold boards on the back of her legs sent shivers down her spine. The warmth had left with the sun and a chill had settled in the air.

Hazel sat beside her. They rested their feet on the steps below. Ruthie linked her arm in Hazel's arm and pulled her close for warmth and comfort. They both stared into the sky. The moon was an orange mass encircled in a glow of white light. It hung in the darkest velvet blue sky. It was a harvest moon, that's what Ms. Williams had called it. Ruthie was surprised she remembered anything Ms. Williams said because her class was such a snooze-fest. Ruthie listened to the crickets begin to tune their instruments and the frogs warm up for the night's chorus. A lone wolf in the distance started to howl its solo. In Hazel's stories, the night orchestra was directed by an old horned owl.

The screech of the screen door startled Ruthie. She twisted her head to see her father standing in the doorway. His eyes glistened in the porch light. He came over to them. Ruthie and Hazel moved, creating space between them. He scrunched his large body in the small space they created and wrapped his heavy arms around them. Ruthie leaned her head into his chest and breathed in. The scent of earth, wood, and sweat filled her nose. Ruthie's father lifted his chin toward the sky. Ruthie looked under his square chin covered in dark hair. She laid her cheek on the soft cotton of his plaid button shirt and listened to the forest's songs. She wondered how Mama could ever want anything more than a life like this. Mama was wrong. Ruthe was nothing like her. She would never leave this place.

Chapter 3

JOEL

Joel sat on the threadbare blanket spread over his bed. His bed was pushed close to the window, so he could look out into the night sky. The full moon lit the darkness. It cast an unearthly glow into his room. If only he could grab hold of a moon beam and soar into outer space. He imagined exploring space and traveling to different planets. In art class, he'd doodle stars and aliens on his construction paper instead of focusing on the projects Ms. June had the fourth and fifth grades working on. Sometimes, because he couldn't help himself, he'd stare at the long, dark hair of the girl sitting in the desk in front of him. She was in fourth grade, so art was the only time he saw her. He'd never spoken to her, even though he wanted to, but he knew her name. It was Hazel. Hazel McKay. He didn't know why, but he thought about her often. Maybe it was because she was kind. He didn't have to talk to her to see that was true. She reminded him a lot of Ms. Angel.

Joel stared at the huge moon and scattered stars. He wondered if his mother was looking down from heaven. He hoped she could see him and that she had met Ms. Angel. He wondered if Ms. Angel would tell his mother how he'd been a good kid. Sadness filled Joel's heart. Every time he thought of Ms. Angel, he felt empty. He'd only lived with her for the first five years of his life, but still he remembered her like it was yesterday. Her rough wrinkled hands rubbing his tear-stained cheeks after he'd fallen. He missed her terribly. When Ms. Angel died, she took any chance of him having a good life with her.

He placed his palm on the windowpane. The chill of the glass made him shiver. The days were starting to get cooler, and the nights were becoming frigid. He looked down at his blanket. He rubbed the thin, soft material. It had yellowed with time. The ends were starting to fray, and the small rips were getting larger. Joel knew he'd need more when winter got here. He let his eyes pass around his sparse bedroom. Except for his bed, a white dresser with scratched edges, an old lamp, and an oval mirror, his room was almost bare. Maybe he'd go to Waldron Gun and Pawn. Mr. Simmons would trade him a thicker blanket and winter coat, if he had them, for the mirror or lamp. A cool wind blew. The old house creaked and rocked on its foundation. He'd go tomorrow after school. He'd see what trade he could make.

Joel's thoughts were interrupted when he heard the crash of the thin plywood door against the wall. His heart leaped into his throat.

skillet around, letting the butter spread evenly over the bottom of the pan. The bacon popped and sizzled when he laid it in the butter. The smell of bacon mixed with the odor of alcohol made Joel crinkle his nose.

"It should have been you," his pa said with his head in his hands. He lifted his head and glared at Joel, his eyes red and raw.

Joel looked away. He tried to focus on the cooking bacon. With a trembling hand, he took a fork and turned over the bacon to crisp the other side.

"It should have been you," his pa repeated. "You should be in the ground rotting and decaying away to nothing. Not my Sarah." He pounded the table with his fist. It rocked. "But you killed her," the words came out like a growl.

Joel's heart sped up. It popped in his chest like the bacon in the grease. He wanted to cry, but he held it in. Only stupid little babies cried, his pa had told him.

"I never wanted you," his pa sneered. "She did. And you took her from me."

Joel laid the bacon on a plate. He'd heard all this from his pa before. Whenever he had a rough day, it was always the same, like a record with a scratch repeating over and over as the needle skipped across the surface. Joel opened the refrigerator and pulled out two eggs. His hands shook as he cracked them over the skillet. Some egg splashed on the counter. He closed his eyes hoping his pa didn't see. He placed the cracked shells on the counter near the stove. Joel stared into the skillet. His eyelids felt heavy as if a sandbag weighed them down. He began to think about how the yolks of the eggs looked like two yellow moons joined together. He took the wooden spoon and broke the yokes. He stirred them gently.

Out of the corner of his eye, Joel saw nothing but a blur, leaving him no time to shield his face. His head flew to the side as his pa's palm connected flat with his cheek. Joel bit his tongue and tasted metal. The blow sent him stumbling. He fell to the floor, his knee slamming hard against the linoleum.

His pa grabbed the skillet and threw it across the kitchen. Eggs and grease went flying. The grease splattered all around him and the floor. Joel covered his face with his arms as burning drops of grease hit his forearms, searing his skin. He cried out. The skillet hit the floor with a hollow *gong* that echoed throughout the house. It spun on the floor, ringing until it finally came to rest.

"How many times I gotta tell you!" His pa screamed, spit flinging from his lips. "I don't like scrambled eggs. You idiot!"

Joel whimpered on the floor. "It's all I know how to do," he whispered, covering his face.

"What did you say to me?" His pa towered over him, pumping his hands into fists at his side. His massive shadow eclipsed Joel's frame. Joel looked at the floor. He knew he should say he was sorry, but he wasn't sorry. A small voice inside told him to stay quiet. Except Joel was his pa's son and he could feel the burning in the pit of his stomach bubbling up. His fear began to morph into a blaze of red-hot anger, and this time, he didn't want to control it. The voice said stay on the floor, but he pushed it away. He wasn't listening to it this time. On shaking knees, Joel raised himself off the floor. His legs quivered underneath him.

"I said," Joel hollered, "that was all I know how to do!"

This time, Joel saw it coming, but he wasn't fast enough. His pa struck his face with a closed fist. Joel heard his jaw crunch from the impact, sending blood and a tooth into the air. His body swooned and he dropped hard to the floor. His mind went blank.

Light peaked through the kitchen window kissing Joel's face. His eyelids flickered open. For a moment, he didn't know where he was. He tried to get up, but pain sent him back down to the cold floor. His head spun. He rested his forehead on the floor, feeling its firmness and letting its cool touch sooth his throbbing head. Sharp pain radiated from his mouth and jaw. He was afraid to move it. For a moment, he wasn't sure what had happened, but when the horrible last moments rushed back to his head, he froze. He worried his pa would be waiting for him to get up, so he could knock him down again. Joel closed his eyes. He tried to listen for his pa, but all he could hear was the pain thumping between his ears. Joel tried to block it out. Finally, he let out a long breath. He could hear his pa's deep, hoarse snores coming from the bedroom next to Joel's. *He's asleep.* Joel's heart slowed and he tried to pick himself up off the floor. He tried to be quiet, but his body ached.

Joel touched his jaw with his fingertips. Pain shot through him. He winced. Joel worried what it must look like. It was getting harder and harder to make up stories to tell his teachers and friends at school. This time, he'd have to play hooky until the swelling went down.

Silently, Joel worked to clean the kitchen. He picked up pieces of egg and wiped up splotches of dried grease from the floor. He threw away the broken shards of the glass vase his pa had shattered. When he bent over to pick up the turned over chairs, something small and white caught his eye. He reached to pick it up. It was his tooth. He rolled it around in the palm of his hand before closing his fist around it. The pointy parts dug into his palm. He pushed the tooth deep into his pocket, holding it in his fist. He hoped another tooth might grow in its place. He hadn't lost many and he usually threw them away. There was no tooth fairy here. In his pocket, he gave the tooth another squeeze. He'd keep this one though. One day, he wouldn't be little and weak. He'd be big like his pa, and he'd show him this tooth and remind him of what he did. Then Joel would make him pay.

Joel went to his room. He sat on his bed and opened the window wide. The morning breeze greeted him, ruffling his hair. It left a nippy kiss on his nose. Orange and pink colors smeared the horizon. The dark blue clouds heavy with rain hung low in the sky. A few birds sang a happy tune. They had no idea what Joel had been through or how his face ached. They darted from the ground to the sparce branches of the trees. The colorful leaves piled in heaps on the ground.

Through the bare tree limbs, Joel could see the little house below the hill. It stood slightly slanted in the center of a circular clearing. Usually, Joel could only see the tip top of the green patched roof among the leaves of the trees, but now he could see it all. The girl with the long, dark hair lived there with her little sister. A twinge of sadness pinched his heart. He'd have to miss art class today, and he'd miss seeing her. He imagined her, living in that little house, with her happy family. He was certain she must have a caring pa and mother. He wished with his whole heart to be there too, or anywhere other than here in his room.

Chapter 4

HAZEL, APRIL 1954

Hazel folded her daddy's work clothes as Ruthie watched. She laid them neatly on his bed near his open duffle bag. Just before church, she and Ruthie had taken them down from the clothesline. As she folded his shirt and laid it on his comforter, her insides squirmed. The weekends with Daddy always seemed to soar by. She knew he had to go to work, but being alone was scary and sometimes watching Ruthie was hard. Ruthie never listened. They ended up fighting most of the time.

"Don't go, Daddy!" Ruthie's voice squalled. She followed him as he walked into the living room, his bag now full of clean clothes hung on his shoulder.

"Ruthie, you girls will be fine. Ms. Faye from church will come check on ya."

Hazel stood in the small kitchen silently clearing the Sunday lunch plates from the long, rectangular wooden table their father had made by hand. Hazel laid her hand on the light brown top. She took her finger and traced a wavy wood streak, following the grain until she reached a round, dark spot. She loved this table. She made a circle with her finger on the spot. She'd chosen the pine tree used to make this table. Picked it all by herself. A wave of sadness passed over her. Hazel remembered that day. Her mother had been especially mean. She brushed and pulled Hazel's hair with a wiry brush. She dragged it through Hazel's tangled brown horsehair. Her mother had screamed and hit the back of her head with the brush when the tangles wouldn't come loose. Her father rescued her that day. He scooped her up, messy hair and all, and took her to the forest.

At first, she was confused about why they were in the forest. When he told her she'd be picking a tree for the family table, a huge lump formed in her throat. *Me?* She couldn't believe he was trusting her, all by herself, to do the picking. *What if I pick the wrong one?* she worried. Hazel didn't want to upset her mama. *What if I pick a rotten tree and the table falls apart?* She put a finger in her mouth and tore at her nail.

"There's no wrong choice girl," her daddy said. "Use your heart."

She tried to do what he said. She'd chosen a tall sturdy pine tree with branches full of dark green needles. He smiled at her and tied a red cord around the tree to mark it. After a few weeks, the table was finished. Her daddy brought it into the kitchen. Hazel ran to it trying to take it all in. It was beautiful. Her daddy stood beside her, admiring his work. He laid a strong hand on her shoulder.

"See girl, even on bad days, something good can come out of it."

Hazel never forgot that day. She ran a hand across the smooth surface and smiled. She'd done good.

Hazel moved the white porcelain dishes from the table to the sink. She let the water run and rolled her eyes when Ruthie started to whine.

"But Daddy, I'm only two years younger than Hazel. Why can't I be the boss sometimes?"

Hazel ran her hand through the stream of water for a few moments. The water was warm, never hot. Hazel wondered if she should say something. Sunday was Ruthie's day to do dishes, but Hazel could tell Ruthie was in no mood to be helpful. She didn't want to start a fight before Daddy left. She had to be the responsible one. She was the oldest. Nothing would ever get done if Ruthie was the oldest.

Hazel picked up a dishrag and began to wash the three plates. After she'd dried them, she returned them to the cabinet where one lonely plate sat waiting for the others to join it. Mama had been gone for six months now. Hazel turned to look at her father and Ruthie. It felt different being three instead of four. Ruthie thought it was better. Mama had gone to California, at least that's what Grandmother had told them. She wondered if Mama was meeting any famous actors or drinking Coke under a palm tree. Her arms felt heavy as she put the plates up. *I'll probably never see her again.* Hazel hurried and wiped her blurry eyes.

Ruthie grabbed Daddy around the waist. She looked into his eyes. "Take me with you!"

"Ruthie, you know I can't take you. You got school, and you can't be buildin' roads. That's man's work and you're too little."

"I'm not!" Ruthie jerked her arms away and folded them in front of her.

He pointed his finger down towards her. "Now, I gotta go. You listen to your sister. You hear me?"

Hazel picked up the dishrag and started to wipe down the table trying to act like she wasn't paying attention to their conversation.

"Don't let me come home and find out you've been misbehavin." He wrapped Ruthie in his arms, forcing her to hug him. "I love you, peanut. Please be good."

Hazel could tell Ruthie was trying not to smile. She could never play mad for long. He gave her a tickle. Ruthie puffed out her cheeks trying to suppress a laugh, but it didn't last. She exploded in giggles and hugged him back. She buried her head in his shirt.

"I love you too, Daddy."

He released her and walked to the kitchen. Hazel continued swiping the dishrag over the table. She blinked her eyes, trying not to let any tears escape. She didn't want him to see her crying like Ruthie. She was the boss now. But every Sunday, it got harder and harder to watch him go. She shivered. They'd be alone in the house from Sunday night to Friday night. She hated it, but he had a job to do, and the town of Waldron didn't have much work for him.

He laid a big hand on Hazel's shoulder, "I left you ten dollars in the coffee can under the sink."

Hazel nodded. He pulled her into a hug. His warmth calmed her. She leaned her face against his chest, breathing in his dirt and wood scent.

"I love you, girl."

"I love you too," she said muffled in his chest.

When he released her, he took his warmth with him. The screen door let out a long screech when he opened it. He shook his head. "I'll fix this old thing when I get back. Don't go too far in the forest and not after dark, ya hear?"

"Yes, Daddy," her and Ruthie's voices echoed in unison.

"Ms. Faye's phone number is on the table next to the telephone if you have any trouble. But come home right after school and do your homework."

"Yes, Daddy," they echoed again.

He turned and looked at Hazel, the door still in his hand. "Hazel, I got you girls some gifts."

Hazel and Ruthie looked at each other. Ruthie clasped her hands together and squealed. Hazel's heart jumped in her chest. *Gifts from Daddy? We never get gifts unless it's a special occasion.*

"I put them on my bed. But you gotta share!"

"We will! We will, Daddy!" Ruthie said, jumping in place.

"Love you girls," he said closing the screen door behind him.

Hazel and Ruthie raced to their father's bedroom. Hazel slid on her socks and Ruthie ran ahead of her.

"Ruthie!" Hazel yelled. She chased her sister into the bedroom.

On their father's bed were two brown packages. One flat shaped like a book and one in a square box. Ruthie was sitting on her knees bouncing in place, the square box turning over on its side on the mattress.

"Stop, Ruthie, you might break it!"

Ruthie stopped moving and stuck out her bottom lip. She snatched the square package and held it tight to her chest.

"Hey, that's not fair," Hazel said, glaring at Ruthie.

Ruthie narrowed her eyes and slowly set the square shaped box back on the bed. She crossed her legs in front of her. She pointed to the square package. "Do you really want to open that one?"

Hazel sighed. "You can open it if you wanna."

"Thank you, thank you!" Ruthie said, smiling bright and big. She picked it up and began ripping the paper off, letting pieces fly through the air.

Hazel picked up the book shaped package. She felt the weight of it in her hands. She could feel the hard cover through the paper. *Yep, a book.* She was certain. Hazel began to pull at the ends of the packaging, savoring every moment. She looked over and watched as Ruthie tore off the last piece of brown paper.

Ruthie sat the box down on the bed. Her fingers rushed to peel the lid open. When it was open, Ruthie sat back on her knees and stared inside the box. Her head tilted to the side.

"What's wrong?"

"It's binklers. Why did he get us binklers?"

Hazel frowned, "What is it?" She laid her partially opened book on the bed and inched toward Ruthie. She peered inside the box. "Binoculars!"

Ruthie furrowed her eyebrows. "Yeah, that's what I said."

Hazel put her hand over her mouth, so Ruthie wouldn't see her smile.

"What was in yours?" Ruthie scrambled to her knees and pointed toward the half-opened gift.

"I don't know. I think it's a book."

"Oh, a book." Ruthie sat back down.

Hazel reached across the bed. She picked up her heavy package and continued to work at the edges of the brown paper. Ruthie scooted next to Hazel. Her knees jittered making the bed shake.

"Ruthie!"

"Sorry, I can't wait!"

When all the paper was laying in long brown sheets on the bed, Hazel laid the book down on the comforter. The front cover was full of colorful birds. Some were flying, some sitting on branches, and others standing in water. Hazel touched each bird. She ran her hand over the embossed title, *Birds of the South*.

"It's a bird book," Hazel told Ruthie. She flipped open the pages.

Ruthie moved closer.

"Look," Hazel pointed at a space in the book. "You can write down the day and place you see each bird."

"I wanna go find birds!" Ruthie squealed, grabbing the binoculars from the small brown box. "They're heavy." She held them to her eyes, tilting them and her head sideways. "Come on, Hazel. Let's go, let's go!"

Before Hazel could say anything, Ruthie slid off the bed and ran out of the bedroom for the front door.

"Wait, let me find a pencil for the book. And be careful with–," but it was too late. The front door popped loudly as the screen door slammed shut.

Chapter 5

RUTHIE

Ruthie's heart raced. The binoculars hung heavy on the strap around her neck, but she held them in her hands to keep them from knocking against her chest. Hazel's footsteps pounded loudly behind her. Hazel yelled. The sound growing louder the closer she got. When Ruthie made it to their special tree, she ducked under a low branch and hid behind the trunk. She peeked around it, trying to keep her breathing quiet.

"I know you're here," Hazel said, standing with one hand on her hip and the other holding the bird book. "You have to share." Hazel panted, face red.

Ruthie poked her head out from around the tree. She held her hand over the binoculars to keep them from hitting the trunk. The weight of the strap dug into her neck. "I call dibs!"

"You have to share!"

Ruthie exhaled, letting a big puff of air escape her lips. "I will, but I wanna go first."

Hazel sighed.

Ruthie chuckled when Hazel's shoulder's slumped in defeat.

"Okay, you can go first."

Smiling, Ruthie came out from around the tree. She ducked under the low hanging branches and sat on the cool ground under the lush leaves. Hazel plopped down beside her placing the book on the ground so they both could see the pages. She opened it, and Ruthie moved closer, propping herself on her knees. Hazel began to flip through the pages. The sun peaked through the tree, illuminating part of the book in dappled sunlight. The ground felt cold and damp under her bare knees. Her skirt not quite long enough to cover them.

"It's so pretty," she whispered.

Hazel nodded. "Why don't you look toward those trees?" Hazel pointed to some tall pines to the right.

Ruthie held the binoculars up and aimed them at the trees. She bit her bottom lip. Something wasn't right. She blinked, but it didn't fix anything. All she could see were smears. The world had blended together into a messy muddle of colors. "It's not working."

"Here let me do it."

Ruthie started to hand the binoculars to Hazel then thought better of it. She pulled them away from Hazel's hands and held them tight against her body. The hard metal pieces dug into her skin. "Promise you'll give them back?"

Hazel's eyebrows furrowed. Her long hair blew in the breeze. Hazel pinched her lips together and held out her hand. "Fine, I promise."

Ruthie lifted the strap from around her neck feeling the relief from the weight. She handed them over to Hazel. Looking through them, Hazel twisted the gray nobs near the eye pieces then aimed the binoculars toward the trees and twisted some more. Ruthie smiled at the way Hazel held her mouth crooked while she worked.

"Got it," Hazel said, handing the binoculars back to Ruthie. "Look at the trees now."

Ruthie snatched them away from Hazel. Hazel frowned, but Ruthie paid her no mind. She lifted the binoculars to her eyes and pointed them to the trees. She felt dizzy at first, until her blurry eyes adjusted. Then as if a dirty film had been washed away, she could see clearly. Her back straightened. *Beautiful.* Her mouth opened. It was like seeing tree branches for the first time. The green pokey pine needles, brown pinecones, the bark on the branches—they all looked clear and new. She moved, scanning the tree. Her heart leaped.

"I see a bird!"

"Shh," Hazel hushed. "You'll scare it away. What color is it?"

"It's so pretty," Ruthie breathed. Its feathers were white speckled with gray. A red line streaked across the top of its head. She felt like she could reach up and touch it. She watched it *tap tap* on the trunk of the tree. She could hear it. The light tapping sound. She handed the binoculars to Hazel. "Look!"

Hazel held them up. "Oh! It's a woodpecker."

Hazel and Ruthie flipped through the book pages until they found the woodpecker with the bright red streak down the back of its head.

Hazel pointed. "Here it is. It's a Red-Bellied Woodpecker. Very common in Arkansas." She took the pencil and began to fill in the blank spaces.

"I thought it was a red bird at first," Ruthie said.

"They're called cardinals," Hazel corrected.

Ruthie stood. She dusted the dirt off her knees and skirt. She ducked under the tree branches and stood in the grassy spot near their special tree. She flipped off her old black flats and curled her toes, feeling the soft green grass. Little yellow dandelions were sprinkled throughout the grassy area like tiny, round yellow suns. She loved when they turned white with seeds. She'd pluck as many as she could and hold them to her lips. She'd make a wish then blow a huge puff of air, sending the little seeds dancing in the breeze to their new homes.

Ruthie made her way to the center of the grassy spot then took a deep breath. She extended her arms out to the side with her palms open toward the sky and made slow circles. She felt the sun warm on her skin.

"Daddy said red birds have only one true love. They go through the trees singing a love song until they find 'em."

"That's just a silly story," Hazel hmphed.

Ruthie stopped spinning and looked at Hazel. "He says when they find their true love, they never leave them. *Forever,*" she said, emphasizing the last word.

"It's just made-up," Hazel said as she flipped through the bird book pages. "Everything leaves."

Ruthie tilted her head back and pointed her chin toward the sky. Her wavy blonde hair falling on her back. Puffy white clouds dotted the sky like tiny pieces of cotton. She closed her eyes and listened. She wanted to hear a love song, but all she heard was the sway of the grass and rustle of leaves in the warm breeze. "I'm going to find my red bird one day."

"Cardinal."

Ruthie rolled her eyes and began to spin. She let her imagination take her miles away. "My red bird will be tall and handsome and hard working. He'll never leave me."

Ruthie peaked over at Hazel. Hazel watched her with one eyebrow raised. The corner of her mouth began to turn up. Ruthie's heart picked up its pace. She kept going. *Smile, Hazel,* she wished. *It's been a long time since you smiled.* Ruthie spun faster. She wanted to be silly for Hazel. "My love is going to be a prince from a faraway land. He'll have so much money, we'll sleep on it like a bed. And I'll sit at home and eat chocolates all day."

Finally, Hazel laughed. The sound pricked Ruthie's heart. Ruthie spun harder. The landscape around her blurring. Her head began to feel woozy, but she held her hands higher into the air. She felt like she might be lifting in the air, floating off the ground. She never wanted to stop. She flapped her arms like wings and kicked her feet. She cupped her hands beside her mouth and called, "Oh prince. Oh prince. Come out, come out wherever you are. Come marry me!"

Ruthie froze, like a statute in a garden. She held her hand to her ear, pretending to listen for her fairy-tale prince. Hazel fell sideways, clutching her side. Her laughter was like a burst of sunshine. Hazel laughed so hard, she started to hiccup. Ruthie spun again and called out louder.

"Oh prince, I'm waiting!" Ruthie ran to Hazel. She grabbed her arm and pulled with all her might. She yanked Hazel off the ground. "Come on, Hazel. Come call your prince with me."

Hazel shook her head, "You're being so silly."

"Come on. It's fun. Please. Come play with me."

Ruthie pulled Hazel from the tree and into the center of the grass. She sat down on the ground, crossing her legs, and watched Hazel as she stood there. Her hands folded in front of her. She pushed the toe of her shoe into the ground.

"Spin, Hazel! Call your prince."

"No, I feel silly."

"Come on! Have some fun."

Hazel dropped her hands to her sides and rolled her eyes. Reluctantly, she closed both eyes and scrunched her face. She started to lift her arms, raising them until they were parallel to the ground. She sighed and began to spin. Ruthie clapped loudly to encourage her.

"Oh, prince," Hazel said quietly.

"Louder, Hazel!" Ruthie shouted.

Hazel shook her head. "Okay, okay." She sucked in a deep breath and started again, shouting. "Oh, prince. Oh, prince wherever you are. Come take me away! I like chocolate and marshmallows. Come get—"

Snap. The sound made Ruthie jump out of her skin. It cut through the air like a knife. The trees rustled with a flurry of wings. Ruthie clamped a hand over her mouth to keep from screaming as a chill ran down her spine. She looked at Hazel, who stood frozen with her arms clenched around her. Neither said anything for a moment. Hazel looked at Ruthie with big eyes. *If only Daddy were here to protect us.*

Ruthie saw a shadow move from behind a tree. She gulped. She opened her mouth, but no sound came out. She raised a trembling finger and pointed to the tree. Hazel followed her finger. The muscles in her jaw tensed.

"H-hello," Hazel said, her words trembled. "Anyone there?"

Chapter 6

JOEL

The branch broke with a sharp crack. *Stupid*, Joel hit his forehead with his fist. *Why am I so stupid?* The hairs of his neck stood, and his insides quivered. He wasn't watching where he stepped. The girl with the long, dark hair usually read or wrote in her notebook. She never played or ran around like her sister. He'd gotten careless. *What have I done?*

Joel jolted when he realized she had said something. He couldn't hear all the words because his heart was pounding between his ears like it was going to explode. He pulled at the bark of the tree with his fingers. He considered turning away and running up the hill for home. But she'd seen him. *What if they told Pa I'd been following them?*

"I-I know you're there," she said, speaking to him again. "I can see your red shirt."

He looked down and saw the thin red material of his long sleeve school shirt. Joel's shoulders slumped. His throat felt tight and dry. He rubbed his forehead with his hand. He knew he couldn't stay behind this tree forever. He sucked in a long, deep breath, pushed his shoulders back, and on weak knees, walked out from behind the tree. With each step, he was certain his knees would buckle, and he'd fall to the ground.

The girl who sat in front of him in his art class last year was staring at him. Her cheeks flushed red. Her younger sister's blonde hair was a tangled mess of curls around her face. Her mouth spread into a huge grin making it easy for him to see she was missing a front tooth.

"It's a boy," she said. "Hazel, you called a prince! Are you a prince?"

"Ruthie!" the girl snapped.

The smaller one scrunched her nose. "Well, he might be."

Joel felt heat in his cheeks. He rubbed his hand through his hair and rested it on the back of his warm neck. "Um," he coughed, clearing his scratchy throat. "I'm no prince."

"How old are you?" the little sister asked.

"Um, I just turned eleven."

"I'm eight, but I act older. And she's ten," she motioned to the girl with the long dark hair with her thumb. "Where do you live? How come I ain't ever seen you before?"

"Ruthie, quit askin' so many questions."

Joel looked at the girl. Her hair was loose, long dark strands flowed in the wind. When she realized he was looking at her, she lowered her eyes to the ground. Her cheeks turned a bright pink.

"It's alright. I don't mind answerin' questions. I live up there," he pointed to his house on the hill.

The little one's eyes grew big. "You live in the haunted house?"

"Ruthie! Mind your manners!"

"Well, that's what everyone calls it," she said, flapping her arms in the air. "He's gotta know that's what everyone calls it."

Joel laughed. "It's okay. I don't mind." He smiled. "It's not haunted. That's just a story kids at school made up. Me and my pa live there."

"Where's your mama?"

"Ruthie!"

Joel gulped and began fiddling with a button on his shirt. He hadn't expected an inquisition. He looked at Ruthie. She stared at him, waiting for an answer.

"Well," he paused. He wished his twisting stomach would settle. "She's dead. She died when I was born. I never got to meet her."

"Oh!" Ruthie frowned. "That's sad you never had a ma."

"Yeah." Joel pushed his hands inside his pockets unsure what to do with them anymore. He gripped the tooth he always kept with him, feeling the familiar point poking his palm. He took in a breath, "But I had a real nice lady who cared for me until I was five. Her name was Ms. Angel."

Ruthie smiled, "That's nice. What happened to her?"

Hazel crossed her arms and scowled. Joel felt a pang in his chest. All of these questions were starting to make him feel uncomfortable.

"She was old. And passed away. Then I came here to live with my pa."

Ruthie shook her head and scratched at the grass with her big toe. "Our mama's alive, but she's gone too. She left us," she said almost in a whisper. "Might as well be dead."

"Ruthie!" Hazel growled.

Ruthie shrugged her shoulders and ignored her sister. "So, what's your name? I'm Ruthie McKay and this is my sister, Hazel."

Hazel scowled and gripped her fingers tight in front of her, the red in her cheeks spreading to her neck.

"I'm Joel Davenport."

"Joel," Ruthie said his name like she was trying out a new word. "I like it."

Joel's heart fluttered. He looked toward Hazel. Her eyes darted toward her feet. "Um, thank ya," he said to Ruthie.

"You wanna look for birds with us? Our daddy bought us some binkul...binokul..." she huffed and ran to a tree. She raced back with a pair of binoculars in her hands and handed them to him.

He took them from her and examined them. He turned them over and dusted some dirt off the bottom. "These are cool!"

Ruthie smiled and Joel could see she was actually missing both front teeth. "Yeah, they're cool," she said, trying out the word he'd used.

Joel chuckled.

"Daddy got us a bird book too. It's cool too." She grabbed his hand and pulled him toward an old tree with low hanging branches.

Hazel followed behind them but kept her distance. The book lay open on the ground. Joel got down on his knees to look at the pages. He saw a picture of a Red-Bellied Woodpecker. There was a pencil lying between the pages of the book. He read the handwriting to himself. *"April 5, 1953. Saw red bellied woodpecker in a pine tree near our magical spot."*

"Magical spot?" he questioned, pointing toward the words written in loopy handwriting.

Hazel hurried around him, bumping him with her shoulder. He wobbled on his knees and put a hand on the ground to keep from falling over. She swiped the book and slammed it shut with the pencil still inside.

"That's none of your business," she snipped.

"Hazel," Ruthie whined. "He's our friend."

"We just met him."

Joel rubbed his dirty palm on his blue jeans. He wasn't sure what to do. He swallowed the lump in his throat. It landed in the pit of his stomach and went cold. *What did I do wrong?* He hurried out from under the tree's branches and stood awkwardly among the dandelions. His eyes darted from girl to girl. Hazel scowled and Ruthie frowned. He looked down at his hands. They felt like they didn't belong to him, so he shoved them back in his pockets and swayed in place. He coughed to clear his throat. "I-I'm sorry." He said the words, but he wasn't sure what he was apologizing for.

"Don't say sorry! Hazel is just being mean," Ruthie said. She crossed her arms.

Hazel rolled her eyes and hugged the book close to her chest as if she was protecting it.

"She loves to write stories in our magical spot. That's what we call that tree over there," she pointed.

"Shush," hissed Hazel. "Don't be tellin' my business." She glared at him. The redness in her face moving up to her ears.

Girls are strange. How could she be upset about writing stories in a special spot? "Writing stories, that sounds kinda neat," he said, making sure he met Hazel's eyes.

Her face softened and she looked down at her shoes. "Thank ya," she said so softly the wind carried the words away.

"I'm thirsty," Ruthie announced.

She reached down and slipped on her shoes. She ran to Joel and tugged at his arm. He winced a little and he hoped she didn't notice.

"Wanna go to our house for a Coke? We got some extra ones. We gotta keep the bottles cause Daddy always puts them in the rack by the Coke machine so he can get us more."

Joel's throat felt dry. He could use a Coke. The corners of Hazel's mouth stretched downwards, and he wondered if she'd say he couldn't come with them. Joel looked toward the sun. The heat of the day beat down on the top of his head, making his hair warm to the touch. A bead of sweat trickled down his back and his school shirt stuck to his skin.

He nodded, "Yeah, sure. I could use a Coke."

Hazel sighed, but she didn't balk or protest. She turned without saying a word and started walking through the woods. Ruthie walked behind her with Joel. He liked how easily Ruthie smiled.

Ruthie fanned herself with her hand. "Joel, aren't you hot? Why you wearin' that long sleeve shirt? It feels like summer already to me."

Joel rubbed his arm where the bruises under his shirt were still sore. The round purple plums on his skin had begun to turn greenish gray. "I like this shirt," was all he could think to say.

Ruthie shrugged, "I like it too."

Joel couldn't help but smile. Her comment helped to erase the memories of a few nights ago.

Joel walked up to the little white house that he'd seen through his window a hundred times. It looked different up close. He could see where the white paint was starting to chip away and where some porch boards were warped from the rain. He touched a rotted place on the steps, pushing it. He felt it give.

"Yeah, Daddy said he's gonna fix that when he gets back," Ruthie said. "But he's gone working."

Hazel said nothing. She walked up the steps and went inside the house. Joel sat on the edge of the porch not wanting to go inside the house without an invitation, especially if the girls' father wasn't home, even he knew that would be improper.

Hazel came out a few minutes later holding three glass Coke bottles. They chimed together. She handed one to Joel, then to Ruthie. She held a small silver bottle opener. She sat her Coke bottle down and opened Ruthie's for her before opening her own. She offered the bottle opener to Joel. His fingers lightly grazed her hand as he took it. Her cheeks flushed crimson, and Joel's heart popped in his chest like popcorn. He tried to act normal and pried the cap off his Coke. The top popped and the bottle let out a small hiss. He kept Hazel in a sideways glance as he took a long pull from the bottle, feeling the carbonation burn his raw throat. Hazel sipped her Coke.

"It's gettin' hot. I bet the summer's gonna be terrible." Ruthie said, breaking the awkward silence.

Joel smiled. She acted so grown up. He nodded and took another long swig of his Coke. Ruthie burped.

"Mind your manners!" Hazel snapped.

"Oops, sorry."

Joel couldn't help but laugh. Ruthie started to laugh too. He glanced at Hazel. A small smile creased the edges of her mouth. With one more swig, Joel's Coke bottle was nearly empty. He held it up. A small amount of brown liquid swished around the glass bottom. He took one last sip to finish the remainder and sat the bottle down on the porch.

"Well," he said, "I better be headin' home. Thank you kindly for the Coke."

"Oh! Don't go," Ruthie begged.

"Ruthie, he said he needed to be headin' home."

Ruthie looked at him with pleading eyes. Hazel folded her arms, propping up the Coke bottle on one of them.

"I really better get," he said, looking at Ruthie.

She stuck out her bottom lip.

Hiking up the hill back to his house, Joel couldn't contain his smile. His body was weightless as he walked the steep incline to his house. He couldn't remember the last time he'd laughed so much. He replayed the moments with Hazel and Ruthie through his mind. *It's been a good day. A great day.* He chuckled to himself when he thought about Ruthie and how before he left, she made him raise his right hand in the air and swear. Hazel didn't like that, but Ruthie made him swear anyway. He'd swore, "I, Joel Davenport, swear with my whole heart to come back again and visit."

Chapter 7

HAZEL, MAY 1954

Hazel tried to work on the long division problems the teacher had written on the chalk board, but today, she was having a hard time focusing. Joel sat in front of her hunched over a wooden desk. His teacher was sick today, so his math class had been shoved in with her class. It bothered her that he was in her space, and she watched as his pencil moved in circles on his paper. *Is he even working on the assignment?* She wondered with a huff. It didn't look like it.

Joel had walked Hazel and Ruthie to their house every day after school since they'd found him in the woods, watching them. Once off the school bus, Ruthie and Joel would walk in front of her. Ruthie talking the whole way home.

"Margarette Ann told me there were hot-rodders burnin' rubber in the parking lot of Piggly Wiggly last weekend," Ruthie had told Joel yesterday.

"You don't even know what burnin' rubber means," Hazel chided.

When they got home, Joel never left right away either. Ruthie would offer him a Coke and he'd take it. They'd sit on the front porch sipping their Cokes, Ruthie's mouth going ninety miles an hour. It made Hazel's stomach twist. One night, when Daddy made his nightly check-in telephone calls, she tried to tell him about Joel. *I'm not tattling. Not really,* she'd told herself. She thought for sure when he learned that a boy was hanging out at their house while he was gone, he'd put a stop to it quick. He'd tell Joel to never come back again. Ruthie would be mad. She'd probably flip her lid, but it'd be worth it. Joel would be gone.

"Joel Davenport's been walkin' you girls' home from school?" Daddy repeated what she told him.

"Yes, a boy! And Ruthie's been giving him Cokes." Hazel told him.

Ruthie's eyes had grown wide when she realized what Hazel was telling him. She charged Hazel and tried to grab the rotary telephone from her hand. Hazel whipped around to keep it away from her. The cord wrapping around her body.

"He lives on the hill, is that right?" he asked.

"Yes, he lives on the hill," Hazel hadn't been sure why it mattered where Joel lived. He was a boy, and he was drinking Cokes at their house when Daddy was gone.

"Well, I'm glad he's there to walk you girls home and to keep an eye on ya. Makes me feel better knowing there's a man around to protect you."

Hazel's mouth had fallen so far open she could have caught flies. Her heart raced and she began to stutter. "B-but he's a boy?" *Daddy doesn't care?* She was so distracted by this absurd turn of events that Ruthie snatched the telephone from her hands and began to divulge all the facts about how they'd met Joel in the woods and how now Joel was her great friend—her best friend. Hazel rolled her eyes and wondered if Daddy had hit his head while he was working and gone bonkers. There was not one good reason she could think of, on the whole face of the Earth, for Joel being around.

Hazel glared at Joel's back as she pressed her pencil into her paper. She sighed when she heard the familiar *crack* of the lead breaking. *This is all his fault.* She wasn't sure how, but it was. Ever since he'd started coming around, she could barely concentrate on her schoolwork. Before, she never paid attention to him. Never noticed him. And now, he was the only thing she saw. Every time he glanced in her direction, every turn of his head, every half grin aimed at her, her stomach would twist in a funny way. Just thinking about all the plans Ruthie had made for them this summer when school let out sent her stomach into her throat. Joel never said no to Ruthie either, even when Hazel made it clear that she didn't want him around. Anger burned inside her chest. She didn't know why he bothered her so much, but he did, and she didn't like it.

She stood up. Her chair's legs screeched across the floor. Joel turned his head to look at her. Hazel felt heat pass through her. The heat irritated her, and it made her cheeks burn. She made a face at him. His eyes went big before he smiled. *He smiled. The nerve!* She turned on the heel of her saddle shoes and huffed toward the pencil sharpener at the back of the classroom. She forced her pencil into the small hole and twisted the handle while holding it firmly in place with her other hand. The familiar grinding sound and smell of wood soothed her.

"If you don't stop, you're gonna grind it to nothin' but a nub," Joel whispered behind her.

She twisted the handle harder. "Leave me alone."

Joel chuckled, "You got a bee in your bonnet or somethin' today?"

Hazel twisted the handle hard one more time. She was going to give Joel a piece of her mind, but when she turned around, she didn't expect him to be so close. She could see little brown specks in his blue eyes. All the snide, cruel comments she'd planned evaporated from her mind. She felt light-headed. Her face, neck, and ears were warm. Too warm. Her hands felt slippery, and she dropped her pencil. Before she could pick it up, Joel reached down and scooped it up.

"Oh, you broke the lead again," he said, holding the pencil up for her to see.

Without thinking, she snatched it from his hand. "I don't need it any way." She hurried around him to the safety of her desk. She plopped down, wanting to bury her face in her arms. *Why does he bother me so much?* She squeezed her eyes tight and tried to force her breathing to return to a normal pace.

The squeak of the seat in front of her made her eyelids flutter open. Joel was back sitting at his desk. His shoulders hunched over his schoolwork like nothing had happened between them. A huge lump stuck in her throat. She wasn't a mean person, but it felt like she couldn't stop being mean to him. He brought it out of her. She sighed and looked down at her unfinished math paper. She sucked in a breath. On top of her paper sat a perfectly sharpened No. 2 pencil with a bright pink eraser. Her eyes darted up to the back of Joel's head. She felt like such a goof, the biggest goof in the world.

Chapter 8

HAZEL, AUGUST 1955

Hazel stared at her reflection in the bedroom mirror. The summer heat wafted in through the open window causing little beads of sweat to form across her brow. The Arkansas summer was in full force, which meant walking outside was like bathing in your own perspiration. Even in her room, Hazel's church clothes clung to her. She wiped at the beads of sweat that had started to trickle down her face, but it didn't help. Long strands of hair stuck to her damp skin. She sighed as she gathered her hair and divided it into two sections. She twisted each section into a low bun and secured the ends with Lux bobby pins. At least having the hair off her sticky neck helped somewhat. She fanned herself with her hand wishing she was swimming in the river with Joel and Ruthie. Her cheeks reddened in the mirror even though she was alone, and she wanted to kick herself.

She wondered what Grandmother would say if she knew for the past two summers, Ruthie and Hazel had been hanging out with a boy. Hazel could still barely believe it herself. No matter how hard she tried to convince Daddy that it wasn't a good idea, he'd say something like, "I'm sorry, girl, it makes me feel better knowing that ya'll have Joel around."

Hazel rolled her eyes at herself in the mirror. She couldn't put a pin in it. *Why am I such a ditz when he's around. He's so annoying.* She hated how she stumbled over her words, how her tongue felt like it had swollen two times its size. Still, she couldn't understand why she cared anyway. Ruthie was no help, calling her a drag all the time. *And right in front of Joel!* Like the day Hazel had been too scared to try the old rope swing hanging from a tree near the river. The rope looked old and ratty, but that didn't keep Ruthie and Joel from using it to fling their bodies high into the air before hitting the cool water feet first. Hazel narrowed her eyes at her reflection, sizing herself up in the mirror like her grandmother would. *I am not a drag... Am I?* Hazel knew Grandmother would not approve of Joel. She'd agree with her, but Hazel wasn't sure how much that was worth since they hardly even saw her anymore since Mama left.

Hazel rubbed her hands down the paisley skirt and straightened her navy top. Her outfit had been a Christmas gift from Grandmother. It was the last time they'd seen her. She'd shoved the gifts in her and Ruthie's arms, gave them half hugs, and tried to hurry out the door even though Daddy had invited her to stay for Christmas dinner. Hazel was surprised at how fast her old legs could carry her. Hazel wondered if the only reason she brought them gifts was because she felt bad about Mama leaving. Because it sure seemed to her that Grandmother didn't like them very much. During Grandmother's quick Christmas visit, Hazel made it a point to ask her about Mama. Grandmother had frowned, making the deep lines at the side of her mouth deeper. She waved a wrinkled hand in the air, "Oh, she's in California now," she'd said before rushing out the door with a "Merry Christmas ya'll."

Even though it'd been almost three years, since Mama'd left them. It was still hard for Hazel to think about. Sometimes at night, questions would pound in her head. *Why'd she have to go? Why weren't they enough? What was she doing all the way in California?* She'd even once considered hoping on a bus to California to find her, but she knew that was silly. She didn't even know where to start.

"Hazel!" Ruthie's scream pierced her memories like a bubble.

"Hazel, come help your sister!" Daddy bellowed.

Hazel ran to the living room. Her heart pitter-patted in her chest. *What in the world is wrong?* She froze when she made it to the living room. Daddy was sitting on their yellow tattered sofa. Ruthie stood between his legs as he held her shoulder. His lips were clenched tight, making a thin red line encircled by dark beard. The hairbrush hung from Ruthie's curls, stuck in her blonde tangled mess. Tears flowed down her face.

"It hurts," she whined.

Daddy hung his head.

Hazel placed her hands on her hips. "I've been tellin' you to brush your hair every day, but you don't listen."

Daddy sighed, "Maybe we should have started this last night. We're gonna be late for church." His face twisted in a grimace as he tried once more to pull the hairbrush from Ruthie's hair.

"Ouch!" she screamed.

He lightly touched Ruthie's shoulders, leaving the hairbrush hanging in her hair before he stood. "I give up. I'll be outside. We gotta leave in five minutes, girl. Do what you can." He walked past Hazel, patting the top of her head. At the door, he paused and looked back at Ruthie. "Sorry, peanut." The screen door squeaked and snapped closed behind him.

Hazel moved to where he had been sitting on the sofa. She situated herself on the bouncy cushion. An old spring poked her leg. Ruthie sniffled and wiped her face with the back of her hand.

"I hate my hair!"

"Shush, I'll fix it. But you gotta start listening and brush your hair every day. You wouldn't have this problem if you did."

"I want short hair like a boy. I want straight hair like you. I don't want hair at all." Ruthie folded her arms.

Hazel shook her head. "Now just be still."

In a few minutes, Hazel had most of the tangles brushed out. She took a small pink ribbon and pulled the sides of Ruthie's hair back into a low ponytail. She tied a bow around the tangle-free section of hair. The tails of the ribbon hung over Ruthie's wavy curls.

"Finished," Hazel said.

Ruthie ran to the bathroom. "I look beautiful!" she squealed. Ruthie hurried back to the living room and grabbed the ends of her dress. She made it swish side to side. "I invited Joel to church today."

Hazel felt her stomach pinch, then she exhaled and picked up the small, tattered Bible sitting on the kitchen table. The cover was torn at the top corner. "You always invite him. He ain't ever came."

"Yeah, but maybe this time."

At church, Hazel held the small brown hymnal down so Ruthie could see it. Ruthie bellowed out the words to "Great is Thy Faithfulness." Hazel moved her mouth, so it looked like she was singing. When the song was over, they sat down in the pew. Hazel shut her eyes. She watched light spots bounce on the back of her eyelids and began to silently pray the same prayer she said every Sunday. *Please, O Lord, please bring Mama home.* When Mama first left, she'd prayed and promised God anything she could think of. She'd do good every day of her life, she'd read the whole Bible, she'd give away all of her things to the poor, even though it wasn't much. Still, God didn't want any of her promises because Mama never came home.

Hazel's prayers were interrupted by the wooden church doors slamming shut. Hazel and Ruthie turned in their seat to see who was late.

Joel walked inside. His head down as he shuffled to the pew in front of them and plopped down.

"He's here," Ruthie whispered, her eyes dancing over her bright smile.

Hazel breathed in. The smell of rancid dead fish filled her nose. She frowned and pinched her nose, trying not to breathe.

"What's that smell?" Ruthie asked too loudly.

People in the pew near them turned their heads, their eyebrows furrowed.

"Shh," Hazel held a finger over mouth then used her hand to cover her mouth and nose. The smell was coming from in front of them. The smell was coming from Joel.

Her father leaned over so he could whisper. "Smells like someone went catfishin' this morning before church."

Hazel lowered her hand to her lap and scrunched her face. She glared at the back of Joel's head. *Why would anyone go fishing and not take a bath before church? Now they had to smell that horrible stench all morning.* Hazel felt the old irritation bubble up inside her. She had started making it a point to be kinder to Joel, but sometimes he bugged her so much. She couldn't explain it. For some reason, Joel got under her skin like a bad itch.

After church, Joel disappeared into the crowd, taking that horrible smell with him. Hazel stuck close to her father while he shook church members' hands and spoke about the weather. Outside the old brick church house, Hazel squinted at the brightness of the sunlight. Ruthie placed a hand above her eyes. She spotted Joel walking toward the road and took off running to catch him like a dog chasing a bone. Hazel frowned.

"Joel, Joel wait!" Ruthie waved her hand in the air to get his attention.

Joel stopped and turned. Daddy walked briskly to reach Ruthie. Hazel trailed behind him. She realized in that moment Daddy had never met Joel. Joel had been to their house a thousand times. He and Ruthie had played in the forest and swam in the river together while Hazel wrote stories and watched, but Daddy didn't even know what Joel looked like. For a minute, she wondered if Daddy planned on getting onto Joel for coming to church smelling like stinky catfish bait. Maybe he'd tell him he needed to take a bath before church or not come at all. But her thoughts were quickly dashed when her Daddy's face cracked into a wide smile, and he extended his hand for Joel to shake.

"So, this is the young man that's been protecting my girls."

Joel stared at Daddy's offered hand. *Did he even know how to shake hands properly?* Hazel thought. *Does he have any manners at all?*

Joel timidly took the hand and shook it.

"Arvel McKay. You must be Joel."

Joel nodded.

"Well son, we were just headin' home to have some lunch. Why don't you join us? It's the least I can do for you for watching out for my girls and all."

Hazel's knees almost buckled. *Had Daddy just invited Joel to come inside the house? Inside her house!* Hazel pulled on Daddy's shirt, but he ignored her. Joel having lunch at the house was a terrible idea. He didn't watch out for them anyway, that was her job. Ruthie started jumping up and down. Hazel scowled. *Oh Lordy, of course, Ruthie would flip her lid about Joel eating lunch with us.* Hazel felt the sun beating down on her head, but it was nothing like the heat that passed through her body and rose to rest on her cheeks. Joel would see inside her house, her space.

"Oh, please come eat lunch with us!" Ruthie squealed. "Daddy can give you a ride, you don't have to walk."

"Yeah, why don't you jump in the truck bed. What else you gotta do today?"

"N-nothing sir," Joel stuttered. "Thank ya for the offer. I sure appreciate the kindness."

Daddy patted Joel's shoulder, "Don't think anything of it. I owe you a debt of gratitude."

Hazel crossed her arms tight across her chest. Joel looked at her and she turned her head.

On the ride home, Ruthie kept turning around in the seat to look out the back window at Joel.

"Ruthie, quit spyin' on that boy. You'll make him wish he never agreed to come to lunch," Daddy scolded.

Ruthie flopped back down in the seat with a *hmph.*

"Why'd we have to invite him to lunch anyway?" Hazel's question came out in a whisper. "He smells like catfish."

Daddy took his hand off the steering wheel and reached over Ruthie to pat Hazel's knee. "A little bit of kindness goes a long way," he said.

"But he smells horrible!" Hazel said louder, unsure if Daddy really understood what she'd said or how big of a mistake he was making.

Daddy sighed. "Hazel, that's Joel Davenport sitting back there."

Hazel turned her head to look out at Joel. He was sitting near the tailgate, staring at the sun-scorched pastures. His hair whipped around his face in the wind.

"He may not be our kin, but he might as well be. His family has always been like family to me." He paused. "And if you only knew what he likely has to deal with on a daily basis." Daddy sighed. "Hazel, he can come over and eat a meal at my house any day of the week."

Hazel wasn't sure what he meant. Joel didn't have a family, not really. It was only him and his pa living on the hill. Joel's mama was gone. Hazel kept her mouth shut. Daddy was mistaken, but there was no sense in correcting him. The fishy-smelling boy was coming over for lunch, and it was too late to stop it. Hazel folded her arms in front of her, matching Ruthie's position. She watched the pastures disappear into trees.

At lunch, Hazel didn't say one word, but it didn't matter. Ruthie filled the table with conversation from silly questions to long dumb stories. Hazel's insides twisted when Ruthie told their father stories about their adventures in the forest. Ruthie told Daddy how Joel was now teaching her how to fish in the small pond not far from the house. Hazel wasn't sure how Ruthie could eat, breathe, and talk at once.

To Hazel's relief, Joel left straight after lunch. Ruthie begged him to stay longer, but he said he needed to get home.

"Thank you kindly for lunch Mr. McKay."

Daddy shook Joel's hand, making him promise to continue to keep an eye on his girls while he was gone. Hazel felt flames burst inside her when Joel nodded in agreement. No matter what she told Daddy, he wouldn't believe her. They didn't need a boy around to protect them.

That afternoon, before Daddy left to head out of town for work again, Hazel saw him put some extra money in the coffee tin under the sink. When he noticed her watching, he shrugged his shoulders and said, "Coke money for Joel."

Chapter 9

RUTHIE

"My shoes ain't working!" Ruthie hollered. She flopped down on the floor and yanked her right shoe off her foot. The back was squished down from where her heel had flattened it. She straightened it and tried to slip the shoe on again. Her hair fell in her face. She huffed and pushed the loose strands behind her ear. "Why do I have to wear shoes anyway? I know for a fact that George Piles gets away with not wearing shoes."

"He can't afford shoes. Now come on! We gotta go. We can't miss the bus on the first day of school! It'll be at the bus stop in an hour, and you know it will take you every bit of that to walk there. If you don't hurry, we'll have to run."

Ruthie huffed again to move the hair that had once more fallen in front of her eyes. She detested running just as much as she detested shoes and hair and George Piles. *Only a dumb boy could get away with not wearing shoes to school.* It wasn't proper for a girl. *Boys!* She hated them all. Joel popped in her mind. *Except Joel. I don't hate him,* she thought. He was different. He was their friend.

"I'm gonna head that way without you if you don't come on!" Hazel yelled from the living room.

"I'm comin', I'm comin'!" Ruthie yelled back.

She forced her growing foot into the tight black shoe. She stood and straightened the bottom of the blue dress Hazel had given her. She wiggled her foot. The shoes pinched her toes like crawdad claws, but it couldn't be helped. She didn't have another pair of school shoes. She ran into the living room and saw Hazel was already opening the screen door. Hazel paused in the doorway before letting out a blood curdling scream. Ruthie's heart jumped into her throat, and she ran to Hazel, half expecting to see something dead laying in the threshold of the door.

"Hazel, what's wrong?" she said, reaching out to touch Hazel's shoulder. Hazel jumped, making Ruthie shriek.

"I-it's a catfish!" Hazel pointed.

Ruthie peeked around Hazel's shoulder. A gray catfish swam splashing in a blue bucket in front of their door.

"Ewww," Ruthie squealed. "Where'd it come from?"

"That silly boy! Who else would be so dumb?"

Ruthie put her hands on her hips. She knew exactly who Hazel was talking about. "Joel's not dumb!" *Why is she so mean to him sometimes?*

Hazel let the screen door go and it shut with a *pop,* startling both of them. "He is too dumb." Hazel said. "Who leaves a catfish by someone's door?"

"He's just tryin' to be nice," Ruthie protested.

"Well, what are we supposed to do with it?" Hazel waved her hands toward the door.

They both looked at the screen door. Through the dark screen, Ruthie could still see the blue bucket and hear the catfish splashing in the water. She bit her bottom lip. "We could take it to school with us."

"It's the first day!" Hazel laid a hand across her forehead. "We can't take it to school. We couldn't carry this bucket a mile down the road to the bus stop. If we miss the bus, and Daddy finds out, we'll be crusin' for a brusin'." Her chest heaved up and down. "And we can't leave it here in front of the door. It's probably gonna be a hundred degrees today. It will cook in the sun and when we come home, we'll have a dead catfish to deal with."

Ruthie's nerves felt jangled. She flung her arms out. "I don't know what to do with it either!" She could feel the desperation building around them. Time was ticking away, and a catfish was swimming in circles on the porch. Her heart raced in her chest. They couldn't miss school. Daddy trusted them to be good girls. She felt the back of her throat tighten and she thought she might start to cry.

Hazel opened the screen door. She bent down and grabbed one side of the bucket. She began to tug it inside the house.

"Wh-what are you doin?"

"Help me," Hazel panted.

Ruthie bent over and helped pull the bucket. *Oh man, oh man, this is bad. What are we doing?* The water splashed over the lid of the bucket onto Ruthie's hand, and she recoiled.

"Come on," Hazel snapped.

Ruthie reached back down and took hold of the side. She couldn't believe they were taking a catfish inside the house. "Why are we doin' this?"

"We can't leave this yucky thing on the porch."

"So, you want it in the house?" Ruthie asked, her mind trying to work out what Hazel was doing.

"No, I don't want it in the house. The only place I could think of was to put it in the bathtub."

Ruthie stopped tugging her end of the bucket. She stood straight as a board. "The bathtub?" Ruthie looked behind her. That's exactly where they were headed.

Hazel grunted as she continued to pull the bucket. "C'mon now! We gotta hurry." Sweat began to bead across her forehead.

If this wasn't such a serious matter, Ruthie knew she'd be laughing. She bit her lip and bent down to help Hazel finish moving the catfish into the bathroom. Once they made it to the tub, Hazel grabbed its white handles and twisted. The waterspout sputtered to life, shaking as the water worked its way out. The water's metallic smell filled Ruthie's nose. Ruthie hoped the catfish wouldn't mind well water.

When the tub was half full, Hazel turned the water off. They stared at the fish, swimming in slow circles in its small enclosure.

"It's okay fella, you'll be fine in the tub," Ruthie said, trying to make her voice sound soothing.

Hazel gestured toward the bucket and they both grabbed an end.

"On three," Hazel directed.

Ruthie steeled herself for the count.

"One. Two. Three!"

Ruthie grunted as they heaved the bucket up. Her arms quivered with the weight.

"Almost there," Hazel panted.

They tilted the blue side over the edge of the tub. With one last push, the contents of the bucket poured into the bathtub, sending water sloshing out of the tub in rolling waves, dousing Hazel and Ruthie. They both screamed. The front of their dresses dark and plastered to the front of their legs.

"We did it!" Ruthie yipped, wiping her hands on the front of her wet dress.

Hazel breathed out a long sigh.

A thought hit Ruthie, "Wait!" she exclaimed. She ran from the bathroom toward the kitchen. She threw open the bread box and grabbed a piece of bread. She ran back to where she left Hazel, her hands firmly on her hips. Ruthie tore the slice of bread into chunks and threw them into the tub. They landed on top, absorbing the water. She and Hazel watched as the catfish swam from one end of the bathtub to the other, ignoring the pieces of sinking bread bites.

Ruthie shrugged. "He might get hungry while we're at school."

Hazel's face went white. "School! Holy smokes! Let's hurry!"

Hazel darted out of the bathroom and out of the house. Ruthie ran after her. The screen door popped closed behind her. Ruthie's skirt clung to her legs, making them feel like they were stuck in plaster. Her shoes squeezed her feet with each step. Within a few moments of running after Hazel, her side ached and her chest burned. She realized she was never going to catch her.

"W-wait," she tried to call but her words were swallowed up by the wind. She didn't have enough breath to force the words out again. She gripped her side and slowed down. Her legs trembled and her stomach felt sick. She hated running.

Hazel turned around, jogging backwards. Ruthie hated how easy running came to her. "We're so close. Not much farther. Come on, you can do it." Hazel said to cheer Ruthie along.

Ruthie shook her head. She couldn't do it. "I can't run anymore. My legs won't go."

"I'll see if I can get the bus driver to wait," Hazel hollered before turning and bolting down the road, leaving Ruthie behind.

Ruthie's feet throbbed and rubbed against the side of her shoes. Her toes so scrunched inside them; she'd probably never be able to straighten them out again. A sharp pain settled in her heel, and she began to limp. *A blister! I bet I've got a blister.* By the time she made it to the last curve, she was certain the bus would have already come and gone. She wondered if Hazel made it and went on to school without her. She moaned, thinking about the long walk back to the house. She'd never stayed home alone before. A tremor ran through her.

A long horn blast jerked her from her worries. The bus pulled to a stop. Its brakes squealed like they were screaming for help. Hazel stood beside the bus, waving for her to hurry. Ruthie forced her legs and feet to work faster until she made it to the side of the dusty bus. Her feet felt like heavy bags of potatoes as she climbed the steps and took a seat near the front. Her body collapsed in the green bench seat. She lurched forward when the bus began to move. She scooted next to the window and stared at her reflection. Her hair was a tangled mess again. She balled her wet skirt in her hands, making it wrinkle. She looked at her reflection in the window and smiled. *There's a catfish in my tub.* Her leg muscles quivered and ached, but she smiled and wondered if they'd ever be able to take a bath again. The thought sent a shot of pure joy through her. She'd give that catfish a name, since now it was living with them. She'd never had a pet. She needed to thank Joel. She turned in her seat to scan the seats behind her, but Joel wasn't on the bus today. She shrunk back down, resting her knees against the seat in front of her. It didn't matter. She'd thank him when she saw him.

Chapter 10

HAZEL

Heat rushed through Hazel's body when she saw Joel sitting in the grass with his friends during lunch break. Other students sat on benches or under nearby shade trees eating sandwiches and talking. It had taken every ounce of willpower she had not to yell at him in the school hallway when she first saw him. He'd not ridden the bus, so she couldn't confront him first thing this morning, like she wanted. *Probably walked to Mr. Simmons' store to make some kind of trade,* she thought. In class, she had tried to focus on her studies and push the nonsense of the morning aside, but the coolness of her damp skirt when it touched her skin scattered goosebumps across her legs and arms, igniting the anger inside of her.

Now her skin felt like it was on fire. Her muscles quivered as she ground her teeth. Any other day she'd have been too nervous to approach a group of boys even if Joel was sitting with them, but today was different. She'd have her word with him, and she'd have it now.

She marched toward Joel. Her hands balled into fists. When he saw her approach, his face brightened, but his wide smile quickly faded when he met her eyes.

"May I have a word with you?" she said, her words were clipped.

Joel hesitated. His eyes flicked from her to his friends. Resolve seemed to settle on him as he cleared his throat then wiped his hands on his jeans. He stood, "Yeah, I can talk to you."

His friends whispered to each other in hushed conspiratorial tones, but Hazel didn't care. She was beyond caring about what silly boys thought or did.

They walked to an unoccupied oak tree at the corner of the school yard. She bit her lip to keep the words inside until the two of them were out of earshot of other students. She didn't need everyone in the school knowing her business. She was certain a catfish in the bathtub was one calamity a girl couldn't live down.

When they were far enough away, she lit into him, pointing her finger in his face. "How could you!" She shouted, tasting the angry words on her tongue.

Joel took a step back. She took a step forward, her finger moving closer to his face.

He stuttered, "I-I don't know what you're talkin' about." A crease formed between his brows and his shoulders sagged like she'd beaten him.

Her father's words came to mind, "If you only knew what he likely had to deal with on a daily basis." Hazel stared in Joel's hurt eyes. All at once, her rage evaporated like water on a hot pan. She whipped around, covering her face with her hands. Tears stung her eyes. She didn't want to cry, but she couldn't stop. He was a stupid boy, just a stupid boy. She jerked her shoulder away when she felt his touch. "Don't touch me!"

He cleared his throat. "I-I'm not sure what I've done to make you so put out with me. But whatever it is. I'm sorry."

Hazel hung her head. A thickness formed in the back of her throat. She turned towards him. Her chin down at her chest so she couldn't look at his crumpled face. She wiped her tears away with the back of her hand and took a deep breath.

"I know you were just bein' nice, but we don't need a catfish." She raised her head, furrowing her eyebrows. Joel's eyes were watery. "Look at my dress," she held out the wrinkled skirt with her hands. "It's soaked. And that fish of yours almost made us miss the bus."

A flicker of something passed across Joel's face and a smile began to play at the corner of his lips. He raised an eyebrow. "I'm not sure I understand. How'd that catfish almost make you miss the bus?"

Hazel pushed her loose hair behind her ears as heat rose in her cheeks. She looked around to make sure no one had moved close enough to hear them. "Well, we didn't know what to do with it. And we couldn't leave it in that bucket. Why'd you give it to us anyway?"

Joel shrugged his shoulders. "At your house yesterday, your father said he liked the taste of fried catfish. He said it's been a while since he'd had any, so I was just...," his words faded. He titled his head to the side. "What do you mean you couldn't leave it in the bucket? Where'd ya put it?"

Hazel knew her face had to be as bright as a ripe tomato. Her body felt so hot, she was sure Joel would be able to see the water evaporating off her dress. She bit her lip, wondering how much she should say. She leaned forward and whispered, "We put it in the bathtub."

"The bathtub!" Joel said loudly.

"Shh," she hushed him. "I don't need everyone knowin' my business."

Joel began to laugh. Hazel glared at him, but that only made him laugh harder. He bent over, hands on his knees. Tears ran from the corner of his eyes as he chortled louder. Watching him become hysterical made Hazel's shoulders relax. It *was* funny. Joel trying to be nice and them putting a catfish in their bathtub. Before she knew it, Hazel began to giggle with him until they were both cackling.

"Ruthie even threw some pieces of bread in with it, 'cause she thought it'd be hungry."

That sent Joel to the ground, holding his stomach, and Hazel laughed so hard she started to hiccup. When she was finally able to breathe again, she asked "So what are we going to do?"

Joel stood up and dusted off the back of his jeans. "I'll come over today and take it back to the river."

Hazel smiled. "Okay, but it may be hard to convince Ruthie it needs to go. I'm pretty sure she's already adopted it."

After school, Ruthie and Hazel sat at the kitchen table doing their homework. Ruthie's stomach felt hollow. Hazel had told her she couldn't have a snack until she finished her math. She bit on the end of her pencil as her stomach growled.

"I can't think about math when I'm so hungry," she complained.

"No snack until your math is done."

Ruthie hmphed and tightened her grip on her pencil. The numbers on the page wiggled the more she stared at them. She hated it when Hazel was the boss. If she was the boss, anyone could have a snack any time they needed one. Her thoughts were interrupted by a small rap at the door. She and Hazel looked at each other.

"You stay, I'll check it," Hazel began to say, but Ruthie didn't wait. She bolted from her chair and sprinted to the door.

"Ruthie!" Hazel hollered after her.

Ruthie swung the door open causing Joel to jump back.

"Joel!" she shouted, pleased he was here to save her from math.

He smiled. Ruthie grabbed Joel's hand and yanked him inside the house. "What you doin' here?"

Joel pushed his hands into his pants pockets and looked down at his feet. "Well, I've come to collect my catfish."

Ruthie's eyes darted to Hazel, who was grinning.

Ruthie frowned and narrowed her eyes at Hazel. *She's up to something*. She turned her attention back to Joel. "You can't take Marvin. He's, my pet."

Joel's eyes darted to Hazel. Ruthie looked back and forth between them. *Something is going on, and I don't like it!* Ruthie glared at Hazel. When Hazel met her eyes, she turned her head. Ruthie was almost sure she saw a little smirk on Hazel's face.

"Why do you wanna take Marvin? He's got a home here."

Joel cleared his throat, "I am sorry. Really, I am." He swayed on his feet. "I- I just needed you to watch him for me for a while, but now I need to take him back to the river."

Ruthie stuck her bottom lip out. She folded her arms in front of her body and shook her head. "I can't let you take him. I love him. He's mine."

A small giggle escaped from Hazel. Ruthie whipped her head around with eyes like daggers. "I do love him."

Joel sighed.

Hazel walked toward her. "Ruthie, we've got to let Joel take him back to the river. We need to be able to take a bath."

Ruthie's eyes began to fill with tears and the room looked blurry. She squeezed her arms tighter around her middle. *No, this can't be. Marvin is mine and they can't take him from me.*

"But I've never had a pet before and I want to keep him."

"But what about his family Ruthie?" Joel said. "His family is probably missing him so much right now."

Hazel walked and stood near Joel. She nodded, "Oh yes, that's right, his family probably misses him so badly. I'm sure his father and brothers and sisters have been crying since he's been gone."

Ruthie narrowed her eyes. *Do fish have families?* She was certain they were lying to her. They thought she was a silly little baby, but she wasn't. Ruthie opened her mouth to protest again, but Margarette Ann's nose, crinkled in disgust, ran through her mind. If even her best friend in the whole world thought having Marvin in the bathtub was disgusting, maybe she should think twice about keeping him. She didn't want everyone at school to think she was some kind of a germ or something. Ruthie loosened her arms and let them hang at her side. She sucked in a deep breath and blew it out. "Fine, he can go home. I'll go get the bucket."

Chapter 11

JOEL, MAY 1956

A light breeze tussled Joel's hair. He bent down and picked up a twisted brown stick, laying on top of the grass and added it to the load in his arms. He adjusted the bundle and winced when an unruly stick poked the inside of his bicep where fresh, round purple bruises the size of his father's fingers had formed. Joel looked at the collection of sticks he had gathered. He had enough for a night alone in the woods. He wasn't going home now or ever again. He'd live off the land and give up on school. He didn't want to be there anyway. His friends teased him all year long about Hazel, calling her his girl. Although he didn't mind their jokes, Hazel hated it. She was always mad at him when he had nothing to do with what they said or thought. So, to keep the peace, he avoided her at school.

They'd barely said four words to each other throughout the whole year. He remembered their only words. On his thirteenth birthday, she'd walked up to him while he stood in the hallway talking to his friend, Ronnie. She'd said happy birthday, and he'd thanked her. And that was it, nothing else. She never approached him at lunch again or spoke to him on the bus ride home. It was like they'd been transported to the time before they'd met. Of course, he'd see her and Ruthie at the house, but it wasn't the same. It'd never be the same again.

Joel stomped to the clearing where he'd pitched his homemade tent. He dropped the sticks on the ground. They landed in a haphazard pile on top of each other. He ran a hand down his face. He had to stop thinking about Hazel. It bothered him how much he thought about her, but he hated that they barely spoke to each other. He knelt down to straighten the pile of sticks but stopped mid-stoop. His ears caught a sound in the distance, a soft wail. The sound stopped almost as soon as it started, and Joel wondered if he'd heard anything at all. He shook his head, *It's just the wind.* He lowered his knees to the ground, feeling the wetness soak through his jeans. He began to arrange his kindling. He shivered when he heard the eerie cry again. It sounded like the hollow howl of a ghost. Joel swallowed. He didn't believe in ghosts. He looked at the trees. They swayed in the wind. For the first time, he felt nervous being alone in the woods.

When he heard the sound a third time, over the beating of his heart, he knew full well what it was. He leaped off the ground and bolted like a jackrabbit through the brush. He knocked briars and limbs out of the way as he rushed to find her. It didn't take him long. Ruthie was on her knees. Her body hunched over. Joel's heart pounded in his head, and he sucked in ragged breaths as he tried to speak.

"Ruthie, you hurt?"

She sniffed and tried to answer but her words got caught between sobs, and he couldn't understand what she was trying to say. He was so focused on trying to understand Ruthie, a rustle in the brush startled him and he jumped. Hazel walked toward them, pushing away the branches. Her cheeks flushed pink when she saw him, then her eyebrows pulled together, and she frowned as she looked at Ruthie.

"What happened?" she asked him, as if accusing him of doing something. Sweat glistened across her forehead like tiny diamonds in the sun.

Joel shrugged. "I don't know. I found her like this."

Hazel lowered herself to the ground beside Ruthie. She laid an arm across her back. "Ruthie?" Her words were soothing and kind. "Are you hurt?"

Joel felt helpless and out of place. He pushed his hands deep in his pockets and wished he'd stayed where he was fixing his campsite for the night.

Ruthie sucked in a deep breath. She stood and Hazel followed her. Ruthie held out cupped hands so Hazel and Joel could see them. "I-I," she sniffed. "I was lookin' for birds." She nodded her head toward the binoculars and old bird book that lay open on the ground. She blinked her red puffy eyes. Her wild blonde hair was stuck to her wet cheeks.

Hazel pushed Ruthie's hair out of her face and behind her ears with her fingertips. "You were lookin' for birds?" Hazel prodded.

Ruthie nodded. "Yes." She dropped her head. "You always find more than me. I just wanted to find my own bird and write in the book." Ruthie paused and sucked in a breath before continuing, "And then I saw this poor baby fall from the tree. He fell straight down and landed on the ground."

Joel and Hazel instinctively raised their heads to look at the top of the trees. Joel didn't like the thought of something falling down on him. Joel glanced at Hazel. Her mouth was pulled tight.

"Do you want to see it?" Ruthie asked.

Joel's heart fluttered, but he nodded and stepped closer to get a better look. Ruthie held her arms out and began to slowly uncurl her fingers until her cupped hands were open. Inside, lying on Ruthie's pink palms, was a small furry creature. Joel moved in. It looked dead, but then he saw its little nose twitch and one black eye opened. Its fuzzy brown tail was longer than its whole body.

"She found a baby squirrel," he said, in case Hazel hadn't figured it out. The tension left Hazel's face and she exhaled.

Ruthie sniffed, "It fell from the tree. It's all alone now. It'll die without its mother." She opened her mouth and a loud sob escaped. The baby squirrel flinched in her hands. "I can't let it die." Ruthie cried. "It needs me. I'm not leaving it."

Hazel's face twisted. "Even if you take it, it's so small. It might die anyway."

Ruthie held the baby closer to her chest. "I can't leave it. Not like she left us. He needs me."

A single tear ran down Hazel's cheeks. She looked at Joel and frowned. She wiped the tear away so quickly; it was like it was never there. "You don't have to leave it," she told Ruthie. Then she turned to Joel, "Stay here with her. I'll be right back in a jiffy." She'd spoken to him without meeting his eyes.

Hazel took off running through the forest. Joel watched her until she had completely disappeared.

Ruthie stared at the baby squirrel. Silent tears ran down her face. Joel stood, not sure what to do. He'd never had to take care of a crying girl. He thought he'd have better luck with the baby squirrel. He scratched his head. Her crying made him nervous. He bit a fingernail, tearing off a piece that was hanging. The sting made him wince. He sucked on his sore finger then shoved his hand in his pockets. Inside, he felt the sticky outer shell of the marshmallows he'd planned to cook on the fire tonight when he was alone.

"Hey, hey look here," he pulled a marshmallow out of his pocket.

Ruthie blinked. Her face was splotchy and red. Her eyes focused on the puffy sweetness he held up in his hand.

"I found some pennies in the parking lot of the Waldron Drug Store today after school. So, I bought me a few of them to roast on the fire. I'll share some with ya, but you gotta promise to quit cryin'."

Ruthie sniffled and nodded. Her bottom lip pushed out.

"Okay, come on. I was startin' to build a fire."

He guided Ruthie through the trees to the clearing where his tent was pitched. While she walked, she held her cupped hands near her stomach to protect her new baby.

"You really sleepin' outside tonight?" she asked after seeing the tent.

"Yep, you sit here," he said pushing an old hollowed out log near the patch of dirt where he was going to build a fire. She sat down on the weathered bark holding her baby close and watched him. Joel began to pick up the rough rocks he'd left near the dirt patch and formed a circle. He took the bigger sticks and set them up like a small tipi in the center of the circle. While he balanced the tipi, he looked at Ruthie. She was petting the squirrel using the tips of her fingers."

"I can't wait for Margarette Ann to see my squirrel. She's gonna turn pea green with envy." Ruthie giggled.

"What are you going to name it?"

Her head jerked up. A silly grin appeared on her face. "Name it?"

"Yeah, a name for the squirrel. If you're gonna keep it, you should give it a name. You know, like a real pet. Not like the dumb catfish. What was his name?"

"Marvin," Ruthie whispered.

"Oh yeah," chuckled Joel.

Ruthie narrowed her eyes and scrunched her nose at him. "This name has to be a really good name," she said.

Joel continued to work on his fire pit while Ruthie bit her lip in thought. He felt better now that she'd stopped crying. His hands moved freely as he filled the bottom of his tipi with twigs and dry leaves. He positioned the smaller sticks on top of them. When he was finished, he stood up and admired his creation, wondering if he should add a few more dry leaves.

"Henry," Ruthie said, shaking Joel from his fire-making thoughts.

"Henry?"

"Yep, that's my favorite name. It sounds so proper. Like a prince's name from a far-off place."

Joel smirked. "Henry it is, I guess." He laid a few more dry leaves on the pile.

"How ya gonna light it?" Ruthie asked, her eyes following his every move as her fingers absently stroked the top of her tiny baby's head.

Joel reached into his back pocket. He pulled out a shiny silver lighter. "I found an old broken radio at the dump. Mr. Simmons said he thought he could fix it. He traded me this here brand-new Zippo lighter for it." Joel held the lighter up and flicked it. A flame ignited and blazed.

"Wow," Ruthie whispered.

Joel got on his knees and began to light the dry leaves and twigs at the bottom of his tipi. It crackled, catching quickly. The leaves curled as they burned. In seconds, he had a glowing blaze. He sat down on the ground beside it, proud he made fire. Maybe he really could live off the land. He flicked the lighter over and over, happy with his trade with Mr. Simmons. Joel and Ruthie looked up when they heard a rustle in the bushes. Hazel walked into the clearing. Her arms full of things. Joel leaped off the ground and went to her.

"You need help?"

Hazel's cheeks reddened. "Okay," she said. She began to hand him some of her load and paused when their hands got close to each other. Joel rolled his eyes and took some of the things from her hands. She scowled at him. "Careful now," she said with clipped words.

"I think you mean 'thank you,'" Joel snapped.

A grin played at the corner of Hazel's mouth. "Fine, thank you."

Joel felt a rush of heat pass over him. *That smile.* She hadn't smiled at him in so long. He cleared his throat. "So, what is all this stuff?"

"Let's go sit, and I'll show you what I got."

Joel and Hazel sat on the ground near Ruthie.

"Did you see the fire Joel made? He got a shiny lighter from Mr. Simmons," Ruthie exclaimed.

Hazel smiled at Joel then quickly looked away. She began to fidget with the things she'd brought. She straightened the items out then began to pick each one up and explain its use.

"I brought this old blanket. It's very soft," she held it so Ruthie and Joel could touch it. It was pale green. It looked like a baby blanket. "You can wrap the squirrel in it and keep it warm."

"Henry," Ruthie corrected her.

"What?" Hazel asked, looking at Ruthie and then Joel, confused.

"She named it Henry," he explained.

The light of the fire danced across Hazel's face. Her grin widened. His stomach flip-flopped. *Oh man, why do I always feel trapped in a Tilt-A-Whirl around her?*

Hazel set the blanket down and picked up the next thing. She held it up, "I found this eye dropper in Daddy's medicine cabinet. I washed it. You can feed it. I mean Henry with it."

Joel picked up a stick and moved closer to the fire. He poked at it, making the embers blaze. Hazel held out a mason jar filled with a thin white liquid. It sloshed around in the jar. Ruthie stared at it.

"It's the goat's milk we get from the Berrett's farm for half price."

Joel crossed his legs in front of him. He watched Hazel show Ruthie how to fill the eye dropper with milk. She and Ruthie sat close together on the log. Ruthie held the eye dropper, biting her lower lip. She begged her little Henry to drink. Joel watched their faces, so serious in concentration and concern for a silly squirrel. He stared at Ruthie. She was a pretty girl with her blonde wavey hair, but his eyes moved to Hazel, and he couldn't take them off her. She smiled as Henry took a sip. For sisters, they were so different. Hazel's long hair fell over her shoulders and her long eyelashes seemed to touch her fire-flushed cheeks.

Hazel must have felt his eyes on her because she looked at him. Their eyes locked and Joel's stomach lurched. He diverted his eyes toward the fire and poked it hard with the stick he was holding. He felt his body grow hotter. He couldn't bring himself to look and see if she was still staring at him. He had to get away. He needed to put some space between him and the girls. He popped up from the ground and dusted his jeans off. Ruthie and Hazel's heads jerked up to look at him.

"I'm gonna go find some sticks to roast the marshmallows," he said, turning and trudging into the woods. He didn't even wait for them to reply.

Chapter 12

RUTHIE, FEBRUARY 1957

Ruthie pressed her nose against the cold, frosted window and shivered. Snow covered the ground in huge white sheets and long, pointy icicles hung from the roof like sharp daggers. Ruthie touched her chest. Ms. Faye had sewn some pockets into the front of several of Ruthie's outside dresses and shirts. Henry lay sleeping curled up inside it. He had really grown, but he was still small for a squirrel, or that's what Joel said. Ruthie thought Henry was perfect.

Ruthie heard the pots and pans banging in the kitchen. Her wide smile reflected back toward her. She loved when it snowed. Daddy couldn't go to work, and she and Hazel couldn't go to school because there was no way the old buses could make it down the small country roads. Because of all the snow, she'd been stuck inside the house for nearly a week. It was the most snow Ruthie had ever seen, and even though it was beautiful, she was starting to get stir-crazy.

"Breakfast is ready, peanut," Daddy hollered.

She pushed her finger into the pocket on the front of her dress and caressed the top of Henry's soft head before rushing into the kitchen. Daddy laid a plate of pancakes on the table. Butter and syrup dripped down the sides. Ruthie licked her lips. She plopped down in front of the stack, closed her eyes and said a quick prayer because Daddy was watching, then started to dig in. She stuffed a huge bite in her mouth when she noticed there wasn't a plate set out for Hazel. Between pancake puffed cheeks, she asked "Where's Hazel?"

A muscle worked in her father's jaw. "She's not feelin' good. She's in bed resting. Why don't you finish up and bring her a glass of water and this here small pancake to eat?"

Ruthie nodded and stuffed more pancake in her mouth. Yesterday, Hazel was fine. She'd promised to go out and explore with Ruthie today. Ruthie was tired of sitting in the house. She wanted to take Henry outside to look at the snow. She wasn't worried he'd escape from her pocket and run off. She'd been outside more than a few times with him, and he always stayed close to her. When she was finished eating, she pushed away from the table and carried the glass of water and plate to Hazel's room. The door was open, and Hazel lay on the bed, her back facing the door.

"Hazel?" Ruthie walked in and set the plate and water on the small bedside table where Hazel kept her books, notepads, and pencils.

Hazel turned over. Her face was flushed, and she was shivering. She looked at the pancake and water. "I'm not hungry right now."

Ruthie walked to Hazel and placed her lips to her forehead.

"What are you doin?" Hazel asked. She tried to push Ruthie away, but after a few seconds of protesting, her arms dropped back onto the bed limp.

"You have a fever. That's how Margarette Ann's mom said to check. You're burnin' up." Ruthie left the room and went to the kitchen. She got a small towel and ran cool water over it until it was damp. She squeezed the excess liquid out and folded it. Hazel's eyes followed her as she returned to the room and placed the cool cloth on her forehead. Hazel shuttered.

"How's that feel?"

Hazel touched it with her fingers. "Good."

Ruthie picked up the glass of water. She came beside Hazel and held it out for her to take.

"I'm not thirsty," Hazel said, lifting her arm to wave her away but dropping it back down again.

"Margarette Ann's mother is a nurse. She said when you're sick and have a fever, you need to drink water. Now you can either drink this glass or I can pour it down your throat."

Hazel's eyebrows furrowed. "You wouldn't dare."

Ruthie pushed the glass toward Hazel's face. "Would you really like to see if I would dare?"

Hazel started to sit up and Ruthie leaned forward to help her. Hazel smiled when Henry poked his head from Ruthie's front pocket. Hazel petted his head with her fingertips. When she was all the way up, Ruthie placed the glass in Hazel's hands, then put her hands on her hips and waited. She watched Hazel like a hawk, making sure she drank every last drop. When she finished, Ruthie took the glass and sat it back down on the table before helping Hazel lay back down. Ruthie repositioned the cloth on Hazel's forehead.

"Thank you," Hazel whispered.

Ruthie touched her arm. "You need to rest."

Hazel gave her a half grin. "Did you learn that from Margarette Ann's mother too?"

"You betcha."

Ruthie sat on the edge of the bed. It took only a few minutes before she could hear Hazel's gentle snores. It made her happy to take care of Hazel. She slid off the bed trying not to disturb her sister. She tiptoed out of the room and into the living room. Daddy was standing at the sink washing dishes. He turned when he heard her.

"How's your sister?"

Ruthie sat down at the kitchen table. "She's sleeping. Would it be okay if I go out explorin' some without her? I'm tired of bein' stuck inside. It's driving me bonkers."

He chuckled. "It's mighty cold out. You bundle up and don't go far. You understand?"

"Yes, Daddy."

Even though Ruthie was bundled in her old coat, mittens, scarf, and hat, her skin prickled from the nip of the cold weather when she rushed outside. She stretched her scarf over her nose and mouth before stepping off the porch and sinking into the untouched snow. Ruthie started to trudge toward the forest. Each step added a footprint to the trail behind her.

In the forest, the trees were beautiful. Tiny icicles hung from the branches. The trees seemed to shimmer and sparkle under the sunlight like they were full of diamonds. *Oh, I wish Hazel were here to see this.* The scene would probably inspire more of Hazel's fairy-tale stories. The thought of Hazel made Ruthie sigh. She hated that Hazel was sick. A loneliness settled over her and she blinked away tears. She shivered hard and touched her chest, worried she may have shaken Henry, but then she remembered she'd left him at home wrapped warmly in his shoebox bed. Ruthie looked toward the hill where Joel's house sat. A thought made her smile, clearing out all the loneliness she felt. She knew exactly what she'd do, she'd go get Joel. Together they could build a snowman outside Hazel's window. Hazel would see it and feel better.

She began to make the hike up the slope to the top of the hill. She thought about Daddy and felt a tightening inside her chest. She knew she shouldn't be going up there. Daddy had given her and Hazel strict instructions to never go to Joel's house. She'd asked why, but his face had grown stern. "Do not go to the house on the hill." He had said each word with force. She'd nodded in agreement with his demand, not understanding. But today, she needed Joel's help. She couldn't build the snowman alone. *It's for Hazel. To make her feel better*, she told herself as she began to climb the hill. Still, Ruthie decided not to outright disobey Daddy. She wouldn't go near the house or even inside it. If she saw Joel out in the yard, she'd ask him to come help her, and if she couldn't see him, she'd turn around and go home. She considered what she'd do if he wasn't in the front yard. *Yelling for him a good ways away wouldn't hurt anything*, she decided.

As she marched up the hill, her toes began to feel stiff inside her boots. The snow was deeper the higher she went. Some snow fell into her boots, wetting her wool socks. She bent to clear some loose snow that had fallen inside before it could melt when a huge explosion sent her falling backwards. The quiet forest around her came alive. Trees shook as terrified birds scattered and took flight. Ruthie's heart danced in her chest, but her body wouldn't move. A man was yelling.

"Get back here you maggot! I'm gonna kill you!"

Another loud explosion made Ruthie's insides quiver, and she was afraid she might lose her bladder. She wished she could bury her whole body in the snow. Her eyes darted to the left and right as a third blast echoed through the trees. She spotted a large log lying on its side. She scrambled on wet knees to hide behind it. When she got to it, she gasped. Joel sat behind it. His breath coming out in fast, white puffs of air. The side of his face was swollen. His red eye was almost completely shut.

He grabbed her, pulling her close to him. She opened her mouth to scream, but he clamped a cold hand across her mouth. "Shh, please," he whispered. He held her close. His body shivered against hers. Ruthie noticed his bare arms were pink. *He needs a coat. Where's his coat?*

Her thoughts splintered and her breath caught in her throat. The crunching footsteps were growing closer and louder.

"I know you're here boy. Come out and face your pa."

Ruthie's nose caught a hint of something sour. It made her stomach turn. She looked at Joel and saw his eyes were wide. They huddled together. Their bodies going ridged. Ruthie squeezed her eyes closed, wishing she would have stayed home with Hazel. She sat there with her eyes closed for what felt like an eternity. When the footsteps grew fainter, she felt Joel shudder. She let out a huge sigh and opened her eyes. She turned to Joel.

"What's happening? Is that your pa?" she whispered.

Joel nodded his head. "He lost his job today."

"But he's shootin' at you."

Joel closed his good eye. "I cost too much money. He doesn't think right when he's been drinkin'."

Ruthie could feel her mouth agape. She closed it, taking in Joel's wet jeans and short-sleeve shirt. He wasn't wearing shoes, just white socks.

"You can't stay out here like this. It's cold." She looked around, "And you can't go home."

Joel shook his head in agreement. "I can't go home. Not right now."

Ruthie listened, straining to hear if Joel's pa was nearby, but she couldn't hear anything over the beating of her own heart. "Come to my house. You'll be safe there."

She started to move, but Joel grabbed her arm. "Let's stay a few more minutes." His teeth chattered when he spoke. "Just to be safe."

Ruthie looked at his wounded face and agreed. *What kind of father would be so cruel?*

Ruthie had never been so happy to be inside of her own home. Daddy took Joel to his bedroom to talk, but before he closed the door, he'd asked Ruthie to warm some hot cocoa for her and Joel.

"We won't be long, peanut. I need to get Joel something warm to wear."

She nodded and began to gather the hot cocoa ingredients. She measured them and added them to a pot on the stove. She twisted her head while she mixed and measured. Daddy's door had been closed for a long while. When she could take it no longer, she tiptoed to the door and leaned an ear to it. All she could hear were their muffled voices. Then there was nothing but quiet, and the doorknob began to turn. Ruthie's heart leaped into her chest, and she bolted to the kitchen. She grabbed the huge wooden spoon and quickly returned to stirring the Baker's Cocoa, sugar, vanilla, and milk mixture that bubbled in the pot.

Daddy came out of the room first. He narrowed his eyes at Ruthie like he'd suspected what she'd been up to. Ruthie smiled. "The hot cocoa is almost ready."

"Well, put some in a mug for me too."

He and Joel took a seat at the table. They watched Ruthie as she carefully poured the hot mixture into mugs. Daddy folded his hands. "Joel's going to be staying with us for a while. So, when we're done can you pull out the old quilts for him and lay them on the couch?"

Ruthie nodded. A spark of excitement filled her. It was going to be like a sleepover, a real sleepover. As she sat a warm mug in front of Joel, their eyes met. His swollen eye barely opened. She bit her lip. Her excitement shriveled up like a leaf baking in the hot sun, and she began to worry. *What if Joel's pa came lookin' for him?*

Later that night, Ruthie snuck into Daddy's bedroom and crawled into bed with him. She sat on her knees on the mattress beside him.

"Daddy?" she whispered, touching his shoulder and giving it a jiggle.

He moaned and rubbed his eyes. He leaned up on an elbow. "Peanut, that you?"

"Yes," she whispered. "It's me."

"You, okay? Did you have a bad dream?" he asked, his voice thick with sleep.

"What if Joel's pa comes lookin' for him at our house and he has his gun with him?" She shivered, thinking about it.

Her father stroked her blonde curly hair. "His pa knows he's here."

A cold, prickling sensation ran down her spine, "He does?"

He patted the bed beside him. She hurried and shimmied under the blankets, pulling them to her chin. She felt his warm skin next to her, but it didn't comfort her.

"I went and spoke to him. He knows Joel is here, but he won't come here and bother us."

"How do you know?" she said, wanting to bury her head under the blankets so Joel's pa wouldn't find her.

"I just know. I've known Mr. Davenport for a very long time. He won't bother us, but if it will make you feel better, you can sleep in here tonight. But no snoring."

Ruthie giggled. "I don't snore, you do."

"Oh yeah, now go to sleep. You're keeping me up."

Ruthie snuggled deeper into the bed and closer to her father's warmth. In no time, her eyelids felt heavy, and the world went black.

Chapter 13

HAZEL, JULY 4, 1957

The crowd pressed around Hazel. A young boy sitting on his father's shoulders swung his foot and kicked her arm. The boy didn't notice what he'd done. His head turned to watch the street, intently waiting for the huge Fourth of July parade. Hazel rubbed her arm and scowled.

"I can't see," Ruthie said, jumping up and down beside her.

Hazel could hear the firetruck sirens blaring in the distance.

"I can't see! And it's starting," Ruthie whined.

Joel tugged on Hazel's arm. She turned.

"Look," he pointed to a raised brick flower bed in front of the Crutchfield Bakery. "We can sit on the ledge."

Hazel grabbed Ruthie's hand and gripped the back of Joel's shirt as they weaved their way through the thick crowd. The smell of cotton candy and hot roasted peanuts filled the air, making her stomach growl.

"Snacks for sale. Get your snacks here," a man called out.

The ten cents in her skirt pocket felt like it was burning a hole, but she didn't dare let go of Joel's shirt or Ruthie's hand. Hazel's hands were slick with sweat. It was hard to keep hold of Ruthie as she twisted and turned in excitement. Hazel gripped Joel's shirt tighter, wrinkling it in her fist.

When they finally made it to the flowerbed, she wiped her hand on her skirt front and lifted her chin to survey the brick ledge. Up close, she realized it was much higher than she'd thought and there was no way for her and Ruthie to climb up it in their skirts. Her grandmother's voice played in her head, "Decent ladies would never do such a thing."

The firetruck siren grew louder, and she bit her bottom lip. She turned to survey the crowd in front of her. There was no way to make it back near the street between the hundreds of bodies smooshed together. They'd end up missing the whole parade if they tried.

"I'll help ya," Joel said, as if he could read her mind. He grabbed Ruthie around the waist and hoisted her into the air. She giggled and plopped down on the ledge. She quickly pulled her skirt over her knees. Sitting high on the ledge, she began to swing her saddle shoes. Their new, polished white leather glistened in the sun. They'd recently purchased them from Ackmon's Department Store in Fort

Smith. Ms. Faye had taken them shopping for new clothes. It had been their daddy's idea.

"Daddy and Ms. Faye sitting in a tree," Ruthie had sung when he'd suggested the trip.

He chuckled. "Now don't you be singin' your song around Ms. Faye, or she may turn around and bring you back without letting you buy anything."

Hazel didn't care if Daddy and Ms. Faye were sweet on each other. She liked Ms. Faye. She'd helped her pick the wonderful blue dress Hazel was wearing. She looked down at the new material. It was wrinkled and splotched. Hazel felt heavy sweat drops run down her back, and she wished she'd had saved her pretty dress for another occasion.

"You can see everything up here," Ruthie yelled.

Joel turned to Hazel, "Your turn?"

Hazel felt a lump in her throat as she swallowed. His closeness was unnerving. She remembered how he'd slept on her sofa for a couple of weeks during the winter. One side of his face bruised. She remembered how no one really talked about it. She'd cooked the meals, and he'd helped her in the kitchen. She shivered as she thought about the first morning he was there, their hands brushing against each other as they both reached for the cast iron skillet to cook some bacon. Her heart had hurt for him because he was in pain, but those weeks were the most uncomfortable she'd ever felt in her own home. The day after her thirteenth birthday, she'd heard him and Daddy whispering about hiding a gun and Daddy told him he could stay, and she thought Daddy meant for forever. But he didn't. Joel left the next day, saying he didn't want to impose any longer. Ruthie had begged him not to go. She latched on to his arm, but he gently shook her off as he headed out the door.

"I'll be fine," he'd said.

Joel cleared his throat. "I can help you get up there, if ya want." His voice brought her back to the present, shaking her memories away. His head was cocked to the side, a silly grin on his face. She felt a flood of heat pass through her.

"Oh, I don't know. It's so high."

"Don't be a party pooper," Ruthie yelled down from the ledge.

Hazel clenched her hands into fists. Ruthie was always embarrassing her around Joel. She swallowed down what she wanted to say. She turned toward the brick flowerbed so she wouldn't have to face him. "Fine, help me up," she said. Her stomach twisted into a knot when she felt Joel slide his fingers around her waist. She sucked in a breath when his grip tightened around her, and then she felt herself lifting into the air. Her bare knees scraped against the brick. She didn't complain. She used her hands to help twist herself into a sitting position on top of the flat surface. She moved to make sure she was stable then pulled her skirt down like Ruthie did to cover her knees.

Joel hoisted himself effortlessly through the air, plopping down in between her and Ruthie. Hazel tensed when his arm grazed hers. Her skin seemed to tingle at the touch. Hazel mentally kicked herself. *I'm so lame. What's wrong with me? It's just Joel.*

"What you think?" he asked.

"Oh, it's a swell spot," she said. "Thank you for finding it."

He smiled and she felt her cheeks grow hot. She looked down at her skirt and dusted off dirt that wasn't there.

The firetruck sirens blared. Everyone's heads spun to the right in anticipation. Hazel could see the bright red truck. It was nearly to Hal's Service Center.

She looked back over at Joel and Ruthie. Joel leaned over and said something to Ruthie that Hazel couldn't hear. Ruthie's head whipped back as she laughed. Hazel felt a burning in her chest as she noticed Joel was different now. He'd changed a lot since they'd met four years ago. He went from a scrawny, scared boy in the forest to a tall, broad-shoulder teenager with a hint of scruff on his chin. He told her next year he was going to play football. He wanted to be a Waldron Bulldog. She had no doubt he'd be good at it. He'd start hanging around the popular crowd, and she knew she'd see even less of him. Before she could dwell on why seeing less of Joel made her feel empty inside, Ruthie began to squeal and clap.

"Look! It's coming!"

The town's firetruck passed slowly by. Men hung off the sides and waved to the crowd. Ruthie waved back. Hazel couldn't help but smile. After the firetruck had gone, the homemade floats began. A shiny blue pick-up truck pulled a flat-bed trailer with the Fourth of July queen. She sat on a wooden throne covered in blue, red, and white crepe flowers. There were so many paper flowers, they seemed to cascade from the throne like a waterfall. Hazel thought the queen looked like a fairy princess. She wished she had paper to write down all the details from the queen's beautiful dress to the way her crown sparkled in the sun. Hazel didn't want to forget a single one.

"Whoa! Look at that nifty Ford F100," Joel said, pointing to the blue pick-up truck pulling the queen's float. "I'm gonna have one of them one day."

"Will you give me a ride?" Ruthie asked.

Joel flashed her a huge grin, "Sure will! It'd be a blast."

Ruthie laughed. *She's floating on cloud nine.* The queen waved at the crowd with a regal open hand wave. Ruthie put her palm in the air, mimicking the wave.

Other floats slowly rolled by filled with people waving and throwing candy to the crowd. Young children ran into the roadway, scooping up the pieces. Hazel's favorite float was the one covered in huge exploding firecrackers made from cardboard boxes stacked high. The firecrackers were painted red with white smoke pouring from them. After the float had passed, the Scott County Woman's Coalition, dressed identically in long red dresses with white belts and a string of white pearls, marched by holding a banner with their name printed in black block letters.

"Oh! I just love their dresses!" Ruthie exclaimed. "When I grow up, I'm gonna join the Woman's Coalition so I can wear a red dress and pearls and walk in the parade."

"They wear green dresses during the Christmas parade," Hazel pointed out.

"I just love them!" Ruthie said, laying her hands across her chest.

Joel rolled his eyes. "Girls!"

Hazel covered her mouth to hide her giggle.

As the women walked past, Hazel lifted her chin. The cloudless sky offered no relief from the bright rays. The top of her head felt hot to the touch, and she wiped her sweaty forehead with her hand. She noticed many women in the crowd were waving paper fans to cool themselves. She wished she had one too.

"I hear them!" Ruthie said, wiggling on the ledge. Hazel couldn't see them, but she could already feel the drumbeats thumping in her chest.

"Can you see him yet?" Ruthie shouted over the noise.

Hazel shook her head. Joel leaned closer to her, so he could talk to her without shouting. Hazel's stomach flip-flopped.

"How long was your dad in the war?" he asked.

"Um, maybe a year," she said, hoping he didn't notice the anxious hitch in her voice. "He got shot on some island." The closeness of his face to hers made her thoughts a jumbled mess as she tried to remember exactly what Daddy had told her and Ruthie. "He said he gave part of his liver and a kidney to the war. And he wants it back."

Joel snorted and laughed. Hazel felt light-headed.

Ruthie leaned over to join in the conversation. "He met Mama when he got back home. They got married quick, and then, surprise! Hazel was here." She giggled.

Joel flashed Hazel a grin and she quickly looked down at her lap to dust off more imaginary dirt.

"I see him!" Ruthie yelled and pointed to the street.

Hazel's head shot up and she followed Ruthie's finger. *I see him too!*

Daddy was marching up the street dressed in his old World War II uniform. Other soldiers in various uniforms marched beside him, all behind boys beating drums in a rhythmic beat. Hazel noticed that a few men wore the same uniform as her father. Each man's uniform looked like they'd seen better days. Some fit snuggly, and others hung haphazardly on the men's frames. The buttons of Daddy's uniform pulled a little taut near his midsection, but overall, it still fit nicely. *He looks so handsome.*

Ruthie waved wildly. "Daddy! Daddy!"

He looked toward the area where they were sitting. Hazel saw his face light up when he found them. He gave a small wave before turning his head and donning a serious marching face. Hazel felt pride soar inside her. Her eyes followed Daddy as he marched with the veterans until he was a tiny dot down the street. A blare of trumpets from the high school marching band made her turn her head back to the parade.

"I love the majorettes," Ruthie yelled.

The majorettes danced and twirled their silver batons. The head majorette threw her baton in the air. Hazel watched it glint and twist in the air before she caught it with one fast swoop of her hand. She tossed it in the air again, higher into the sky. Hazel followed it, squinting as sunlight reflected off the metal handle. Before the baton hit the majorette's hand, Hazel saw a glimpse of her mother in the crowd across the street. She blinked. Her heart felt like it stopped beating. Her eyes scanned the crowd again, but she couldn't see her. *It wasn't her. It couldn't be her.* Hazel shook her head. *No*, she told herself, but she'd recognize that smile anywhere. *It was Mama!*

"Down."

"What?" Joel said a little too loudly beside her. His eyes glued to the parade.

"I need to get down now!" she yelled.

He finally turned his head to look at her. His eyebrows pulled together. "Okay, I'll help you." He leaped down from the ledge and turned, taking Hazel's hands.

She hardly felt his touch as she jumped down. She pushed his hands away from her.

"Hazel, where are you going?" Ruthie called.

"I saw her!"

"Saw who?"

"I saw Mama." She had no time for explanations.

"But grandmother said she's in California."

"It was her," Hazel said not waiting for Ruthie to respond. She turned and began pushing her way through the bodies of people cheering and waving. She pressed into the crowd chin to chest, using her elbows. Grunts and grumbles filled her ears.

"Hey, watch it," someone said, but she didn't stop to apologize. She kept pushing her way through the crowd of bodies. When she finally made it to the street, she felt like she couldn't breathe. Too much time had passed, she had to get across the street. With only the thoughts of her mother filling her mind, she ran into the road. A loud horn honked, making Hazel scream.

"Get out of the street girl!" an angry man pulling a float yelled.

"Sorry. Sorry," she said, holding up her hands as if in surrender.

People muttered for her to move it along and to get out of the street, but she didn't listen. Her leg jiggled as she waited for the float to pass. Once she could move behind it safely, she bolted to the sidewalk. She threw herself into the crowd. She stood on tiptoes. Her eyes scanned the area, but she couldn't find her mother. Her stomach began to hurt. A huge sweat drop ran down the side of her face. The heat from the sun and the bodies pressing around her made her dizzy. Tears began to sting her eyes. *It was her. It had to be her.* She looked at each face around her, searching for her mother's face, searching for the face she'd been praying to see again.

"Mama," she sobbed. "Mama."

She began to maneuver her way around the cramped bodies until she reached Goodman's Soda Shop. She felt lost even though she knew exactly where she was. Through the huge glass window, she could see Goodman's was empty of patrons. Everyone was outside watching the parade. She pressed her back against the glass window. The heat from the pane soaked through the thin material of her blue dress. Colorful words written in block letters announced a new bubblegum flavor. Despite the crowd, she felt alone. She slid to the hot cement and sat with her head in her hands. It felt like her mother had left her all over again. Hazel began to doubt herself. Doubt what she'd seen. *Mama's in California like grandmother said. She's having fun under palm trees and on sandy beaches. Fun without me.* Anytime Hazel attempted to ask Grandmother about her mama, she'd shake her head and say, "No more questions about it. I've told you time and time again, she's gone to California, and she won't be comin' back." For the first time, Hazel let that reality sink deep into her heart. It was time for her to accept it. She'd never see her mother again.

"Hazel?"

Hazel wiped her eyes with her forearm. She titled her head up. A shadow covered Daddy's face, and she couldn't read his expression. He held out a hand. Her head dropped.

"Come on girl. Get up. You're gonna get trampled."

"But I ruined your parade."

Daddy's laugh was big and hearty. It made the buttons near the midsection of his uniform pull even tighter. She lifted her head, and he stuck his hand out closer to her.

"It's not my parade, and you didn't ruin anything. I see your sister and Joel comin'. Come on, wipe your face and let me buy my girl some ice cream."

She wondered if she should tell him what she'd thought she'd seen. The hand in front of her was calloused and creased from hand work. She grasped it, letting its strength pull her up. She decided to bottle up her past. Her mother was gone, but he was here. She straightened the skirt of her dress with her hand and ran an arm across her face to clear away any dried tears. Daddy wrapped his arm around her shoulder and pulled her close.

Before Ruthie and Joel made it to them, he whispered in her ear. "I love you, girl."

Chapter 14

HAZEL, MAY 1958

Hazel walked down the school hallway with an arm full of library books. Two rows of silver lockers extended down the beige walls. Above the lockers were huge black and white photographs of the graduating classes going back to 1910. Balancing the stack of books in her left hand, she opened the latch of her locker with her right. She pushed the heavy novels into the crowded space. She smiled, thinking about all the years of Mrs. Honeycutt's kindness. How every year since fifth grade, Mrs. Honeycutt would allow Hazel to check out as many books as she wanted, way above the library's three-book limit. Then she'd allow her to keep them for the entire summer break. The end of a school year always made Hazel feel sad, except on the day she got to choose her summer books. She straightened her summer selection in her locker, running her fingers along the spines and making mental notes of which ones she wanted to read first.

The class bell sounded its long, high-pitch clang, and the hallway began to fill with students. Hazel sighed, wishing she could open one right now and read a chapter or two.

"I gotta say, Hazel, if you keep staring at those books, people around here are gonna begin to think you're a wet rag."

Hazel shook her head. Alice swayed toward her and leaned against the lockers. Alice wore a long plaid skirt and a fitted black button up shirt. A cream headband pushed her dark brown hair back, but her bangs fell perfectly across her forehead, just above her eyebrows. Her blue eyes were bright as Hazel scowled at her.

Alice had been her best friend for as long as she could remember. Even when they were little, Alice had always given Hazel a hard time about keeping her nose in a book. Alice wanted to do and see things. Hazel liked to write and dream.

"Just because I like to read doesn't make me a wet rag. It makes me smart."

Alice flashed a wild grin while she leaned close to Hazel conspiratorially and whispered, "Did you hear they put out the list of boys who made the football team already?"

"Already? I thought they did that during the summer." Hazel felt her heartbeat pick up. She knew Joel was planning on trying out now that he was old enough. He'd said as much the last time she saw him, but that was a while ago. Surely he wouldn't have changed his mind.

She wanted to ask Alice if Joel had made it, but the words wouldn't come out, so she bit her lip and listened as Alice continued talking.

"I heard they did tryouts early this year. Going to start having the new players learn plays and drills before summer practices begin. I heard they believe we've got a really good chance of beating Booneville."

Hazel narrowed her eyes. "Where are you getting your information from?"

Alice giggled and shrugged, "Around."

Hazel rolled her eyes. She had no doubt the information Alice was hearing came from Nancy Graham, the biggest mouth around. Hazel slammed her locker shut. Alice took her arm and pulled her close as they walked down the hall to their typing class. She leaned closer, speaking in a low tone, "I heard Joel made the team."

Hazel's heart pounded in her chest, and she blinked. She tried to keep her face straight. "Oh?" she said, forcing herself to sound casual. She hoped Alice wouldn't read anything in her tone.

Alice nodded, "Yep, I have it on good authority that he made the team."

Hazel felt a hard ball form in the pit of her stomach. She couldn't understand why she didn't feel comfortable confiding in Alice, her best friend. They told each other everything, and she longed to tell her about the strange feelings she had when Joel was around. How her whole body grew hotter, and her stomach turned itself in knots when he looked at her, but she was too afraid. Afraid Alice would read too much into it and think Hazel was sweet on Joel. And she wasn't. Or at least, she didn't think she was. Everything was so confusing right now. *Joel's my friend. We are just friends.* Hazel cleared her throat, "Well, that's good news."

Alice whistled a low sound, "Have you seen him lately? I know he used to hang around with you from time to time."

"Who? Joel?" Hazel swallowed hard.

Alice gave her a wicked smile and nudged her with her hip. "Yes, of course Joel!"

Hazel shook her head, "Not really. Well, not lately anyhow. I'm not sure what he's been up to." And that was true. Of course, occasionally, he'd show up to the house on the weekend when Daddy was home and ate dinner with them. Still, even then, he never really stayed for long. She wondered if he'd outgrown her and Ruthie. If he'd rather hang out with his buddies instead of two silly girls.

Alice sighed. "Well, that's too bad, because let me tell you, that boy is lookin' good. Turning into a real dream boat, he is."

Hazel felt her face flush.

Alice lowered her voice, "I hear Nancy is really head over heels for him. She's practically falling over her feet to get him to ask her out on a date. I guess they would make the perfect pair. He's a football boy now, and she's bound to wind up being the head paper shaker one day."

Hazel's insides turned to acid. A burning feeling rose in her chest. Her mind swirled with madness. She wanted to pull Nancy's blonde ponytail out of her head. She shook her head. *What is wrong with me?*

Alice released Hazel's arm as they walked through the open door of their typing class. Hazel stomped to her desk and plopped down in front of her Royal Quiet Deluxe typewriter in light pink. Alice sat in front of an eggshell-blue one beside her. Alice leaned over and poked her side. Hazel jolted.

"Hey, what's eating at you?" she asked. "You look like you swallowed a bee."

Hazel felt her cheeks grow hotter. She shrugged. "I just don't want Nancy leading Joel on and usin' him. You know how she is."

Alice chuckled, "I'm sure Joel can take care of himself. I'm not so sure he'd care if Nancy used him. I saw him eyeing her yesterday at lunch."

Hazel's stomach dropped. She could barely process what she'd heard. "H-he was eyeing her?" she stammered.

Alice nodded as the teacher walked to the front of the class, hushing the students. Hazel could barely hear what the teacher said as she directed the class to turn to page twenty and begin. In a daze, Hazel flipped through the book propped beside her on a small stand. The letters blurred together as she felt her eyes begin to fill with tears. *Why do I care if Joel was eyeing Nancy? What does it matter to me?* But for some reason, she realized, it did matter. Her feelings were a jangled mess. She tried to concentrate on her typing, but her accuracy was way off. Her fingers felt like stiff tree limbs as she fumbled over the keys. She sucked in a sharp breath and paused. Her hands resting on the keys.

In her mind, Hazel pictured Nancy in her tight hot-pink sweater, her red lips pouting as she clung to Joel's arm. In an instant, Hazel's confusion and sadness transformed into something red-hot and fuming. She needed to put blame where blame lied. It was Joel's fault she felt like this. If it wasn't for him being so nice to her or always looking at her then turning his head, she wouldn't have these strange feelings. She flipped to the next page in the book a little too hard, making it rock on the stand. Alice looked over at her, but Hazel narrowed her eyes. Her focus landed on the typewriter in front of her. *This was all Joel's doin'*. She hoped he got what he deserved. As far as she was concerned, Nancy and Joel were perfect for each other. Hazel bent over the keyboard. A newfound blaze ignited her fingers, and with a click and clatter, little black typeset letters began to soar across her typing paper.

Chapter 15

Ruthie, December 1958

"Are they here yet?" Ruthie said running to the window. She pulled the floral curtains to the side. Her leg jiggled as she stared into the darkness.

"Why are you so excited?" It's just the Sutherlands?" Daddy chuckled.

"Maybe Mrs. Anne will teach me some things too."

"Ruthie," Daddy said, pulling the small ham out of the oven and setting it on the top burners. "You are too young to wear makeup. Mrs. Anne is helpin' your sister."

Ruthie felt anger boil inside her. She watched him pick up the baster and fill it. He slowly squeezed the juice over the pink meat. He leaned over, taking in the smell of roasted ham. She folded her arms in front of her, but her stomach growled. It didn't matter how angry she was, she could always eat, and she was plain starving right now. She tried not to pout. Pouting was for babies, and she was too old for that. Still, she couldn't shake the whine in her voice. "I'm nearly a teenager! Hazel's only two years older than me!"

She looked at Hazel, hoping to get some help convincing him, but Hazel said nothing. *Of course.* Ruthie rolled her eyes. Hazel continued setting out the fancy porcelain dishes they never used, not since Mama had left. Hazel loved the pink painted roses on the edge of the plates. When they were little, Hazel thought Mama would come back for the dishes one day.

"She has to come back. She wouldn't leave something so valuable."

Ruthie had put her hands on her hips and shouted, "She left me and you too! Aren't we worth more than some plates?"

Ruthie hated those plates. She hated anything that reminded her of her mother. It should be Mama teaching them things like how to put on makeup, even though Mrs. Anne was kind to fill in the gap she left. *Mrs. Anne would do a better job anyway.*

"Feed Henry and quit poutin'," Daddy said, returning the ham to the oven. "He has to be starving."

Ruthie looked at the top of the floral curtains. Henry sat on the edge of the curtain rod. His little paws passed quickly over his face. Ruthie couldn't help but smile. She felt the tightness inside her loosen. He was adorable. His fluffy brown tail, huge black eyes, and tiny nose.

"Come on down here Henry," she said and made a clicking sound with her tongue. She patted her shoulder. Henry's eyes darted down toward her. His paws washed his face two more times, then he leaped from the curtain to the back of the sofa. He scrambled from the sofa to her leg and climbed up until he was perched on her shoulder. Ruthie giggled when his soft fur tickled her cheek. She reached into her skirt pocket and pulled out a little pecan. His little hand took it from her fingers and began nibbling. He turned the pecan over and over in his tiny paws.

Ruthie's heart leaped when she heard the gravel crunching outside. "They're here!" she squealed, sending Henry leaping from her shoulder. He scurried back to the sofa. His nut tucked safely in his puffed cheek. "Sorry Henry."

Hal and Anne Sutherland entered the house with hands full of goodies. Mr. Hal was still in his uniform, a blue shirt and gray pants, from the garage he owned downtown. The Hal's Service Center patch visible on the right side of his chest. In his grease-stained hands, he held a freshly baked pumpkin pie and peach cobbler. Mrs. Anne was dressed in a sensible long-sleeved wool dress with a brown plaid pattern. Her short, dark bob sat perfectly in place. She was carrying a huge dazzling gift bag covered in red and green shiny ornaments. Ruthie's heart raced. She was dying to see what was in the sparkling bag.

Daddy hurried to Mr. Hal and took the peach cobbler from him.

"It sure smells good in here," Mr. Hal said, sniffing loudly. He followed Daddy and sat the pie on the kitchen counter. "When do we eat?"

Mrs. Anne chuckled, "Dear, you had a snack before we left."

Mr. Hal gave Daddy a toothy grin and they shook hands.

"The ham is nearly finished. Would you like some coffee while we wait?" Daddy gave Ruthie and Hazel a head nod and they headed to the kitchen to brew the coffee.

"Coffee would be lovely," Mrs. Anne replied, before her husband could comment.

While Ruthie and Hazel worked in the kitchen, the grown-ups moved into the living room. Ruthie watched Mrs. Anne sit on the sofa. She sat the bag near her feet. Hazel began to boil the water, and Ruthie slid the tin coffee can toward Hazel.

"What do you think is in the gift bag?" she whispered.

Hazel shook her head. "I don't know, but I'm dyin' to see."

When the coffee was ready, Hazel pushed two mugs toward Ruthie. "Can you give Mr. and Mrs. Sutherland theirs? I'll hand Daddy his," she directed.

Ruthie smiled when she saw the light blue coffee mugs. Daddy had bought them in Arizona one week at work. He'd found them at a small coffee shop. He told her and Hazel, he'd bought them because the color reminded him of the sky back home. Hazel had asked, "Isn't all the sky the same color?"

He'd laughed and said, "Nothing is better than the little patch of sky over your own home."

She and Hazel walked carefully into the living room, trying not to let the hot brown liquid slosh out of the mugs. She handed the mugs to Mr. and Mrs. Sutherland.

"I just love your Christmas tree," Mrs. Anne commented as she blew on the coffee to cool it.

"Thank you! Daddy cut it last week and we popped popcorn all day to string up."

Hazel giggled, "It took us all day because we ate so much of it."

They all laughed, and Hazel blushed.

"Ya'll girls are a gas," Mr. Hal said, taking a huge swig of coffee. "So, Ruthie, where's that squirrel of yours? I told Anne all about it."

Ruthie looked around the living room. She scrunched her nose when she couldn't spot where Henry was hiding. She clicked her tongue. "Henry. Come here, Henry."

Henry bolted from her and Hazel's bedroom. He scurried up her leg until he was perched on his favorite place, her shoulder. He burrowed under her blonde hair. "He's shy." She explained as she took a pecan from her pocket and held it out so Henry could take it.

He swiped it from her hand.

"Well, I'll be," Mrs. Anne said. "He's adorable. And I love his name."

Ruthie smiled and leaned her face toward Henry. His head popped out from under her hair, and he rubbed his furry head against her cheek. She handed him another pecan.

"How long do you think till the ham is ready?" Mrs. Anne asked.

Daddy looked at his wristwatch. "Maybe a little less than an hour. Faye should be here around that time too."

Mrs. Anne stood up, flattening her dress. "Good. Hazel lets go into your room. I've got some things I want to show you," she said and bent over to pick up the shiny gift bag. She looked at Ruthie. "Why don't you come too? I got a few things for you as well."

It was all Ruthie could do not to leap up and run to the bedroom. Inside the room, Mrs. Anne asked Ruthie to shut the bedroom door because this was "women's time." Ruthie's heart tip-tapped in her chest. No one had ever called her a woman before. Mrs. Anne set the gift bag on the end of the bed. Hazel and Ruthie sat on the pillows and watched wide-eyed as Mrs. Anne began to remove things one by one and lay them on the end of the bed.

"Now, Avon is the best brand out there," she said in an informative tone. "Believe me girls, I've tried lots of different brands, and Avon is by far the best."

She began to pick up items she'd set on the bed and hold them out for Ruthie and Hazel to see. "You've got your skin freshener. You want to use this every night after you wash your face. Oh! And this here's moisturizing cleansing cream. It will help smooth out your wrinkles." She looked at the girls and pursed her lips. "Although, you don't really need to worry about that right now. And here's face powder." She opened the small compact and held it so they could see the mirror inside. "You can slip this in your purse. This mirror helps so you can look at yourself while you freshen up."

The compact mirror cast a small circular reflection of light onto Hazel's forehead. Ruthie giggled.

Mrs. Anne touched each item on the bed and listed off what they were. "I've got fingernail polish, mascara, blush, lip liner, eyeshadows, lipsticks." Her voice trailed off. She stared at the gift bag. "Your dad made me promise to not put you in red lipstick. So, I brought these." She rustled in the bag and took out two more small golden tubes. She held out one for Hazel to take, "Luminous Pink," she called it, then gave Ruthie the other tube, "Hot Coral."

Ruthie's hands almost shook as she took off the golden case and twisted the lipstick until the colorful stick rose out of it. She stared at it in awe.

"Now Ruthie," Mrs. Anne said, taking the lipstick from her hands and twisting it down to slip the golden case back over it. "Your daddy said you're too young for makeup right now."

Ruthie felt the air leave her lungs. Her chest deflated as she watched Mrs. Anne return the lipstick she was holding to its place on the end of the bed. She opened her mouth to protest, but Mrs. Anne held up her finger and quickly glanced at the shut bedroom door. She turned back to the girls and whispered. "But I can keep a secret if you girls can."

Ruthie almost yipped in excitement. She looked at Hazel who sat wide-eyed. *A secret from Daddy? What a scandal!* They both looked at Mrs. Anne and nodded.

"Good, don't tell your daddy." She looked straight at Ruthie. "But I brought you some light pink blush and lip gloss. It's not lipstick." She opened it. "But it does have a little hint of color."

Ruthie's heart soared. Her very own makeup. She greedily took the items Mrs. Anne held out. They felt like precious gold in her hands. Hazel looped an arm around Ruthie's shoulder and hugged her. Ruthie couldn't wait to show Margarette Ann. She was going to die of jealousy!

Mrs. Anne showed Hazel how to expertly apply her makeup. Ruthie closely watched each move of the wand or flick of the brush along the cheek. She wanted to know exactly what to do when she got old enough for her own blush and lipstick. Hazel bit her lip as she tried to apply the mascara with a steady hand. She dropped the mascara stick, and it hit her face, leaving a long black smear. Ruthie laughed so hard she thought she might be sick. Hazel and Mrs. Anne laughed too.

It felt like no time had passed when a knock at the bedroom door made them jump.

Daddy opened the door a crack. "Dinner's ready, girls."

Mrs. Anne told Hazel to wait. She wanted to announce her, so she could make a grand entrance to show off her beautiful face. Ruthie walked out of the room and was surprised to see Joel sitting on the sofa. He smiled, a Coke bottle in his hand. She rushed to him and plopped down on the sofa.

"What ya doing here?" she said then slapped his arm.

"Ouch!" he said and rubbed his arm. "What's that for?"

"It's been too long since you've come by. I was missin' you."

Joel's smile was easy. "I've been busy with football. Your dad asked me to come last week. Said he wanted to introduce me to his friend, Mr. Hal."

Ruthie opened her mouth to ask Joel another question, but she was interrupted as Mrs. Anne made her big announcement. "Now introducing the sweet and beautiful Ms. Hazel McKay."

Hazel slowly opened the bedroom door and walked out. Her eyes cast toward the floor.

Daddy cleared his throat, "Well, girl, you sure look mighty pretty."

Hazel looked up through long black eyelashes. Her smile crumbled and her eyes grew wide when they fell on Joel sitting on the sofa. Hazel's face transformed into a bright red globe. Her eyes darted back to the floor. An awkward silence hung thick in the air like summer heat after the rain.

Mrs. Anne coughed, "Doesn't she look beautiful, Hal?"

Mr. Hal stood up, "Yes, so beautiful, and so grown-up."

Joel scrambled to his feet. "Yeah, y-you look mighty nice," he agreed, stumbling over his words.

"Thank you," Hazel whispered, gripping her hands tightly in front of her.

Oh Lordy! Ruthie felt embarrassed, and she wasn't even the one standing in the middle of the room with all eyes on her. She could practically feel the heat radiating from Hazel's red face.

Everyone jumped as the screen door popped shut as Ms. Faye entered the house.

"Sorry I'm late," she said with a worried look on her face.

Daddy hurried to her, taking her purse from her hands to lay it on a small table near the sofa.

"Good to see you, let's eat." He clapped his hands together and quickly shooed everyone to the table.

Ruthie made sure Hazel didn't have to sit beside Joel. She wasn't sure what was going on with her sister. They'd barely seen Joel. She should be happy he was here, but Ruthie didn't think she was. The conversation around the table was filled with talk of football, work, and Christmas.

"I heard that last game against Booneville was a real close one," her father commented to Joel.

"Yeah, we lost by a field goal. I hate when we lose, but I really hate when it's to Booneville."

Everyone laughed.

"Booneville has been a rival of ours since I can remember," Mr. Hal chuckled. "I sure love when the Bulldogs have those Bearcats for lunch."

Everyone nodded their heads in agreement.

"I wanna be a cheerleader one day," Ruthie said, wanting to join in the conversation.

Daddy's eyebrows furrowed. "A cheerleader? No ma'am. I don't think so."

Mrs. Anne swatted him. "She'd be a lovely cheerleader."

Ruthie smiled at Mrs. Anne. "In two years, I'll be old enough to tryout."

"Well maybe in two years, you'll change your mind," Daddy said, pointing the end of his fork at her.

"I think when Ruthie gets something in her mind, there's no changing it," Joel said and flashed her a quick grin.

Ruthie's heart fluttered. She could feel Hazel shift in her seat beside her.

"So, Joel, you think you want to start this Saturday? You can come after football practice, and I'll start teaching you some basic mechanic skills. When football season is over, you can start work right after school," Mr. Hal said.

"Work?" Hazel whispered.

"Yep, Joel's gonna start working with me at the shop. I could use the extra hand."

Joel looked at Mr. Hal, "I'll work hard. I can promise you that."

"Good, good," Mr. Hal chuckled. "You're gonna need some spending money to pay for all those dates you're gonna get now that you're on the football team. Cheerleaders sure love football players. How do you think I got Anne?"

"Oh Hal."

Mrs. Anne shook her head, and everyone laughed. Everyone except for Hazel.

Chapter 16

Hazel, August 1959

Hazel sat alone under her favorite tree reading a library book. She wiped away the sweat drop that ran down the side of her face. The air surrounding her was thick with heat and moisture. Even the shade of the leaves failed to provide any type of coolness to soothe her hot skin. She wished for a cool breeze, but everything was as still as a dead man in a casket. She stood and brushed the dirt from the back of her damp skirt. She couldn't handle it any longer. She'd go home, strip down to her underwear, and cook on the sofa. She was by herself anyway. Ruthie had gone to Margarette Ann's house and Daddy wouldn't be home until Friday evening.

Hazel ducked under a low hanging limb. As she passed under it, her long brown hair wrapped around a rogue branch. She tugged, but her hair wouldn't come loose. She tugged again. She tried to turn her head to see what was happening, but she couldn't see behind her. She dropped the book on the ground and began to feel with her hands. She felt a tangled knot with a branch sticking out of it. She sighed and began to try to blindly work her hair free.

"Got some trouble there?" Joel said, walking toward her.

She tugged harder on her hair, but it only seemed to make the knotted mess tighten on the tree branch. "Nope, I've got no trouble at all." The back of her neck grew hotter, and she hoped it was because of the sun.

Joel stood in front of her. One eyebrow raised. "It looks like you're stuck."

"I'm not stuck. What are you doing here anyway? Don't you have something with football or work?" She tugged harder on her hair, feeling a dull ache in the back of her head.

Joel watched her. "Nah, we practiced this morning because of the heat, and Mr. Hal gave me the day off. I was coming to visit you girls."

Hazel yanked again, but nothing loosened. "Well, it's just me. Ruthie's at her friend's house."

"Are you sure you don't want any help?"

"No, I don't need any of your help." Hazel gritted her teeth and pulled hard. A sharp pain made her wince. She stopped pulling.

In two steps, Joel was standing so close to her, she could smell the clean scent of his aftershave. *When'd he start wearing aftershave?* Her heartbeat raced under her shirt. She was certain he could see it beating through her skin as he touched the side of her face and gently moved her head to the side. Her cheek tingled where his fingers had been.

"Let me get a look at what's going on," he said, biting the side of his lip and narrowing his eyes.

"I said I don't need any help."

"Sure, you don't. Now be quiet and let me get a look here."

Hazel huffed.

"Whoa, it's really tangled. What did you do?"

"If I knew what I did, I wouldn't have done it," she snipped.

He chuckled. "I could cut it."

Hazel felt all the blood rush from her face and her warm skin went cold. She didn't much care for her looks, except for her hair. Even though Mama had hated her long horsehair, she'd grown to love it. And for as long as she could remember, it had never been cut. She didn't want her first haircut to be at the hands of Joel. "No, please don't." She felt tears start to sting her eyes. "Please don't cut it."

He moved his head to the side to meet her eyes. She tried to avoid his gaze, but her hair pulled, and she grimaced. His sky-blue eyes locked onto her.

"You'd rather stay here? Stuck to this tree, then let me get my pocket knife out and cut your hair?"

She started to nod but remembered the movement would only make things worse. "Yes," she whispered.

He rolled his eyes, "Girls. I don't get it." He said it like he was talking to himself. He touched her face again and positioned it so he could get a better look at the knot.

She stood between his arms. His hands worked behind her head. She felt a small tug here or pull there. Some bringing her closer to him. She saw sweat run from his chin, down his neck, and to his chest until it disappeared under his shirt collar. His breath tickled her ear.

"Almost got it."

A jerk from behind sent her stumbling into him. His arms clasped around her to catch her. She sucked in a sharp breath as he held her close. She stayed there for a moment, feeling his hard body against hers, before she realized she was free. She pushed away from him, her face on fire and her head dizzy. She patted down her damp skirt to straighten it, afraid to meet his eyes.

"Thank you," she said, unsure if the words came out or if she only thought them.

He passed a hand through his hair. "No problem."

She wasn't sure why the next words came out of her mouth. Later, she'd blame the heat. "So, I guess you better be going, Nancy wouldn't take kindly to you hanging out with another girl."

He was silent, but she saw a flicker of something pass across his face. He sighed and in a low tone said, "She's not my girlfriend you know." His throat moved when he swallowed. "I mean, we've went out on a couple dates, but that's it."

She shrugged. Unable to stop herself, she continued, "That's not what she thinks, but what do I care? I don't care if you and Nancy are an item. You deserve each other."

His face twisted and his words came out with heat, "W-well at least, I'm getting out and having fun. You, you," he gestured to her book laying on the ground, "you're just a wet rag."

Her mouth hung agape. "I am not!" the volume of her voice grew louder.

"Yeah, you are! You'd never go out with me even if I asked you, and I'm not going to sit at home and wait on you."

"Wait on me!" She pointed to herself, knowing she should bite her tongue. But something had loosened it more than it had ever been before, and she didn't want to control it. She opened her mouth and words spilled out, "You never asked me to go anywhere with you! You know why? Because you have a reputation to uphold now that you're on the football team. Everybody knows football boys only go out with paper shakers. You don't even hang out with me and Ruthie anymore. It's not because you're too busy. It's because you don't want people to know we're friends. It would damage your precious image." She sucked in a ragged breath and shook her head. "But it doesn't matter, I'd never go out with you. Even if you did ask. Not ever!"

He opened his mouth and shut it. He did it again, like a fish in water releasing bubbles. Hazel folded her arms in front of her and glared at him. Her eyes went blurry as they filled with tears, but she wouldn't cry, not in front of him. Without saying anything else, Joel turned around and walked away.

Chapter 17

Joel, October 1959

"Three, two, one!" the audience counted down. The loud buzzer resonated throughout the stadium. There was a split second of silence where all Joel could hear was the sound of his heartbeat between his ears. Then came the deafening roar from the crowd. It took over, surrounding him, making it hard to process what had just happened. Joel stood up and felt light as a feather. The game was over. He released a long breath and took off his helmet. The cool breeze of the night hit his damp hair, sending chills down his body. He looked up toward the sky. The stadium lights blurred his sight and blocked out any stars in the sky. He couldn't believe it. He saw the cheerleaders running toward them from the sidelines. Nancy Graham leading the way with a huge smile across her bright red lips.

They had won. He felt like he was in a dream. She grabbed him and kissed him on his cheek before moving on to plant more kisses on other players' faces.

Joel was shaken from his daze when a big hand patted him on the back, knocking him forward. "We did it! We won!" Ronnie said, hitting his back harder a second time.

"I can't believe it. We beat the Bearcats!" Joel said still stunned. He turned and grabbed Ronnie's shoulder pads. They jumped up and down. "We beat the Bearcats!" they yelled in each other's faces.

They were engulfed in a crowd of players and cheerleaders. The smell of body odor and sweet perfume sent Joel's head spinning. He could still hear the shouts and whoops of the crowd. The cheering transformed into song as the crowd began to sing the high school's alma mater. It had been over ten years since the Bulldogs beat the Bearcats. Joel knew he wouldn't sleep tonight. His eyes searched the bleachers on the home side for familiar faces. Hazel and Ruthie stood in front of the first row of bleachers near the railing. Ruthie was waving wildly at him, and Hazel was smiling. *A second miracle of the night*, he thought. They hadn't really spoken since the summer. He replayed their encounter in the woods over and over in his head almost every day. The smell of her skin. The heat of her body when she fell into him. The fact that she said she'd never go out with him. But she was smiling, and her eyes were on him. He started to push through the crowd of bodies.

"Where you going?" Ronnie called out.

"Be right back. Need to say hi to some friends."

He grabbed Joel and spun him around. With rough fingers, Ronnie wiped Joel's face with his bear paw of a hand. "You got some leftover red lipstick there." He laughed, "Don't forget Judy's Drive-in."

Joel nodded and thanked him. He put his helmet under his arm and jogged toward the bleachers. Ruthie beamed down at him from above. She leaned over the bleacher rail with her hand outstretched. Joel reached up to touch her hand.

"I just needed to make sure I wasn't dreamin," she said.

Joel understood what she meant. The night felt unreal.

"I can't believe we won! You played great! Even Hazel was jazzed!" Ruthie bumped Hazel with her hip.

Hazel's cheeks and nose were already pink from the cool wind, but he could still see her blush.

"You were great," she said so softly, he almost didn't hear it.

His stomach fluttered and he felt stupid. She was a lost cause. She didn't want to be with him, she'd said so herself. *Never.* "Thanks," he said unable to meet her eyes. "I can't believe we won. I thought we were done when they scored that last-minute touchdown at the end of the third quarter. Their defense was rough. Can't believe we pulled it off."

"Joel, come on!" Ronnie called from the middle of the field.

Joel turned and waved him off. He turned back to Hazel and Ruthie. "Hey, we're going to Judy's Drive-in to celebrate. You know, have hamburgers and milkshakes. Wanna come? I could give ya'll a ride home in Mr. Hal's truck."

Ruthie's face lit up. "Oh! I'd love to!" she squealed.

Hazel looked at Ruthie and glared. "We can't. Alice's mother gave us a ride here." Hazel looked at Joel. "They're waiting for us at the car. We just came to say hi. But we really gotta go."

"Come on Hazel!" Ruthie cried. "We haven't gotten to hang out with Joel in forever! He's been so busy. Alice wouldn't care. Come on, please!"

Hazel shook her head and sighed.

"Just tell Alice's mother we got another ride," Ruthie begged.

Hazel frowned. "No. We better get going. Daddy wouldn't want us to go hangin' out after curfew with a bunch of football boys."

Ruthie crossed her arms and huffed.

Joel felt deflated, but he made himself smile. "Ruthie, I promise once football season is over, I'll come bird watchin' with you. Okay?"

She didn't respond.

"Hazel's right, your dad wouldn't like you girls traipsing around with us football boys without him knowin'. And I sure don't want to get on his bad side. He'll never let me come over again."

Ruthie rolled her eyes. "Fine, but promise you'll come over and visit."

Joel took his finger and made an invisible "X" across his chest. "Cross my heart."

Ruthie and Hazel smiled. Joel felt as light as air. He watched them leave the bleachers and turn the corner to the parking lot. He watched until he couldn't see them anymore.

When Joel turned toward the football field, there were only a few stragglers left on the field. Most of his team had already gone to shower. He began to jog toward the locker room when he heard his name being called.

"Joel, wait up."

He turned to see the assistant coach running toward him.

"Hey, um, I hate to tell you this, but there's been sort of a situation."

Joel's stomach twisted. "Situation?"

"Yeah, with your dad."

Joel squeezed the helmet closer to his side. The bars across the front dug into his side. The assistant coach scratched his stubbled chin.

"He was in some kind of altercation at the Whisky Joint."

Joel's shoulders slumped. The assistant coach continued.

"He was injured and taken to the hospital. He's causing a ruckus there, and they were hopin' you could come get him."

Joel rubbed his arm across his sweaty forehead. He thought about Ronnie and all his friends at Judy's Drive-in, celebrating their big win. He had half a mind to leave his pa at the hospital. The assistant coach must have sensed Joel's hesitation.

"Well, what ya gonna do?"

Joel wanted to scream. He wanted to let his pa suffer, but he knew the hospital folk would be the ones suffering. "I'll go get him," Joel said. He jogged to the locker room, leaving the assistant coach standing in the middle of the field.

In the locker room, he punched his metal locker, leaving a dent the size of his fist. He looked at his knuckles, and small dots of blood rose to the surface of his skin before running in small streams across his hand. This was the last time he helped his low-down stinkin' pa, he vowed to himself. He showered. His anger burned off with the steam of the shower. When he'd dressed, he felt drained and tired. His pa always seemed to suck away any piece of happiness he had.

At the hospital, Joel learned his pa's leg was broken, along with a few ribs, during a bar fight. Apparently, his pa had lost. A female nurse with short brown hair helped Joel get him into Mr. Hal's truck. He cursed and spit at them the whole way. Joel tried to hold his breath, but the smell of booze seeped from his pa's skin and clothes. Joel thanked the nurse for her help.

She waved a finger at Joel. "I never want to see the likes of him ever again. You hear me!"

"Yes, ma'am," Joel said, completely understanding how she felt. He got into the truck and the smell of stale booze and vomit filled the enclosed space. Bile rose in the back of his throat. He wanted to jump out of the truck and run away, but instead he put the truck in gear and pulled out of the parking lot to drive his good-for-nothing pa back home.

"You steal this truck boy?" his pa spit the question out like it tasted bad. Saliva hung from his lips. He wiped it away roughly with the back of his hand.

"No sir, Mr. Hal let me borrow it. He said it would be easier for me to get from home, work, and school."

"So now we take charity? We don't take charity from anyone. Let alone Hal Sutherland! He owes me much more than a truck," his pa roared.

Joel had no idea what his drunk pa was talking about, and he gripped the steering wheel tighter until his knuckles turned white. His pa crossed his arms and looked out at the night sky.

"Ya'll win tonight?"

Joel couldn't be sure, but it sounded like actual interest in his pa's voice. It made something blossom inside him. "Yes sir, we sure did."

"Hmph," his pa said. "Guess I lost five dollars on that game then. I knew I should have bet on you, but I couldn't believe your dumb team would pull it off."

Joel felt confused at his pa's words. *He should have bet on me?* It was the nicest thing his pa had ever said to him. Joel felt a warmth spread through him.

His pa turned his head and stared at him. "You wanna say something, don't you stupid?"

In an instant, any good feelings Joel had toward his pa burned away as rage filled his chest. Joel tried to bite his tongue, but maybe it was the high from the win, he didn't know, and before he could stop himself, the words escaped from his lips. "Don't call me stupid."

His pa's eyes grew wide, and his face twisted into the same ugly grimace that Joel had seen a thousand times. He snarled. "How dare you disrespect me!" He lifted his balled fist in the air to back hand Joel.

Joel caught his pa's wrist mid-swing with his right hand and squeezed. He dug his strong fingers into his father's wrist. Joel wasn't weak anymore. Playing football and working with Mr. Hal had given him strength. His pa winced and ripped his arm away from Joel's grasp. He rubbed his wrist, eyeing Joel with a side glance.

Joel didn't raise his voice, but said firmly, "You will never hit me again. I'm moving out."

His pa frowned. The lines around his mouth set deeper than Joel had noticed ever before. "You're only sixteen," he said as he continued to rub his wrist, and Joel wondered if in the morning there'd be bruises where his fingers had gripped.

"Yes sir, but there's good duplex housing around the railroad tracks."

"Where the vagrants and rejects live?" his pa spat on the floor.

"I've already seen it for myself. There are good houses, and the people that live there are good too. I've been saving the money Mr. Hal's paid me. I'll get a place in the duplexes there. I'll give up football and work three jobs if I have to, but tomorrow, I'm gone."

His pa opened his mouth like he wanted to say something, and Joel half wondered if he'd try to convince him to stay. Instead, he didn't say anything, but shook his head before turning toward the window. The night sky rolled by in a long, dark blur. His pa's shoulders slumped like he was collapsing into himself. He leaned his head against the window. Joel looked over at him and saw his eyes were closed. For a moment, Joel thought maybe he was dead, but the sound of his pa's snores reverberated from his lips, and Joel realized he was just sleeping. He shook his head. He didn't know if his pa would be able to make it on his own, but that wasn't his problem anymore.

Chapter 18

HAZEL

The girls giggled in the back of the sky-blue Oldsmobile. Hazel could see the streaks of colorful lights illuminating the sky from the Ferris wheel.

"I'm going to ride that," Ruthie said, pointing out the window.

"Me too!" Alice squealed.

Ruthie ticked off her to-do list one by one on her fingers. "I'm going to ride the bumper cars, eat a candied apple, go through the house of mirrors, see the winning pie, pet the blue-ribbon calf. Oh my! There's so much to do."

"Oh, and don't forget the football boy's booth!" Alice snickered. "I'm so happy they won last Friday. And when I heard at school what kind of booth they were having, I practically flipped my lid!"

Alice's mother looked back in the rearview mirror, "What kind of booth do they have this year?"

Hazel scooted lower in the seat. "I can't believe the school let them do it," she muttered.

"I bet they make loads of money for equipment," Alice smiled, giving Hazel a little push. "I'm going to give them all my money."

Alice and Ruthie laughed.

"So, what is it?" Alice's mother pressed.

"It's a...," Hazel felt her cheeks grow warm, and she had trouble finishing her sentence.

"A kissing booth," Alice interrupted to finish her sentence.

Alice's mother chuckled, "Oh! Neato!"

Hazel frowned. She thought Alice's mother would have better sense. It was a terrible idea.

Alice's mother slowly turned into the dirt parking lot in front of the fairgrounds. Alice and Ruthie began to bounce on the long back seat. Alice linked her arm with Hazel's, causing her to join in on the bouncing. Hazel couldn't help but laugh. Alice's mother drove down a line of cars to look for a spot close to the entrance to the park.

"Mom, can we please just get out?"

"Hold your horses. I think I see a spot." Alice's mother finally found an open dirt patch near a rusted Chevy truck. Before she could shift to park, Ruthie flung open the door and she and Alice started to get out.

"Girls!"

"Sorry mom. See you later tonight?" Alice asked as she leaned her head back inside the car. She reached across the back seat and grabbed Hazel's hand and yanked her out the door.

"Yes, yes. I'll be back by nine. You have your money?"

Alice patted her small brown handbag with a golden clasp.

"Be good," her mother called after them, but they were already halfway to the fairground entrance, and her words were swallowed up by the carnival sounds.

Inside, Hazel breathed in the aroma of buttered popcorn, funnel cakes, and cotton candy. Her stomach growled. The laughing, beeping, and whirling sounds made her head spin. Ruthie saw someone in the distance and began to wave wildly.

"Can I have my money?" she asked, holding out her hand.

Hazel began to reach into her floral cloth handbag to find the money Daddy had given them to share. "Aren't you goin' to stay with us?"

Ruthie pointed, "There's Margarette Ann. I'll come find ya'll before we leave."

Hazel thought about protesting, but she didn't want to fight. Not here, when tonight was supposed to be fun. Ruthie was thirteen now but acted grown. Hazel found the money and reluctantly held out half for Ruthie. Ruthie snatched it away.

"Promise you'll be at the front when it's time to go?"

"Yes, I'll be there," she rolled her eyes.

Margarette Ann ran toward them. Her cheeks flushed. She held a gooey caramel apple. The caramel dripped down the stick and onto her hand. She held her hand up and licked it while she talked. "Ruthie, come on! Let's go through the haunted house."

Ruthie squealed and they skipped off without saying good-bye.

"Ankle biters," huffed Alice.

Hazel chuckled and let her eyes take in the blur of action surrounding her.

"What do you want to do first?" Hazel asked.

"I've been dying for some cotton candy."

"Oh yes! Let's get some."

"And ride the Ferris wheel while we eat it," Alice suggested.

Hazel followed the Ferris wheel with her eyes as it rose higher in the air.

Alice grabbed Hazel's arm and pulled her close. "We'll be able to see the whole carnival," she said, pointing to the top of the Ferris wheel.

On the Ferris wheel, Alice wiggled her feet in the air and pulled cotton candy off the stick with her teeth. Hazel tried to keep her body still like a statute. The end of her paisley skirt danced in the wind. Her high ponytail swished back and forth. She pulled her navy cardigan a little tighter around her front.

Halfway up in the air, a gust of wind swayed the seat of the Ferris wheel. Hazel's stomach turned. She gripped the stick, holding her pink cloud of cotton candy tighter. "I'm not sure this was a good idea," she whispered, finding it hard to breathe. She squeezed her eyes shut when the Ferris wheel stopped with a jolt at the very top. The seat squeaked and swayed back and forth.

"But look," Alice said, her mouth full of cotton candy.

Hazel slowly opened one eye and then the other. What she saw took her breath away. She could see all the activity of the carnival. The people looked like tiny ants rushing around. Beyond the bright lights of the carnival, Hazel could see her little town. It sat in the darkness. A few white lights, scattered like a sparsely starred sky, encircled the carnival sun.

"Look," Alice said. She excitedly pointed toward the ground.

The whole seat rocked, and Hazel's stomach leaped into her chest. "Oh, dear Jesus," Hazel whispered as she grasped the cold metal bar in front of her. When the swaying had slowed, she let her eyes look down to follow where Alice's finger was pointing.

"It's the football boys' booth! Let's go there next!"

Before Hazel could object, the Ferris wheel rocked forward, moving their seat onward again through the loop. Butterflies swarmed and circled inside Hazel's stomach, but she wasn't sure if it was because of the ride or Alice's wish to stop at the kissing booth.

Back on the ground, Hazel's knees felt wobbly. She took her time throwing their cotton candy sticks away. She struggled to come up with an idea to distract Alice from the kissing booth.

"Let's go see the winning pie. I heard Ms. Faye won with her famous cherry rhubarb this year."

"Yes, yes," Alice said, batting her words away like flies. "We'll see it later. Look." Alice pointed toward the booth. "The line is already long and getting longer by the minute." She took Hazel's hand and began to drag her.

Hazel tried to make Alice slow down, but Alice was as determined as a hunting dog treeing a squirrel. They made their way near the end of the long line, filled with about twenty giggling girls, all waiting to pay money to be kissed. *This is terrible! I can't do this!* Hazel pulled her hand free from Alice. "I don't want to do this."

"Don't be such a party pooper," Alice said, stepping into the line.

"You can't want to do this," Hazel whispered and leaned closer to Alice, "be kissed like this I mean."

Alice's face fell. Her wide smile gone. She glanced around to make sure no one was listening and cupped her hand around Hazel's ear. "I do want to do this. I've never been kissed before."

Hazel almost laughed, "Me either. So, what's the rush?"

Alice dropped her hands, a perplexed look on her face. "But we're fifteen. It's kinda embarrassing. Don't you think?"

Hazel furrowed her eyebrows. *Is it embarrassing? Have all the other girls in our class been kissed but me and Alice? How did that happen, and how didn't I know?* Hazel folded her arms in front of her. "You want your first kiss to be from a kissing booth? Isn't that kinda Mickey Mouse? And not special at all?"

Alice sighed. "Special?" She shook her head and flashed Hazel a wicked grin. She pointed toward the long line of girls. "What does that matter? We'd be just like them! We'd have our first kisses and have something to talk about at school on Monday."

Hazel noticed for the first time that most of the girls in line were in her and Alice's class. She thought about Monday when all the girls would be talking about the kissing booth and all the fun they'd had. She and Alice would be the only goofs there without anything to say.

Hazel's shoulder's slumped, "Fine, I'll do it too."

Alice's face lit up. She squealed, grabbing and squeezing Hazel's hands. "I'm so excited!"

The line moved quickly, which annoyed Hazel. Her heart sped up with every step closer. Alice was holding her arm, anxiously jiggling her. The closer they got, the more Hazel could see the booth. A white banner painted with the words "Kissing Booth" in red fancy letters hung between two boards. The boys stood under it and behind a wooden box painted with red and white stripes. In the center of the box was a sign that read "10 cent smooches." Hazel folded her arms, *Highway robbery, if you ask me!*

Before she could think of a plan to escape, it was their turn. Alice went first. Hazel felt a cold sweat break out over her body.

The boy at the booth said, "That'll be ten cents."

"Oh yes," Alice's voice shook as she dug in her handbag for a dime.

Hazel narrowed her eyes at the boy. She'd seen him in the hallway at school. His name was David. She didn't know him very well, but she was certain he wasn't very smart. She'd overheard him say once he needed to get his grades up, or he wouldn't be allowed to play football. But overall, he wasn't bad looking. He wasn't dreamy like Alice said, but he'd do, Hazel guessed, for a first kiss. Alice found her dime and handed it to David.

"Thank you," he said and deposited it into a little cardboard box with a hole cut out of the top. "Um, you ready?" he asked, raising his eyebrows.

"Oh!" Alice said. Her body went rigid.

"She's ready," Hazel said, giving Alice a little push closer to the booth.

"Um, well then just–well lean your head in, pucker your lips, and close your eyes," he directed Alice like he was a professional.

Hazel rolled her eyes, but Alice did what she was told. David leaned in and gave Alice a very quick peck on the lips. Alice stood there frozen in place. Her eyes were still closed. David looked at Hazel like he wasn't sure what to do. Hazel shrugged. David looked back at Alice. His eyebrows furrowed but he leaned in and gave Alice another quick peck on the lips. Alice's eye lashes fluttered opened. Her face split wide with a huge grin.

"Hey, hurry up! We want in on the action too," someone behind them yelled.

Hazel turned around to see Nancy Graham anxiously waiting in line. She should have known. Hazel humphed at Nancy and turned back around, but David was gone. Joel stood there, leaning forward, his hands flat on the booth.

"Is it your turn?" he asked.

Hazel felt her stomach drop and all the blood rush from her face. She didn't know what to say. She started to stutter, "I-I was just h-here for Alice."

"Well, since you're here, you might as well stay for a kiss. It's for a good cause you know." He gave her an easy smile.

She looked down at her shoes. Her cheeks blazed hot. She felt him lightly touch her face. He lifted her chin, so she was looking into his blue eyes. He leaned closer to her, and she could feel his warm breath on her skin. Her heart pounded in her chest. She saw him close his eyes and turn his head. His lips began to part slightly as he moved toward her. Before his lips could graze hers, Hazel jerked away.

Joel's eyes popped open. His mouth turned down in a frown.

"I-I'm sorry," she said before turning to run away.

It was Ruthie that found her sitting alone on a hay bale next to the prize-winning calf. Ruthie held a red box full of popcorn toward her, "Popcorn?"

Hazel wiped at her wet cheeks. The buttery popcorn smelled delicious. Hazel reached up and took a handful. She popped some kernels into her mouth. "Thanks."

Ruthie sat down beside Hazel. She scooted near her until they were hip to hip. They sat on the hay bale, neither speaking for a long while. Finally, Ruthie broke the silence.

"It's okay, you know."

Hazel looked at her, "What's okay?"

"Alice found me and told me what happened. It's okay if you weren't ready and wanted your first kiss to be special."

Hazel sniffed, "Yeah, I guess. But it was embarrassing. People will be talkin' about me at school."

Ruthie looked at her, "You don't know?"

"Know what?"

Ruthie smiled. "Nancy Graham's skirt blew up clean over her head when she rode the parachute drop. She tried to push it down with her hand, but then it'd catch the wind and be up over her head again. And she wasn't wearing regular underwear. They were red! With lace!"

Hazel covered her mouth. "You're joking!" she said between her fingers.

"I'm not," Ruthie said, her face serious.

Hazel felt the tickle of a wet nose on her arm. It startled her. The prize-winning calf pushed its black and white head between them, and with a long pink tongue, it licked up a big bite of popcorn from the box Ruthie was holding. Hazel and Ruthie laughed until Hazel's side ached.

Chapter 19

Ruthie, April 1960

Ruthie clapped her hands together on each beat she counted. She tried to keep her shoulders back, her head up, her arms straight, and a fake smile plastered on her face. There was so much to remember. "Go dogs go, beat the Bearcats," she chanted, moving her arms the way she'd learned during practices.

"Ruthie, have you even done your homework yet?" Hazel scowled. She sat on the front porch with her feet resting on the steps below. A big book and spiral notebook lay in her lap. Hazel pulled a pencil resting behind her ear out and scribbled something in her notebook.

Ruthie dropped her hands tightly to her sides. "How can I think about homework at a time like this?"

"Cheerleading tryouts hardly give you a pass at doin' your homework."

Ruthie groaned. "You just don't get it." She wished Hazel would leave her alone. Tryouts were tomorrow and she was still having problems with the main cheer. Every time she missed a move or forgot a word, anxiety built up tighter in her chest, making it hard to breathe. She looked up to the sky. Endless blue stretched above her with out a cloud in sight. *Now what was the next word in the cheer*, she thought, but her mind was blank. She pushed her arm above her head, but she wasn't sure that was the right move. She stamped her foot. "Shoot! You messed me up. I can't remember the stupid moves now." She kicked at the gravel, scattering little rocks everywhere. She stomped to the porch and plopped down beside Hazel.

As she dusted dry dirt from her leg, she could feel Hazel's eyes on her.

"Why do you wanna be a cheerleader anyway? You know Daddy doesn't approve."

Ruthie looked down at the rolled-up legs of her blue jeans. She couldn't meet Hazel's eyes. "Well, Margarette Ann told me, and it's true, you know, because I've noticed it...," her voice trailed off."Not iced what?" Hazel pressed.

Ruthie scratched her nose. She leaned back on the porch using her elbows to prop herself up. Maybe if she put some space between her and Hazel, it would make her admission less embarrassing. She twitched her toes in her shoes.

Hazel turned to look at her. Her mouth a straight line. "Ruthie, are you okay? I've never seen you like this before."

Ruthie bit her bottom lip. She muttered, "It's just that the football boys only ask cheerleaders to the movies or the soda fountain or to go cruisin'."

Hazel furrowed her eyebrows.

She's thinking I'm a big dummy. Ruthie felt her chest deflate.

"Why do you care if they only ask paper shakers on dates?" But as the question slipped from Hazel's lips, Ruthie saw the realization pass across her sister's face. It was like watching the string being pulled on a lightbulb as it sputtered to life, illuminating the space around it. Hazel gasped and covered her mouth. Her book and notebook tumbled from her lap onto the ground.

Ruthie collapsed onto the porch. Her back pressed against the worn porch boards. She laid her hands over her face.

"You've got a crush!"

Ruthie felt her face burn and she couldn't reply. She nodded her head yes. Her mouth wouldn't admit what her heart knew. She was in love, and he didn't even know she was alive. She had turned into a nitwit. Her whole school days were spent worrying about how she looked and how to get his attention. But as far as she was concerned, if she wasn't an inflated brown ball that could be kicked over a goal post, he wasn't interested. Becoming a cheerleader was her last hope. Trying out for a boy was the stupidest thing she'd ever done in her life.

Hazel's eyebrows pulled inward, causing creases to form in the center of her forehead. "Who is it?"

Ruthie shook her head side to side, feeling the grains of the wood under her hair. "I don't want to say. I'm such a dummy. But I think about him all the time. I can't get him out of my head, ever since I saw him helping the elderly lunch lady pick up some trays off the floor in the cafeteria."

"You really do like whoever it is, don't you?" Hazel's voice rose to a higher pitch. "Whoa, this is big."

Ruthie stretched and grabbed Hazel's arm to pull her down, so she laid on the porch beside her. They stared at the paint chipped awning above the porch. "I do. I like him so much. When he talks, his voice sounds like apple butter to me. He's so dreamy and kind. When did I get so mushy?" she chuckled.

She felt Hazel's body tense beside her. Her voice lowered, "Is it Joel? I mean, it's okay if you like him."

Ruthie shot up on her elbow, turning to face Hazel. "Oh goodness no! Don't be crazy! He's like a brother to me."

Hazel's face relaxed and she let out a sigh. She propped herself on an elbow and turned to face Ruthie.

"It's not crazy," Hazel commented. "You guys always got along so well. I know we haven't seen him much this year, but I just figured," she paused. "I mean, maybe you were missin' him or something."

Ruthie stared at Hazel's long brown hair. It fell onto the porch like a cascading waterfall, pooling on the chipped boards near her elbow.

"I do miss him. But Hazel." Ruthie waited until Hazel's eyes met hers. "He likes you. Did something happen between you too? I just wondered 'cause he never even comes for dinner anymore."

She saw a flicker of something pass across Hazel's face and her cheeks pinkened. Hazel shook her head, "No, nothing happened between us. Why do you ask?"

Ruthie narrowed her eyes. Hazel was a horrible liar, and she knew Hazel was lying now.

Hazel scrunched her nose. "I don't know why you think he likes me. I'm not pretty like you. I'm just regular. He'd be better off with someone popular like Nancy Graham."

Ruthie scoffed, "Nancy's a floozy."

Hazel giggled, "You shouldn't say things like that," but the huge grin never left her face. "And anyway, Ms. Ruthie, why are you trying to change the subject and embarrass me when it's you who's supposed to be divulging her deepest, darkest secret. So, who is it? Whose got you so hot and bothered."

Ruthie gave Hazel a little shove and she wobbled on her elbow. Hazel laughed.

"Come on now. If you can't tell your sister, who can you tell?"

Ruthie knew Hazel was right. She did need to tell someone. She was terrified to tell Margarette Ann. She dropped her eyes to the porch and picked at wooden splinters with her finger. She licked her lips.

"It's Ronnie. Ronnie Hartley."

Her eyes darted to Hazel's face, expecting to see shock, but Hazel was smiling.

"Ronnie's very nice. Daddy would like him. He works hard."

Ruthie felt a calmness wash over her. "Yeah, maybe." She laid back down on the hard wooden planks and sighed. "But he'll never notice me if I don't make cheerleader."

Hazel pulled on one of Ruthie's blonde curls, "Have you tried just talking to him?"

Ruthie shook her head side to side. "Not really," she admitted. She sat up and propped her elbows on her knees. She rested her head in her hands and swayed back and forth. "I'm a hopeless cause."

Hazel patted her back. "You're not a hopeless cause." Hazel rested her head against Ruthie's shoulder.

Sunlight reflected off one of the flat rocks in the middle of the road, making it appear white. Ruthie remembered, long ago, a white piece of paper that lay in the dirt. The memory brought back something Margarette Ann had told her last week, and she wondered if she should tell Hazel. She decided she couldn't keep the information to herself. "I forgot to tell you, Margarette Ann told me her aunt said she saw Mama shopping in Fort Smith last month."

Hazel's head jerked up. "What? When?"

"I don't really know. She just said last month sometime."

Hazel's face fell. "That can't be. Grandma said she's in California. She has no reason to lie."

Ruthie thought about that but didn't respond.

Hazel went on, "Plus, lots of people shop in Fort Smith. She probably just saw someone that looked like Mama."

Ruthie wanted to remind Hazel about the Fourth of July all those years ago, when Hazel thought she'd seen their mother, but Ruthie could see the sadness in Hazel's eyes. *I shouldn't have said anything.* "Yeah, you're probably right. It was just someone who looked like her. Plus, Margarette Ann's aunt does get a little tipsy from time to time."

Hazel rolled her eyes, but Ruthie saw the corner of her mouth turn up. "You're crazy. Now get up and let me see your cheer. How are you ever going to catch your hunky dream boat if you don't practice?"

Ruthie gave Hazel a little bump with her shoulder and leaped from the porch. She stood straight and placed her hands tight to her side.

"Maybe one day you can write a story about me and Ronnie. How I found my prince in the school cafeteria, and we lived happily ever after."

Chapter 20

JOEL

Joel made his way up to the bleachers, squeezing in between his teammates until he reached the open space Ronnie had saved for him. Before he sat, he saw Nancy Graham in her cheerleading outfit. She moved her fingers in a seductive wave. Her usual bright red lips puckered to send him an invisible kiss through the air.

Ronnie leaned over, "Whoa, she's got the hots for you something bad."

Joel shook his head. "Yeah, tell me somethin' I don't know."

Ronnie shoved him in the arm with his elbow, "Ladies man."

Joel laughed. Donald White, the team's second-string tight end, gave a long low whistle.

"Would you get a look at all those dollies?" He put his hands behind his head and leaned back. "Hot mamas. The paper shakers have some prime meat to choose from today."

Joel felt the hair on the back of his neck prickle. Donald was annoying and stupid, but Joel left it alone. He was exhausted and didn't have the energy or patience to deal with Donald today.

Joel watched as different girls got up from sitting on the grass, dust off their skirts or pants, and walk to the middle of the football field. Even from the stands, he could tell from their posture they were nervous. They stood in front of the current cheerleaders and performed the cheer routines they'd learned for tryouts. All the girls did the same thing. They moved their arms and body in the same way and repeated the same words.

"Swing those hips," Donald catcalled. Other members of the football team laughed and joined in the whooping and hollering.

"Idiots," Ronnie whispered.

"Oh, look there's Sally," Donald said. "She smells just like a garbage can. We don't need garbage-can Sally stinkin' up the paper shaker's pom-poms. Boo. Boo," he called.

The other team members laughed.

"Give it a rest," Joel said. He was getting tired of Donald's mouth.

"Don't be such a lame duck, Davenport. I'm just goofin'." Donald narrowed his eyes.

Joel shook his head and looked back at the field, ignoring Donald. When his eyes caught sight of Ruthie, his heart caught in his chest. He'd forgotten she was old enough to try out this year. His mouth went dry, and he felt twitchy as he watched her with the other girls.

He glanced around the football field to see if Hazel was there too. He saw her standing at the bottom of the bleachers, biting her fingernails. Her long brown hair blew in the wind. Joel felt his chest tighten when it was Ruthie's turn to begin the routine.

She stood facing the cheerleaders, her hands placed on her hips. Her smile was bright. She began to clap, "One, two, three," to start the cheer. She held her arms out straight. Her moves were precise. Joel felt the tightness in his chest loosen somewhat. She wasn't half bad, and she was doing the same moves the others did, but better.

"Hmmm, I think I want some of that action," Donald murmured to a player beside him. "I hear she's easy. Yep, fast, and easy. Give me some of that!" he yelled.

Red-hot anger ripped through Joel. It seared him from the inside out. He leaped off his seat and grabbed Donald by the shirt collar. His hand raised behind him in a fist.

"Don't you ever talk about her like that! You hear me!" he shouted inches from Donald's face. Spittle escaped from his mouth and landed on Donald.

Donald's face went white. His eyes grew round like saucers. He held up trembling hands.

"Hey sorry man, don't flip your lid. I was just jokin'. You know goofin'. I didn't mean nothing bad."

Joel felt someone grab his arm. He gripped Donald's shirt tighter and whipped his head to the side, ready to fight anyone trying to stop him, but the anger fell off him like a heavy coat when he realized Ronnie was holding his arm. Ronnie spoke in a low calm voice. "He's just goofing. Come on, Joel. You don't want to get yourself into any trouble with the coach. Look at him. He's sorry."

"Yeah, I-I mean it. I'm sorry. I didn't know she was your girl. Sorry, man," Donald stammered.

Joel slowly lowered his raised fist. He breathed out, letting the rest of his anger leave his body. He looked straight into Donald's eyes. "If you ever say anything about her again, I won't care what coach does. I'll give you more than a knuckle sandwich. I'll break every one of your teeth."

"Sure, man, sure. I get it." Donald waved his hands.

Joel released him with a shove, causing Donald to plop back down on the bleachers. He glanced around at his teammates. Their eyes were wide and their mouths hung open.

"I'm goin' get some air," he said to Ronnie.

Ronnie nodded and let him go.

As he walked to the edge of the bleachers, he tried to calm the fury that still bubbled inside him. He clomped down the bleacher steps. At the bottom, Hazel stood facing the field. He wondered if she'd heard or seen what happened. Joel pushed his hands in his jean pockets to try and act normal—casual.

"Hey, she did really good," he said, walking to her.

Hazel looked at him. He saw pink creep across her cheeks. "Oh yeah, she did great. Problems?" she raised her eyebrows and looked toward the bleachers where the football team sat.

Joel felt his face grow hot. He kicked at the dirt with his shoe, "Nah, just a few guys can be real jerks."

Hazel nodded like she understood.

Joel cleared his throat. "I didn't realize she'd be trying out today."

"Yeah, she's been practicing that silly cheer for weeks. Even tried to get out of doing homework last night to practice."

Joel chuckled. "She's always trying to get out of homework."

Hazel flashed him a smile and he felt his stomach flutter. When she turned to look back toward Ruthie, he couldn't take his eyes off her. He stared at her profile. He wanted to say something else, to talk to her some more, but nothing came to mind. He forced his eyes to look away. Ruthie was sitting on the green grass, her legs bent underneath her. Her friend, Margarette Ann, was beside her. He saw Margarette Ann lean over and nudge Ruthie with her elbow during another girl's cheer.

"Are you staying to the end?" he asked.

She answered him without taking her eyes off Ruthie. "Yes, Margarette Ann's mother is giving us a ride home after tryouts. Are you working today?"

He couldn't help but watch her. He knew she'd get embarrassed if she saw him looking at her, but he couldn't help himself. He wondered if she missed seeing him. He hadn't been around a lot because of work, but work wasn't the only reason. If he was truthful with himself, her running away from him at the kissing booth last October bothered him more than he'd like to admit. Of course, he made a joke about it with his teammates that had been with him at the booth. He'd said something lame about how his good looks must have scared her away. They'd all laughed, but inside, he'd felt like something had crumbled and broken. He'd figured the less she saw of him, and he saw of her, the better.

When he didn't answer her question, Hazel turned to look at him. He felt heat pass through him when their eyes met. *I have to quit staring. I'm going to scare her off for sure.*

He ran a hand through his hair to break eye contact. "Yeah, gotta work every day."

She nodded her head then turned back to watch what was happening on the field. When the last girl had finished the cheer, Nancy had them sit down in a group on the grass. She then huddled with the other cheerleaders a short distance away. Joel could see they were discussing the girls because Nancy and the others would periodically steal glances at the nervous girls that sat on the grass. Joel wondered how long it would take for them to decide. Every second felt longer than the last. Finally, the group broke away from each other and Nancy approached the girls.

"This is it," Hazel said, gripping her hands together. "I'm so nervous for her."

Joel felt his stomach twist. He wanted so badly for Ruthie to make it.

"Ya'll did a fabulous job today." Nancy held one hand on a hip that jutted out and her other hand waved in the air. "This was a very tough decision. But if I call your name, please meet me and the other cheerleaders over there on those benches." She pointed to the wooden benches where the football boys sat to rest during games. "We'll give you all the details about practices, uniforms, and other things. Okay?"

Joel saw all the girls nod their heads in unison. His heart pounded in his chest.

"Okay, so," Nancy said.

Hazel laid her hand on her chest. "Oh my, I don't think I can handle this."

"We'd like to welcome Margarette Ann Williams, Brenda Miller, and Ruthie McKay to be Waldron Bulldog cheerleaders." Nancy and the other cheerleaders clapped their hands. "Congratulations, girls!" she squealed.

Joel felt his heart soar. He released the huge breath he'd been holding. Hazel turned to him. Worry in her eyes. She reached out and gripped his arms with her hands. Her fingernails dug into his skin.

"Did she say Ruthie's name? Did she? My heart was pounding so hard, I couldn't hear a thing."

Joel couldn't help himself. He grabbed her and pulled her into a hug. "She made it!"

"My goodness! I can't believe it!" Hazel squealed.

Joel felt like his heart stopped when her arms reached around him and squeezed him back. Her warm body pressed close to his. He laid his cheek on the top of her head and felt her soft brown hair tickle his face. He wished they could stay like this, but Hazel pulled away. It left a hollow space between them. Her face was crimson. She ran a hand across her forehead and gave him a sheepish smile.

"I'm just so happy for her."

Joel nodded, "Yeah, me too."

Not knowing what else to say, Joel looked back toward Ruthie. She was sitting with the other new cheerleaders on the wooden bench. Nancy Graham held out pieces of paper for each one to take. Ruthie stared at her paper.

Joel felt a tug. He knew he needed to go. He wanted to stay here with Hazel and celebrate, but he was going to be late for work. He decided he'd wait, just a few more minutes, to tell Ruthie congratulations. Mr. Hal wouldn't care if he was a little late, especially when he told him the good news.

"Here she comes," Hazel squeaked. A smile spread wide across her face.

Joel blinked his eyes. He watched Ruthie storm across the field. Her steps were more like stomps. Her eyebrows furrowed and her mouth was pulled in a tight line. *Something is wrong.* He wondered if she'd heard Donald's stupid remarks. *But how could she have heard him from the bleachers?* Joel shook his head. Ruthie came toward them.

"Congratu-," he started but Ruthie walked right past him.

He and Hazel looked at each other. Together they ran to catch up with Ruthie. Hazel grabbed Ruthie's arm, spinning her around. The paper Ruthie held flapped in the air.

"What?" she snipped.

"Ruthie! We're so happy for you. Joel was trying to tell you congratulations."

"What does it matter? I'm quitting."

"B-but you just made it," Hazel stuttered.

Joel tried to read Ruthie's face, but all he could see was anger. "What's going on?" he asked. "Did someone say something to you?"

Ruthie frowned, "No one said anything to me. Now both of you leave me alone," she pushed pass Joel, bumping him with her shoulder.

He and Hazel watched her as she stormed toward the parking lot where Margarette Ann stood hugging her mother. Ruthie took the paper she was holding and wadded it into a ball. She threw it at the silver trash can. It hit the side and bounced off onto the ground.

"I don't understand," Hazel whispered.

Joel looked at the wadded-up paper on the ground. He jogged toward it and picked it up. He gently pulled the crumpled paper open and smoothed it out until he could read it. When he read it, he realized the problem. He held the paper out for Hazel to take.

She took it from him and read it out loud. "Uniform forty dollars." Her mouth fell open. "Oh, that's an awful lot. But Dad's going to be back on Saturday. He'll surely come up with a way to get the money."

"No," Joel pointed at the paper. "Look at when it's due."

Hazel leaned closer and used a hand to hold the edge of the paper down. She looked up from the paper. Her eyes were watery as they met Joel's. "Tomorrow?" she said it like a question.

Joel nodded.

"We've only got ten dollars in the coffee can. Why do they need it so soon?"

He didn't have an answer, so he shrugged. Hazel held the paper to her chest. Her face looked pale and solemn. He laid a hand on her shoulder. He wanted to say something comforting, but nothing came to him. He swallowed. "Hey, I gotta get to work. Do you still have a ride home? I can be late if you need a ride or something." His heart raced in his chest. He hoped she needed a ride.

She stared at him like she hadn't heard him. Her eyes not registering what he said.

"A ride?" she repeated.

Joel nodded, "Yeah, do you need a ride. I really don't mind."

She looked down at the paper. "No, no, I have something I need to do first. I'll be fine, thank you."

Chapter 21

HAZEL

Twenty, only twenty miles until home. It wasn't a huge number. Not fifty, but still more than ten. When she'd first thought about it, walking twenty miles home seemed doable. She looked down at her feet. They already ached inside her shoes. They had no give, and her feet throbbed as they rubbed against the sides. Now she wondered if she'd even walked a mile yet. She had no way to gauge how far she'd gone except for the fine dust that had caked onto her shoes, making them appear brownish-gray instead of black. *What have I done?*

A car sped by, blowing her skirt. It fluttered hard against her legs. She wondered if Ruthie was home worried about her. If she wasn't worried yet, Hazel knew she would be once it got dark. She imagined

Ruthie calling the motel their father was staying at this week. A long-distance call would cost a pretty penny. He'd be worried. *Would he get in his truck and head home to find her?* His job might fire him if he left. She pulled at her fingernail with her teeth.

Brilliant reds and oranges painted the sky. She paid no attention to the beauty that surrounded her. Her stomach was tied in knots. She knew the beauty was fleeting, and after it came the dark. Thin wispy clouds tried to hold onto the red until the last bit of light was gone. Before long, she'd be alone in the night and there was still so far to go.

When the sun was gone, she was enveloped in darkness. There were no streetlamps out here in the country. The only light came from the sliver moon and scattered stars that looked like salt sprinkled on a black cloth. She began to make up stories in her head to keep her mind off the rustles in the bushes near the road and the long howls in the distance. It'd been so long since she'd written a story. It made her fingers tingle at the thought, but she'd been so busy, she barely had any time at all. When she did find a moment to herself, she'd sneak off to her and Ruthie's magical spot to write, but she always got distracted. Even in the cool air, she felt her cheeks warm because she knew most of those distractions were because she was thinking of Joel, but her thoughts about him were confusing.

She grimaced as a sharp pain settled in her heel. She had no idea what time it was, but she knew it had to be close to dinner. Hunger began to claw at her from the inside. Her throat tightened and felt raw with thirst. She needed water and food. A light breeze kissed her skin and gave her goose bumps. She rubbed her arms. What had she done?

Behind her, a brightness appeared, and she heard the crunching of tires on rocks. The light made her shadow stretch far in front of her until it was ten feet tall, but she didn't turn around. Her blood had run cold, and her heart thumped hard. Her mind was flooded with horrible thoughts of news headlines of kidnappings, rapes, and murders. Sad stories of missing women found dead in grassy fields or dense abandoned forests. There was no one here to help her. She was alone without a house for miles. She could hear the faint conversations of people talking around an empty casket meant for her.

"She was too young to die, but old enough to know she shouldn't have been walking alone at night on a county road."

The rumbling engine stopped, and the silence made her hair on her arms lift. She made her sore feet move faster. Whoever it was had stopped for her, and she didn't want to stay around and find out why. She needed to get away. Her breath caught when she heard the vehicle's door squeak open. She readied herself to run.

"Hazel?"

The voice sounded familiar, but she couldn't be certain. She could barely hear it over the blood rushing through her head.

"Hazel, is that you?"

She turned, putting her arm over her eyes to shield them from the bright glow of the vehicle's headlights. The figure in front of her was nothing more than a black silhouette. She squinted to see. When the figure walked closer to her, she took a step back.

"Hazel, it's me." The figure held out his hands like he was surrendering.

"Joel?" Realization dawned on her, releasing a flood of peace that made her body slump in exhaustion.

"What are you doing out here? On the dark road?"

She bit her bottom lip. Her eyes stung with tears as she felt everything now. The pressure in her feet, the aching hollow pit in her stomach, her raw throat. She pressed her eyes closed to keep the tears from falling. She couldn't answer him. She didn't know what to say.

"Are you hurt?" he asked, coming toward her.

She shook her head. Her voice wavered, "No, I'm fine. I'm fine."

He wrapped an arm around her. The lights from Mr. Hal's truck made her blink. "Let's get you in the truck. I'll give you a ride home. You shouldn't be out here by yourself." His voice sounded like he was scolding her.

She could feel uncontrollable tears streaming down her face. She couldn't even argue with him. She shouldn't be out here alone. She nodded and let him guide her to the passenger side. He opened the door and helped her inside. Her muscles already felt sore as she stretched them to lift herself into the open door.

When he got inside, he turned on the overhead light to look at her. She didn't want him to see her.

"Are you sure you're okay?"

Then his eyes grew wide. There was no way she could miss the shock on his face. Her heart fell. *I'm hideous. Dirty, smelly, and ugly.* She felt heat spread from her chest up to her neck, and she wished with everything in her that he'd just stop looking at her and take her home. But he wouldn't stop looking at her. His mouth hung open.

"Say somethin'," she croaked.

He reached up and touched a strand of her hair with his hand. He ran his fingers to the end of it, where it touched the bottom of her chin.

"You cut your hair?"

More tears began to flow. She didn't want to cry in front of him, but there was no stopping them. They came without her permission, dripping from her like rain drops running off a tin roof. She wanted to explain to him why she'd done it, but she couldn't find the right words.

"I-I cut m-my hair," she sobbed.

He leaned over and pulled her to him. The movement was quick and unexpected. She gasped. He was so close to her, she could smell the oil and dirt from the garage. He wrapped his arms around her and held her. Her body went stiff and then relaxed in his warmth. She laid her head on his shoulder and cried.

She stayed like that until her tears ran dry. She could feel Joel's heartbeat under his navy T-shirt, and she wondered if he could feel hers beating just as hard. She pulled herself back from his embrace and shivered. She wiped her face with the back of her hand. She looked into his blue eyes to tell him thank you, but without any warning, he pressed his warm lips to hers. Butterflies erupted in her stomach and her head went fuzzy. She tasted her salty tears mixed with the sweet taste of Juicy Fruit gum. He laid his hand behind her head, bringing her mouth even closer to his. Warmth spread through her body. She forgot about her aching feet, cramping muscles, and short hair. Joel was kissing her.

His lips slowly pulled away and she felt like she'd woken from a dream. But it wasn't a dream, she could feel his warm breath on her skin. It sent electricity tingling through her.

He whispered, "I'm sorry. I should have asked you first, but you looked so beautiful."

Hazel blinked. A strange sensation formed in her chest. *No one has ever called me beautiful.*

She forced herself to speak the only words she knew at that moment. "Thank you."

He grinned and she couldn't help but grin back. They stayed there. Close to each other. It felt like time had stopped, and she never wanted it to start again. A car sped by and honked its horn. They jolted in the seat. Joel hurriedly moved back to the driver's side and took the wheel.

"Um well, I guess I better be gettin' you home."

Hazel felt dazed. She wasn't sure what had happened, but whatever magic had entered the truck was now gone. She moved back over to the passenger side. The seat felt cool, and it made her shudder. Home was the farthest thing from her mind, but she agreed with him. It was time to get home.

He reached up to switch off the dome light, but before he did, he turned in his seat to face her. The light illuminated his face, but she couldn't look at him. She felt his eyes on her, watching her. He reached out and took her arm. She noticed his hand was rough and dark in places where he hadn't quite scrubbed all the grease off from the shop. But his touch sent her heart fluttering.

"It'd be okay with me if you sat next to me on the ride to your house."

She twisted her head to look at him. The corners of his mouth were turned up.

"It'd really be okay with me if you always sat next to me."

In the light, she saw his cheeks turn a shade of pink and she knew what he was asking her. She couldn't believe it. Joel was asking her to be his girl.

"What about Nancy Graham?" The question slipped out before she could catch it. She could kick herself for saying anything, and she wondered if the magic of the moment was ruined.

Joel chuckled and shook his head. "I don't care about her. I never did. Hazel it's always been you. Since the first day I saw you in the forest acting like a dancing lunatic."

She gawped at him then slapped the hand that held her arm.

He laughed hard. The sound came from deep inside. He gripped her arm and tugged her over beside him. Her body scooted close to his side. She felt the excitement pop inside her like a lightning streak setting the sky on fire. She felt her smile widen, and there was nothing she could do about it. He gave her a light kiss on the nose before he turned off the dome light and shifted into drive.

As Joel pulled into the driveway, Hazel saw Ruthie run onto the porch. Her face was white, and she squinted from the glare of the truck's headlights. When he put it in park, he leaped out and offered his hand to Hazel. She slipped her hand into his, feeling his rough skin. Her head felt light and dizzy as he helped her out of the truck. Before she could thank him, Ruthie ran from the porch and lunged at her. She wrapped her arms around Hazel. She squeezed Hazel's neck, cutting off her air.

"I was so worried! Where have you been? I thought something terrible had happened."

Hazel patted her back. "I'm fine. It's okay."

Ruthie pulled back. Her head shook back and forth, and her nostrils flared. "No, I called everyone. Alice hadn't seen you or heard from you. Ms. Faye either."

Hazel's heart dropped, "Did you call Daddy?"

Ruthie stopped and looked at Hazel for the first time. Her eyes grew as big as saucers. "Your hair! You cut your hair?"

Hazel felt panic rise in the back of her throat. "Ruthie, did you call Daddy?"

"No, no, I was about to though."

Hazel released a long breath and her heart started to beat again. Joel came and laid a hand on her shoulder. She turned to face him.

"I better be getting home. Thank you for the company."

Hazel felt her cheeks grow hot.

"Did you know about this?" Ruthie asked Joel.

He kicked at the gravel in the driveway. "Nope, but I sure think it looks good. I'll be seeing you soon Hazel. Have a nice night, Ruthie." He nodded his head at them, then got in his truck.

Hazel could feel Ruthie side-eyeing her, but she didn't care as they watched Joel pull out of the driveway. When Hazel walked toward the house, Ruthie was on her heels. Inside the house, Ruthie talked with her hands and paced around the living room. Hazel sunk into the old sofa. She barely felt the hard spring dig into the back of her leg.

"You have no idea how worried I was. I've never been that scared in my whole entire life." Ruthie paused and looked at Hazel. "I can't believe you cut your long hair."

Dazed, Hazel reached up and touched the end near her chin. "You don't like it?"

"I love it! You look just like Sophia Loren in that movie we saw with Daddy." She snapped her fingers. "*Houseboat*, that was it. I just can't believe you didn't tell me, and you let me worry so much. Why would you do that? I just don't understand."

Just then, a jolt of memory hit Hazel. "Oh! I nearly forgot," she said and reached into her skirt pocket. She pulled out a wad of bills and held them out to Ruthie.

Ruthie took the money. Her mouth pulled tight. "What is this?"

"It's thirty dollars. I noticed last week a sign in Ms. Debbie's store at the Clip and Cut. She was offering to buy hair so she could make fancy wigs. You know, the ones she ships to New York."

Ruthie's mouth dropped open. "You cut your hair for me?"

"She said she needed long, healthy hair. That's why she gave me so much. She said she'd get two wigs from what she cut. With the money from the coffee can, you'll have enough for your uniform. It's due tomorrow, right?"

Ruthie almost tackled Hazel on the sofa. She was crying and hugging her. Hazel's back protested, already sore from the walk.

"Thank you! Thank you! Hazel, this is too much."

Hazel patted Ruthie's back. "You just promise me one thing."

"Anything!" Ruthie cried.

"You find Nancy Graham a boyfriend and keep her away from Joel."

Chapter 22

RUTHIE, FEBRUARY 14, 1961

"Please Ruthie," Hazel begged as they folded the clean laundry on the sofa.

Ruthie rubbed her forehead with her hand, then reached down into the wicker basket they'd used to bring the clothes in from the clothesline. She picked up a pale-yellow towel. It was dry, but still felt cool to the touch. She held it in her hands, gripping it tightly. It reminded her of sweet Henry.

He used to cuddle in the towel, and no other towel would do. It was as if his favorite color was yellow. Some days, she didn't think about Henry at all, and other days, memories of him cuddling with her on the sofa and eating from her fingers invaded her mind, making her sad. She missed him, but she had to think he was happier now, free and in love.

Ruthie thought about the two weeks she had with him before he ran off. She remembered how that same small brown squirrel kept coming to the house and sitting on her windowsill. How the female squirrel knew Henry was there, Ruthie would never know, but she and Henry spent hours sitting and staring at each other through the window. Finally, when Ruthie could stand it no more, she opened the front door. She hoped with all her heart that Henry would ignore the open door. But he hadn't. He ran out of the house and joined the other squirrel. They jumped and played before they ran off into the forest together. *There might as well have been a sunset like in the movies.* She never saw Henry again. She hurried and folded the towel into a fluffy square. As she set it on the sofa, she could feel Hazel's eyes boring into her.

"Please," Hazel begged again.

Ruthie didn't want to go with Hazel and Joel on their Valentines date. It was embarrassing being the third wheel all the time, but she knew if she didn't go, then no one could go. That was Daddy's rule. If she refused, Hazel and Joel would be upset with her.

"I just hate being the chaperone. You and Joel don't need one. Ya'll have been together for almost a year now and you both are as boring as apple pie."

Hazel got a dreamy look in her eye. "We're not that boring."

Ruthie picked up a ragged washcloth that was lying folded on the sofa and tossed it at Hazel. It hit her in the chest. "Yes, ya'll are. So, what's playing anyway?"

"*Spartacus*," Hazel said. She picked up the washcloth, folded it again, and placed it on the sofa. She picked up their father's folded clothes and took them to his room.

Ruthie bit her bottom lip while she continued to fold. She'd been hoping to see that movie with her own Valentine's Day date, but no one had ever asked her, not even Ronnie. At school this week, she'd made sure to accidentally run into him at least two times in the hall. She'd even brought the movie up in conversation and twirled her hair while telling him how much she wanted to see it. If she wasn't so worried about him thinking she was easy, she'd have asked him herself, but who was she kidding? No one ever asked her out, and even if they did, Daddy would force her to take a chaperone. Hazel was seventeen years old, and he still made Ruthie tag along every time she and Joel went out. Ruthie wasn't sure what would be worse, never going on a date with Ronnie or going on a date with Ronnie, Hazel, and Joel.

When Hazel came back into the room to pick up the folded towels to take to the bathroom, she gave Ruthie a pouty face, making her bottom lip stick out. Ruthie rolled her eyes.

"Fine, I'll go," she sighed. "But only because I've been itching to see that movie."

Hazel set down the towels and ran to Ruthie. She pulled her into a tight hug that crushed all of her ribs.

"Okay, okay, don't make a big deal out of it."

The telephone began to ring, startling them. Ruthie pushed Hazel out of the way and rushed for the telephone.

"Hey!" Hazel yelled.

"Snooze you lose," Ruthie laughed. She grabbed the telephone headset off the receiver. The white rotary phone fell off the side table and hit the floor with a crash. She picked it up off the ground and wrapped the spiral cord around her wrist. She held the receiver to her ear.

"Hello," she spat out breathlessly. She turned around to avoid Hazel's glare. "Oh, hi Daddy." Out of the corner of her eye, she saw Hazel plop down on the sofa. Hazel crossed her arms frowning.

"Hi kiddo, any big plans for tonight," Daddy's deep gruff voice sounded in her ear and made her heart twinge. She missed him. She always missed him when he left for work. *He sounds too tired.*

She sucked in a breath and sighed, "No plans for me, but Hazel and Joel have a date."

"I guess it is Valentine's Day," he said.

"Yep, they're going to see *Spartacus* at the drive-in movie."

"Together?"

Ruthie couldn't help but laugh, "Of course they'll be together, but don't worry. I'm going with them."

"Oh good, peanut, that's what I like to hear. You had me worried for a pretty minute. Can I speak to your sister? Love you."

"Love you too, Daddy. Miss you."

Ruthie held the phone out to Hazel. She looked worried as she made her way over to the telephone. She pushed a strand of her brown hair out of her face and placed the telephone to her ear. Her fingers nervously twisted the spiral cord as she listened.

"Yes, Daddy, we won't be out late. Yes sir. Love you too."

After Hazel hung up the phone, she went straight to the kitchen. Ruthie followed her. Hazel reached under the sink and got five dollars out of the rusted coffee can. She handed it to Ruthie.

"Daddy said you could buy popcorn and a coke. He wasn't sure Joel would have enough," she looked down. "You know, for both me and you."

Ruthie silently took the money and went to her bedroom to get ready. She laid the five dollars on the bed. Another reminder that she had no one to share this romantic holiday with. Her own father had to buy her popcorn and coke.

An hour later, Ruthie watched as the knock on the front door sent Hazel into a flurry. It made Ruthie's heart hurt. Hazel and Joel had been going steady for almost a year now, and they'd known each other almost their whole lives, and still Hazel got jumpy when he came over. Ruthie hoped one day she'd find someone that would send her into a fluster every time he was near.

Joel came in, closing the screen door slowly to keep it from slamming shut. His garage blues traded for khaki pants and a long-sleeve gray and white striped button-up shirt. His hair looked a shade darker from the product he'd used to slick the sides back. In his hands, he held two very small bouquets of red roses. Hazel took the bouquet he handed her. Her face beamed. Joel then handed the second bouquet to Ruthie. She leaned her head down and breathed in the sweet fragrance from the crimson red blossoms.

"Thank you," Ruthie said, her voice wavering.

He smiled, "Happy Valentine's Day."

She nodded, feeling the pricks of tears in her eyes, and she quickly blinked them away. Her sister's boyfriend had to buy her roses. She took Hazel's bouquet from her and went to the kitchen to put the flowers in water. Ruthie closed her eyes as the vase filled with water from the sink. She breathed in and let the air out slowly through her nose. She felt lonely. Everyone had a boyfriend but her. Hazel had Joel. Alice had David. Even Margarette Ann had started dating. She and Bill Seymour had been going steady for a month. He was too nerdy, Ruthie thought, but when she said that much to Margarette Ann, she'd just blown her off with a wave of her hand.

"He's smart and worships me, and that's why he'll be a good husband one day."

Ruthie didn't want a husband. She wanted a boyfriend. She wanted someone to kiss. She was fifteen for goodness sakes, and she still hadn't been properly kissed by anyone. She didn't think the peck on the lips Donald White gave her under the bleachers counted, even though she knew for a fact he'd told everyone he'd put his tongue in her mouth. She wouldn't have minded his tall tale if it would have made some other boys interested in her, but it didn't work. She just couldn't understand it. *How'd I end up being a dateless paper shaker?*

"We ready?" Joel asked.

His question shook her from her thoughts. She put both bouquets in the glass vase and set it on the wooden table. She and Hazel grabbed their coats. Joel helped Hazel with hers.

Outside, a breeze of chilly wind nipped at Ruthie's nose. It sent a shiver through her body. The sunlight faded into dusk as they squeezed into Mr. Hal's truck. Joel drove, Hazel sat in the middle, and Ruthie sat near the door. The metal door handle dug into her side. Ruthie's reflection in the window frowned back at her.

At the drive-in, they pulled into the space a few rows away from the huge, white screen that stretched far across the dark, flat dirt. Joel rolled down the window, letting cold air inside. Chill bumps ran up and down Ruthie's arms. Joel reached over and unhooked the speaker off the pole. He pulled the speaker into the truck. The black wire stretched from the pole. He rolled up the window as far as it would go without flattening the wire. Joel propped the large silver speaker up on his leg and leaned it against the door.

The white screen filled with color and light. The speaker sputtered to life, making Ruthie and Hazel jump. A little elf sitting on a treasure chest under a rainbow began to dance and sing across the screen. He opened the treasure chest, and it was filled with candy bars, different flavors of soda, and popcorn. The elf encouraged the audience to go to the concession stand and purchase the treats.

Hazel turned to Joel, "I'm going to run to the restroom and stop by the concession stand."

"I'll get you something from the concession stand," Joel protested.

Hazel touched his hand, "No, it's okay."

Joel dug into his pocket and pulled out a five-dollar bill. He handed it to Hazel. "Well at least let me pay for it."

She smiled and kissed him on the cheek as she took the money. "Popcorn and a Coke?"

He winked, "You know it."

Hazel looked at Ruthie, "Want anything?"

Ruthie gave Hazel the coffee can money, "Sure, I'll take the same." Ruthie opened the door and slid out. Hazel bounced across the seat then slipped out the door. Her chin length hair flowed in the wind.

"Be back in a jiffy," she said, walking toward the red building near the back of the drive-in. The huge cutout windows glowed with yellow light. It was already hopping, as people formed a long line in front of the building to purchase their concessions.

Ruthie shivered and hurried to get back inside the truck. Joel stared at the movie screen, then fiddled with the volume knob on the speaker.

"Can I ask you a question," she said her head down.

Joel turned the volume down then turned to look at her. "Question?"

She nodded and turned in the seat to face him. His eyebrows raised and she took it as an invitation to go on. She swallowed, feeling it stick halfway down her throat. She sucked in a breath then blurted out what she wanted to ask.

"Is something wrong with me?"

Joel's face contorted in a combination of confusion and alarm. "Wrong with you?"

She nodded. "Yeah, wrong with me. I've tried so many times to show Ronnie that I'm interested in him, but he ignores all my efforts."

The corner of Joel's mouth turned down. He shook his head. "Ruthie, there's nothing wrong with you."

Ruthie crossed her arms. "Then why does he ignore me. And all the other boys do too. No one ever asks me for a date."

Joel reached over and tugged on her sweater near her elbow. He yanked it a couple times, making her roll her eyes and smile.

"Don't take this the wrong way, but Ronnie's too busy for girls. Even nice ones like you."

She leaned her head to the side and frowned. It sounded like hogwash to her. *How could someone be too busy for a date?*

Joel shook his head and continued, "It's true. He's determined to join the army right after we graduate in May. He wants to serve like his pa did years ago. And a girlfriend would slow down his plans and make it hard to leave."

Her shoulder's slumped, "It's not just him. Why won't anyone ask me out." Her voice sounded thin and small to her ears.

Joel turned his whole body to face her. His face was serious. "There is nothing wrong with you, Ruthie McKay," he said sternly. "You have to understand, I care for you like a sister. But you are a very pretty girl. And that can be, well, intimidating to guys."

Ruthie reached up and touched her blonde wavy hair. "I'm pretty?"

Joel smacked her lightly on the arm. "Don't be stupid. Of course you are."

She couldn't stop the smile that spread across her face. She felt the heaviness weighing her down lighten somewhat.

Joel turned to look out the back window toward the concession stand. He leaned closer to her and whispered, "Okay look, I need to talk to you about something important." He reached into his jacket pocket and pulled out a tiny maroon box. He pushed it in Ruthie's hands.

The box felt soft like velvet. She didn't know why, but her hands trembled as she opened it. Inside was a thin golden band with the tiniest round chip of a diamond in the center. With her finger and thumb, she pulled the slender band from the small pillow encasing it. She turned it over in her fingers, hardly believing what she was seeing. She saw something written on the inside of the ring. She held it closer so she could read it. The words were written in beautiful calligraphy and read, "*My Forever Love.*" She quickly put the ring back inside the box and snapped the lid closed. She could hardly speak. "Oh my," was all that she could think to say. She knew what this meant, but the thought made her head spin. Hazel and Joel married.

Before she could dwell on the thought, he snatched the ring box from her hand and shoved it back in his pocket.

"So, what do you think?"

When she didn't answer, he continued.

"I've loved her ever since I first saw her. I graduate in May. Mr. Hal wants me to work full-time with him and take community college classes at night in Fort Smith. I'm going to take business classes. He wants me to run the shop one day. The duplex I moved into is small, but would be perfect for the two of us. And my neighbors, Milton and Sandra, they're just great, and I know they'd get on with Hazel. Do you think she'll like the ring?"

He stared at Ruthie. She could see the desperation in his eyes as he waited for her to say something. Her thoughts bounced around in her brain. Marriage meant babies. She'd be an aunt one day. She wondered how long Joel had been thinking about proposing. He must have saved every dime he got to buy that ring. Joel wanted to marry Hazel. Her heart ached for that kind of love.

Joel turned quietly to face the steering wheel. His head down. "I think I'll make a good husband. I mean, I'll try with everything in me."

Ruthie felt guilty for being so focused on herself and her problems. She cleared her throat then smacked Joel on the shoulder. He winced and rubbed the spot.

"You will make a wonderful husband. Don't be stupid."

He smiled and continued to rub the spot.

"I'm sorry. I was just shocked. It's a big step. Hazel will love the ring."

His face brightened.

She pointed a finger at him, "But you better not do anything until you ask Daddy's permission for her hand."

Joel grimaced, "Yeah, I know."

Across the gigantic screen, huge clay hands appeared clutching swords as the opening credits began to roll upwards. The door screeched open, letting in a rush of cool air. Hazel stood there, cheeks and nose rosy from the frigid weather. Her pink fingers filled with two large bags of popcorn and two large drinks. Ruthie stepped out of the truck and Hazel handed her one of the popcorn bags and a drink.

She smiled, "Did I miss anything?"

Joel flashed a look at Ruthie.

Ruthie coughed. "No, ya missed nothing. Nothing at all."

Chapter 23

JOEL, MARCH 1961

Joel bent over to put the final touches on the white Pontiac Tempest. He had changed the oil, aired up the tires, and waxed the exterior. He rubbed a hand over the white, shiny hood, feeling the slick wax coating. *It looks good.* Over the last few months, he'd worked overtime repairing everything wrong with the Tempest, and it had been a lot, but now it was finished. Joel jogged to the front of the shop where Mr. Hal's office was located. The door was open, but he knocked on the door frame anyway.

"Hey, Mr. Hal."

Hal Sutherland looked up from a pile of paperwork on top of his desk. His glasses sat crooked on his nose, and a pencil perched behind his ear.

"Bills," Mr. Hal said, blowing out a gush of air. He reached up and scratched his full salt and pepper beard.

"Need any help?" Joel asked, hoping he didn't.

Mr. Hal raised an eyebrow. "The Tempest ready?"

Joel felt heat move to his face. He nodded.

Mr. Hal chuckled. "Get out of here, boy. Take the rest of the day off."

Excitement flooded in Joel's chest. He wanted to run out of the garage and not look back, but he paused. He didn't want to slack on his job. He owed Mr. Hal so much. He'd given him an opportunity when probably no one else would, and he worked with him, letting Joel play football and go to school and never complained when Joel came in late from practice.

"I can come back if you need me."

Mr. Hal looked down at the papers and waved his hand in the air. "Go. Have fun. Before I change my mind."

Joy surged through Joel, and he took off, not giving Mr. Hal a chance to say otherwise. He jogged to the Tempest and slid inside onto the smooth, tan-and-white-striped bench seat. He took hold of the large steering wheel with both hands. Although the ring and box in his pocket weighed mere ounces, it felt like a fifty-pound brick.

Joel looked in the rearview mirror to back the car through the garage door opening. On the road, he had to resist the urge to stomp on the gas pedal. Today, he was going to ask Hazel to be his wife. As he drove, his mind played through what he would say. He thought about his conversation with Mr. McKay over a month ago. He'd came to the garage to visit Mr. Hal. Joel remembered how his legs quivered as he asked Mr. McKay if he could speak to him privately in the office.

"What's all this about, Hal?" Mr. McKay asked.

Mr. Hal just grinned and shrugged. He knew exactly why Joel wanted to speak with Mr. McKay. Mrs. Anne had helped Joel pick out Hazel's ring. Joel's heart raced as he listened to Mr. McKay stomp behind him toward Mr. Hal's office. In the office, Joel couldn't get the words to come out. His tongue felt thick and heavy, like it was a piece of rubber. His words came out in blubbering stutters.

"Sir, I-I'd like to a-ask for your p-permission to ask for Hazel's hand."

Joel released the steering wheel and used his knees to drive as he wiped his sweaty hands on his garage blues. The memory still made him nervous. He gripped the Tempest steering wheel tighter.

Mr. McKay had frowned. Joel remembered his heart felt like it dropped to the floor. He worried Mr. McKay thought he wasn't good enough for Hazel. Joel knew he wasn't, not really, but he'd give his all to make her happy.

"What are you trying to tell me, boy? You want to marry Hazel?" Mr. McKay's eyes narrowed on him like a hawk about to attack its prey.

Joel swallowed hard.

"My Hazel?" he asked, pointing to his chest.

Joel nodded, "Y-yes sir." He felt like his insides might fall out. His stomach clenched tight, and for a moment, he thought he might vomit in Mr. Hal's silver trash can. Standing under Mr. McKay's piercing stare made Joel wish he'd just punch him and get it over with. The silence that spread between them felt heavy. *Just spit it out*, Joel thought. *End my misery*. He wondered if there was anything he could ever do in a million years to show Mr. McKay that he was worthy of his daughter. He felt like a part of him was dying with every silent second that passed.

Mr. McKay coughed to clear his throat. "Well, I know my Hazel thinks an awful lot of you."

Joel gritted his teeth waiting for the dreaded shoe to drop.

"And Hal tells me you're a hard worker and a good boy. I mean, good man."

Mr. McKay ran a hand through his dark hair streaked with gray at the temples. Joel tried to keep his hands pressed tightly to his sides, hoping Mr. McKay wouldn't see them trembling. Mr. McKay looked down at the office floor. *This was it. The moment he says no.* Joel couldn't look him in the eyes because he knew his heart was about to be torn from his chest, and his fears that he wasn't good enough would be made real. This was the moment his future died.

"I only ask you for one thing."

Joel blinked unsure what he was hearing. He looked back up to meet Mr. McKay's eyes. "Anything. I'll do anything," he blurted out.

Mr. McKay nodded. Joel wasn't certain, but was Mr. McKay smiling? At the corner of his mouth, his lips had begun to curve upward.

"You can propose to my Hazel, but all I ask is wait until she finishes high school to get married. It's just until next May. I want her to get her diploma. I know what happens when girls get married and babies start a-coming."

A cascading wave of relief washed over Joel. He thought he might drop to the floor. Mr. McKay gave him his blessing. Joel wanted to run through the office door and shout it for everyone to hear. His mind was in a flurry.

"You hear me, boy?" Mr. McKay had asked.

"Yes. Yes!" he said with more force than needed. "Of course, we will wait until she graduates to marry."

Mr. McKay walked toward him with his hand outstretched. The room around Joel got brighter, the colors more vivid, like he was in a dream. He shook Mr. McKay's hand. Mr. McKay squeezed his hand tightly.

"I guess I should say, welcome to the family."

Joel swerved the Tempest to keep from running off the road. His heart flew into his throat. He rubbed his face with his hand. He had to get a hold of himself, but his nerves were on edge. By the time he turned onto the dirt road to Hazel's house, his stomach was tied in knots.

Hazel ran onto the porch. Her short hair bobbed as she rushed down the porch steps. She looked beautiful, and just seeing her and her bright smile calmed him in a way he could not explain. She waved her arm in the air. He parked the car and got out.

"I didn't know you were coming over today," she said, hugging him.

He breathed in her lavender freshness. He closed his eyes and squeezed her close. She looked up at him and rested her chin on his chest.

"You got a new car?"

He smiled, "It's not new, and it's not mine."

Her face scrunched in an adorable way. She pulled away from him. She walked over to the car and laid her hand on it.

"It's a real beauty. Are you test driving it for someone?"

Mr. Hal had taught him to test drive every vehicle he repaired to make sure it worked properly before returning it to its owners.

He couldn't help but chuckle, "Yeah, in a way."

Hazel whipped around to face him. "What do you mean 'in a way'? This is a ways out for you to be test driving it here, ain't it?" She tilted her head to the side.

He held up the keys and rattled them before handing them to her.

She held them out like they were a feral kitten trying to scratch her. "What's going on?" she asked her eyes narrowed.

"It's yours."

Her mouth fell open, and he couldn't help but laugh.

"What do you mean it's mine?" She turned to look at the car again. "How?"

He came and stood beside her. He looped his arm around her shoulder. "Your dad found it months ago and bought it. He brought it to the shop and hired me to repair it for you. He wanted it to be a surprise. He said, when it was ready, to bring it over to you. I just finished it today."

"You've been working on it?" she asked with raised eyebrows.

Joel felt a flush run over him. "Well, yeah. At night and on my own time."

She looked down at the keys in her hands. He saw a wide smile spread across her face. She turned and squeezed him until he couldn't breathe.

"Thank you."

"Don't thank me. It was your dad. He hated ya'll having to bum rides. He wanted you to be safe."

Hazel buried her head in his chest. "Yeah, but you fixed it up."

She turned in his arms to face the Tempest. Joel's arms draped around her. Her back pressed against his chest.

"I can't believe it's all mine."

He felt her body go rigid in his arms. She turned around to face him. A worried look replaced her smile. "Joel, I can't drive. What am I going to do?", her forehead crinkled.

He laughed hard. Hazel pulled away from him and swatted at him.

"Quit your laughing. This is a serious matter. I can't have a car if I can't drive."

He touched her hair, running his hand gently across her cheek. He felt her shiver. He leaned down to let his lips graze hers before he pressed them firmly against Hazel's ruby mouth. She leaned into him. He pulled away, not wanting to stop, but knowing he had too. They were alone here, and that was too dangerous.

"Mr. Hal gave me the whole afternoon off."

"He did?" she said in a slurred tone.

"Yep, I'm going to teach you to drive."

Her eyes opened wide in alarm. "Oh my!"

"Yep, I hope no one in town is outside. It could get very dangerous for them."

He felt a sharp elbow jab him in the ribs, and it took him a bit to catch his breath between chuckles. He pushed his hands in his pocket and felt the smoothness of the ring box. Today, he was going to teach his future wife to drive.

Chapter 24

Hazel

Hazel felt her insides tremble. Although the inside of the Tempest was stuffy, making it hard to breathe, she felt a cold surge pass through her when she gripped the steering wheel for the very first time. The hard, stiff metal in her hands made her feel nauseous. This car belonged to her. Daddy had bought it for her, and Joel repaired it. Excitement mingled with fear. She felt so small inside it. She looked over at Joel, sitting on the passenger side.

"I don't think I can do this."

He smiled, "You can."

His optimism did little to alleviate her anxiety. She had no idea what her feet were supposed to do. *Are my hands in the proper place on the steering wheel? What if I need to stop? To go? I'm not going fast. I'm just going to take it easy. I can do this, right? Yes. No. Yes! Definitely!* She looked at the numbers on the dashboard. They stretched in a straight line from zero to one hundred and twenty. She felt her lunch rise in the back of her throat. The round silver center of the steering wheel stared back at her, judging her. She gripped the cold metal tighter. She felt like she was gasping for air as her chest rose and fell with rapid speed.

"I don't think I can do this," she said again.

Joel's response was to lean over and point at the pedals on the floorboard. "The long one on the right is the gas pedal. The one beside it is the brake."

"What's that third one over there?" she pointed to the tiny pedal looking thing on the left. "I only have two legs."

Joel chuckled, "That's the parking brake. Don't worry about it now. You're only going to use your right foot to work the gas and the break."

"Only my right foot?" she said with alarm.

"Right now, let's go slowly. First, let's start the car."

Hazel shook her head. "No."

Joel furrowed his eyebrows, "What?"

"No, I will not start the car."

Joel sighed and ran a hand down his face. "Hazel, grab the key. Twist it and start your car." His voice sounded firm, but he gently touched her shoulder. "You can do this."

She didn't believe him, but she didn't want to act like a scared baby in front of him either. Her heart pounded rapidly in her chest as she reached down and took the key in her quivering hand. She thought her heart might burst out of her chest when she twisted the key. The sound of the engine roared to life, which practically made her jump out of her skin. She looked over at Joel while she twisted the key farther.

His eyes grew wide and his face grimaced when the engine started to grind. "No! Stop! That's too much!"

She released the key like it was on fire and had scorched her skin. His chest rose as he sucked in a deep breath. She was going to kill them both today. Joel closed his eyes and took another deep breath. When he opened his eyes, his voice was calmer.

"Okay, this is an automatic. You're going to put your foot on the brake and take the gear selector right there," he pointed to the stick-looking thing on the right side of the steering wheel, "and move it to D for drive."

Hazel nodded. She tried to repeat back to herself everything he'd just said, but the blood rushed in her ears.

"You ready?" he asked.

She wasn't, but she said nothing and bit her bottom lip.

"Okay, let's split," he said like she had just learned everything she needed to know about driving this death trap.

She moved the stick to drive and felt something underneath her shift. She sucked in a breath and held it.

"Now breathe, then slowly lift your foot off the brake and lightly, I said lightly, press the gas."

Hazel did what she was told. The car slowly lurched forward, and they were off.

An hour after driving on dirt roads, Hazel's clothes were drenched, and her back ached from sitting so stiff.

Joel turned on the radio. He twisted the knob, passing through random stations and static.

"Can you please turn that off?" Hazel said. Her voice sounded harsh to her ears.

He reached back over and turned it off then leaned back against the seat, crossing his arms in front of him. "I don't know what you're worried about. You're doing fine."

She released a huge breath. *At least we're on back roads.*

Joel turned to her. "Let's head to town. I could use a hamburger and a shake. I'm starving."

Hazel felt her stomach drop. She wasn't even close to being hungry. How could Joel be hungry at a time like this?

"Town?"

"Yeah, you're ready. Plus, you gotta take me back to the shop so I can get the truck."

"I have to take you to the shop? That's downtown, where people will be!"

Joel laughed. "How'd you think I was gettin' back?"

Hazel's knuckles turned white as she clenched the steering wheel harder. Real people were going to be in danger now. Not just cows and chickens, but actual people.

In town, Hazel drove under the speed limit. If the speed limit was thirty, she went twenty. Sometimes fifteen. She could feel Joel squirming in the seat beside her.

"You know, you could drive a little faster," he chided.

"Do you want a burger, or do you want to die?"

In her peripheral vision, she saw Joel's mouth tighten. He leaned back in the seat and didn't say anything else until she pulled safely into Judy's Drive-in. When she turned the car off, she wrapped her arms around herself, so thankful to be in one piece. Joel grinned at her before leaning over to kiss her cheek.

"You did wonderful."

She shook her head and opened the door, anxious to be out of the car.

Her legs felt weak as she slid into the red booth seat across from Joel. He laid an arm across the table with his hand palm up. She laid her trembling hand inside of his. He rubbed his thumb in slow circles against her skin, sending chills through her hand and up her arm, loosening her tight muscles. She wanted to kiss him, but she noticed he was frowning as he stared at the hand he was holding.

"Hazel," he whispered.

His voice sounded strange, and she worried something was wrong.

"Yes?" she said. Not sure she wanted him to answer.

"We've been having a real blast together."

She nodded and worried about where this conversation was going.

"And you know that I love you," he said so softly she almost didn't hear.

"I love you too, Joel."

"Well, I've been meaning to," he sucked in air. "I've been wanting to say, or really, ask you something for a while now."

"Hazel!" Alice's high-pitched squeal could be heard across the restaurant. Alice ran over and bounced into the booth next to Hazel, breaking her and Joel's hands apart. Alice wrapped her arms around her and squeezed.

"David!" Alice yelled, motioning with her arm. "Come over here."

David squeezed into the booth beside Joel.

"Hey," he said. Hazel nearly laughed. David was a man of few words, and Alice had so many. They were a match made in heaven.

"I had no idea you were here," Alice said. "I didn't see Mr. Hal's truck."

Joel broke into a wide smile, "That's because we came in Hazel's new car."

"Get outta here," Alice shrieked.

Joel pointed outside the huge rectangular window, "It's that white Pontiac Tempest sitting right there."

Alice and David both rose from the booth to see out the window.

"Far out," Alice said.

"And she drove it here all by herself," Joel said, winking at Hazel.

Hazel felt her cheeks flush, and she couldn't help but grin. *I did drive it here. My very own car.* She hardly believed it herself.

Alice turned to her, "Driving here must have been a real blast."

Hazel pursed her lips, "Well, I wouldn't say a blast, but we lived."

"That's just groovy," Alice said, reaching over Hazel to grab a menu from its place between the napkin holder and condiments. "I'm starving. What are ya'll having?"

Hazel noticed Joel's face twist in a funny way before he shook his head. "I'm going to have a bacon cheeseburger and a chocolate malt."

"Me too," David said.

Hazel knew something was wrong with Joel. He'd wanted to ask her something before they were interrupted. She wondered what it could be, but looking at his face now, she knew it wasn't something good. Maybe she didn't really want to know. She looked over at Alice and was glad for the disruption.

"So, what are you wearing to prom? Don't tell me you haven't been thinking about it. It's next month."

Hazel had been thinking about it. Ruthie had been talking about prom nonstop.

"Ms. Faye is taking Ruthie and me to Fort Smith this weekend to shop for our dresses."

"Ruthie?" Joel asked. He apparently had been eavesdropping while he and David discussed cars. "She's a sophomore. I thought only juniors and seniors were allowed at prom."

"Unless" Alice chirped, "a junior or senior asks you to the prom as their date."

"She has a date?" Joel asked, his eyebrows raised. The corners of his mouth turned down. "With who?"

Hazel shrugged, "She wouldn't say. Someone on the football team I suppose, but I don't know."

"Is your dad gonna let her go? Surely not." Joel asked, his frown growing longer.

"She asked him last night when he called, and he said yes. She was beyond excited. Of course, she'll have to come with us."

"I bet she's excited," Alice said. "I'd have died and went to heaven if I could have gone to prom as a sophomore."

Hazel and Alice spent the rest of the meal talking about prom dresses and who was going with whom. Joel and David occasionally added tidbits to the conversation, but Hazel could tell Joel wasn't happy. He tried to act like nothing was wrong, but she could see through his facade. He was angry. Whether it was the news about Ruthie going to prom with a guy on the football team or the fact that he'd never gotten to talk to her about what he wanted to discuss, she wasn't sure. But he wasn't himself, that she knew.

By the time they all stepped out of Judy's Drive-In, it was dark. The night sky was illuminated by the full moon and a blanket of stars. Hazel looked at her car. The dim streetlight by the parking lot cast a bright yellow glow on the hood, but the inside was pitch black. She shivered knowing she would have to drive it home by herself in the dark. She and Joel said their good-byes to Alice and David then crawled inside the car. She turned the overhead light on to help her see enough to stick the key in the ignition.

On the way to Hal's Service Station, Joel was quiet, like he was in another world. She wanted to talk to him and ask him what was wrong, but she could only focus on one thing, and that thing was not killing them. She pulled up near the truck and put the car in park. Her heart still pounded, and she was certain she'd never get used to this driving thing. She turned to Joel and saw he was watching her. His face serious.

"Did I do something wrong?"

He cupped her face in his hand, and she felt a jolt of energy surge inside her. Even with only the light of the moon, she could see his eyes were soft.

"Of course not, you are learning quickly. Just, tonight didn't really go as I'd planned."

She wasn't sure what he meant. *Was he disappointed Alice and David sat with them?* Her face must have revealed what she was thinking because Joel chuckled.

"Don't worry, I had fun." He leaned in and kissed her lips. Heat washed over her, evaporating her worries. Her lips parted, wanting more of him, but he stopped before she was ready. He touched his forehead to hers. She felt his warm breath on her skin and something deep inside her stirred. He pulled away, and it was all she could do not to outwardly groan. She could see he was trying to keep himself in control.

"You better get home."

She didn't respond but breathed in the faint scent of his Brut cologne that still hung in the air between them. She wanted more of his mouth. More of his hands on her. It wasn't proper the thoughts she was having, but she couldn't help it. She was helplessly and deeply in love with him.

When she could speak, she confessed, "I'm not sure I can do this by myself."

He leaned in, and she felt her breath catch, but he only gave her a light peck on the cheek. "You can do it. I believe in you."

She rolled her eyes.

On the way home, she gripped the steering wheel so hard, her hands felt stiff. She knew the speed limit was forty-five, but she felt twenty-five was sufficient. Joel told her he thought she was already ready for her driver's test, but she didn't feel ready. He also told her he believed she could make it home all by herself, but he'd lied. She looked back in the rearview mirror at the familiar headlights that had been following her for the last ten miles. She wasn't sure if she should be frustrated or comforted by him following her.

A pang caught in her chest. In less than two months, Joel would be graduating. They'd never really discussed their future or what would happen after graduation. *Would he leave Waldron?* He'd told her how he hated being in a town where he could run into his pa at any time. He'd also confessed to her that he felt many of the townspeople judged him based on his pa's actions or because he was his son. *Maybe he'd want to start over some place where no one knew him.* Mr. Hal had taught him many valuable skills. If he left, she knew Daddy would never let her go with him. She still had another whole year until graduation. She wondered if that was what he wanted to talk about—their future.

She looked in the rearview mirror. Joel's headlights glared behind her like two glowing eyes. She'd never make it without him. He was the one she wanted for life. She just hoped he felt the same about her.

Chapter 25

RUTHIE, APRIL 1961

"Okay, get together," Daddy said as he motioned with one hand while trying to hold his Kodak Brownie 127 camera in the other.

Ruthie pulled at the pink-laced bodice. She felt constricted, and it was hard to breathe. The sheer puff sleeves made moving her arms difficult. She reached up and touched her hair. Mrs. Anne had secured it in a loose updo. She moved to stand next to Hazel and Joel on the porch. The pink netting of her dress scrunched into the pale-blue netting of Hazel's dress. They'd found their dresses at Lora Lee's in Fort Smith. They were exactly the same style except for the color, and they were on sale. She ran her hands down the netting to straighten it.

"Oh, Hal, don't they look lovely," Mrs. Anne said, her hands laid across her chest.

Ms. Faye stood beside their father. Her eyes glistened.

"Yes, lovely," Mr. Hal said, taking a swig of Coca-Cola.

Ruthie looked at Hazel. Her short hair was pulled back using a rhinestone headband Ms. Faye had let her borrow. Ruthie had borrowed one of Mrs. Anne's beaded barrettes to secure her updo. She also borrowed the matching beaded necklace. The beads sparkled in the porch light.

Ruthie glimpsed at the white orchid corsage fastened to Hazel's wrist above her gloved hand. Its center was streaked with dark violet. Hazel was smiling, holding the corsage hand to Joel's chest as she leaned into him for pictures. His bowtie a pale blue to match Hazel's dress. Ruthie looked down at her empty wrists. He'd have a corsage for her, surely. *There's no reason to worry, right?*

"Okay, smile everyone," Daddy directed, getting her attention.

Ruthie looked toward him and forced a smile. This was supposed to be a happy day. She was a sophomore going to prom, but for some reason, she didn't feel happy.

"Daddy, we better get going," Hazel said.

He reached into his pants pocket and took out a few dollars. He pressed the money into Hazel's gloved hand.

"Make sure you share with your sister."

Hazel leaned up on her toes and kissed him on the cheek. Ruthie went to him and kissed him on the other cheek.

"Thanks, Daddy."

"Your date is meeting you there?" he asked again for the millionth time. His eyebrows knit together, making creases across his forehead.

"Yes," Ruthie said. She tried to think fast for an excuse about why Donald White wasn't picking her up. He'd never actually explained that he wouldn't be coming to get her when he asked her to prom three weeks ago. *He had a good reason*, she told herself. She grasped the first thing that came to her mind. "He said he had something at home he had to do before the dance, and he couldn't get out of it."

Joel narrowed his eyes. He didn't want her going to the dance with Donald. He'd already pulled her to the side and given her a "be careful with that cat" speech. But Joel didn't know him like she did. Donald was obnoxious sometimes, sure, but he was also silly and sweet. He made her laugh, and in the words of Margarette Ann, "he was a real hunk."

They loaded into Mr. Hal's truck. Hazel scooted next to Joel. Ms. Faye helped Ruthie push the pink netting inside so it wouldn't get stuck in the door when it closed. They waved good-bye to them all and took off. Ruthie's fingers tingled, and she felt light-headed. *This is it. I'm going to prom.*

On the road, Ruthie looked over at Hazel and Joel. They held hands, and smiles beamed across their faces. She sighed and looked out the window. The blue sky was dotted with dark gray clouds, and the trees dripped with leftover rain. The truck tires raced over puddles, splashing the bright green grass. In the distance, the sky transformed into a hazy orange as the sun began to set. *Would tonight be the night? Would Donald ask her to go steady?* Although she hadn't really spoken to him much since he asked her to prom, the weeks prior to that he'd practically been all over her. Flirting with her. Going out of his way to find her. He loved making her laugh. Once he even snuck a kiss on the cheek in the school hallway. She'd been so tickled pink when he asked her to prom, she almost fainted. She looked at her reflection in the window. *We are going to look so cute together.*

Ruthie looked over at Hazel and Joel. Hazel leaned her head on his shoulder. Ruthie hoped tonight she'd have someone to love too.

At the school, Joel parked in the gymnasium parking lot. He'd found a spot not far from the brick building. He helped her and Hazel out of the truck. She and Hazel helped each other straighten the netting on their dresses.

Ruthie looked around at the cars and trucks arriving. Students were getting out of vehicles dressed in beautiful attire—fancy dresses and suits with jackets and ties. All the pretty updos and sheer, shiny material of the dresses made Ruthie's stomach twist with excitement. She walked slowly behind Joel and Hazel, letting her eyes scan the school parking lot for Donald or his truck. She didn't see either. They walked toward the double doors of the gym. Balloons and crepe paper decorated the entrance. At the door, Joel reached out to push the bar to open it, but Hazel laid a hand on his arm to stop him.

She turned to Ruthie. "Do you see him?"

Ruthie shook her head, "No, but I'm sure he'll be here soon. Maybe I should wait inside for him. It's kind of cool out here."

Hazel nodded and they entered.

The entrance of the gym was filled with music. Elvis Presley's rich voice singing, "Are You Lonesome Tonight?" echoed from the basketball court and into the opened entrance space. A faux green, blue, and orange coral arch extended above the entrance to the basketball court, creating the illusion that all who passed under would be magically transported to a world under the sea. It reminded Ruthie of one of Hazel's stories. The one with the mermaid who never wanted to leave the ocean. A few stray blue balloons rolled out from under the arch and bounced near the check-in table that sat near the concession stand.

Nancy Graham and another cheerleader sat at the table in their silk lace dresses, checking in the attendees. Nancy's lips were stained bright red to match her dress. They pulled across big, white teeth as she smiled.

"After you and your dates are checked in, please take one of these voting slips and pencils and vote for prom queen and king. The prom queen and king can only be seniors. The voting box is inside near the clam shell," Nancy explained. "Place your ballots in there and don't forget. Voting is very important."

Hazel and Joel got in line to wait to be checked in, and Ruthie stood behind them. Her eyes darted back at the door they'd come through, hoping Donald would push them open and announce in some silly way that he had arrived. She hoped he'd apologize for being late by sweeping her off her feet and kissing her right on the lips.

When they made it to the check-in table, Nancy went through her speech again. She handed Hazel and Joel a voting slip, then they moved to the side to allow Ruthie access to the table.

"Hi, Ruthie!" Nancy said, smiling. "Don't you look lovely tonight." Nancy's smile faded as she twisted her head from side to side. "Who's your date for tonight? You know sophomores can't enter without their dates. It's the rule."

Ruthie gripped her gloved hands together. She felt her throat tighten. She looked toward Hazel and saw concern in her eyes. Ruthie cleared her throat. "Oh, um, Donald White invited me." She heard the waver in her voice. "I don't think he's here yet. Or I didn't see him. I wondered if he'd said anything to ya'll."

Nancy looked toward the wide-eyed cheerleader that sat beside her. "Have you seen Donald yet? I thought you checked him in earlier."

The other cheerleader looked as if she might cry. Ruthie felt her face burn. She thought she might cry too, and she didn't want to do that in front of everyone here watching her. Nancy looked down at the papers she'd been marking. She shuffled through them, examining them closely. Ruthie shifted uneasily from one foot to the other. Nancy pursed her lips to the side and tsked before she looked up to meet Ruthie's eyes. She didn't have to say anything, Ruthie already knew the answer. A heaviness settled in her chest.

Nancy leaned forward and said in a low voice, "Ruthie, I'm so sorry. There must have been some kind of misunderstanding. Donald has already checked in, and he brought Betsey Marsh as his date. He's only allowed one date." She paused. Her eyes flickered back down to her papers. "That's the rule."

Ruthie's head went fuzzy, and her mind reeled with images of Betsy Marsh's huge bosom and round face. The cheerleader sitting beside Nancy bit her bottom lip, and Hazel covered her mouth. Joel balled his hands into fists.

"I'll kill him," Joel hissed.

Ruthie felt like the air had been kicked out of her. *How could I have been so dumb?* There was no misunderstanding. Donald asked her, but he'd found a better date with bigger bosoms. She'd been so excited to be invited, she never suspected anything was wrong. He'd kissed her and flirted with her. *I should have known something wasn't right when he never called me or spoke to me about picking me up. I'm so stupid. Worse than stupid. I can't handle this!* She felt her lunch creeping up her throat. The blood rushed through her head, making it hard to think. Her knees became weak, and she swayed on her feet. Hazel rushed to her and grabbed one arm. Joel grabbed the other.

"We're going to step outside for some air and work this all out," Hazel told Nancy.

Nancy nodded, "I'm so sorry, Ruthie."

Ruthie walked in a daze. She could feel Hazel and Joel guiding her out the gymnasium doors. Everything around her moved slowly, like she was trapped in a horrible nightmare. People in line stared at her. Heat rose from the back of her neck to her cheeks.

Outside, the cool air hit her like a brick wall. She blinked and her whole body shivered. But the brisk wind brought her back to herself. Forced her to focus.

"Let's get you in the truck, so we can head home," Hazel said. She pulled Ruthie toward the parking lot.

Ruthie's mind snapped, and she jerked away from Hazel and Joel's arms.

Hazel gasped, "What are you doing? Don't you wanna go home?"

Ruthie closed her eyes and sucked in a ragged breath. She shook her head. "No, if you take me home, you'll miss the whole dance."

Hazel tilted her head. "That's alright." She looked at Joel. "We don't mind."

Joel nodded, "Yeah, Ruthie, we don't mind. Let's get you home and I'll take care of Donald later."

Ruthie stomped her foot and hugged her arms around herself. "No, I will not let Donald White ruin this night for ya'll too. It's your senior year, Joel!"

"It's really okay," he said, reaching for her hand. She drew back away from him.

"No!" she said loudly. "Give me the truck keys. I will sit in the truck. This whole situation has exhausted me, and I need to rest."

Hazel and Joel looked at each other with uncertainty.

Ruthie stuck her finger out, "You are not missing your senior prom because of some stupid incident. You know I mean it. And you can't change my mind when I mean it."

Hazel sighed. Her shoulders slumped forward. Joel handed Ruthie the keys.

"We won't stay long. Promise," Hazel said and leaned in to hug her.

Ruthie watched them go back through the gymnasium doors. She wished she could go inside and find Donald. She'd punch him right in the face. She gripped the keys in her hand. The edges dug into her palm. The sky had changed to dark blue, and the lights surrounding the gym flickered on. Bugs began to dart and buzz around them like they'd been waiting for just this moment. *What am I going to do?* She gripped the keys harder. *How can I ever show my face in school again?* She'd be the laughingstock of all the football boys. *This is a nightmare!*

"Ruthie?"

She jumped when she heard her name. Her face heated when she saw Ronnie Hartley standing near her dressed in a white suit jacket, black slacks, and a long, thin black tie. His rust-colored hair was slicked back at the sides. He looked dreamy.

"What ya doin' out here? You waiting for someone?"

She felt her body grow hot. She didn't want to tell Ronnie what had happened. It was mortifying. She twisted the truck keys around in her gloved hands. Her eyes focused on the sidewalk as she spoke.

"I was waiting for someone, but it was a misunderstanding, so no," was all she could manage to get out before her throat constricted.

"Oh," Ronnie said. "Well, you sure look nice."

Ruthie's eyelashes fluttered. On any other day, a compliment from Ronnie Hartley would have made her swoon, but tonight her emotions were all tangled in knots. She felt raw and exposed. She felt herself withering under Ronnie's stare. She'd come to prom without a date.

Ronnie cleared his throat. "So, I was thinkin' since you aren't really with anyone 'cause of the misunderstanding and all. And I don't have a date. If you'd—well, I'd love if you came to the dance with me. If you wanna, but I understand if you don't. It's no sweat, but I think we'd have a gas."

Ruthie was sure her mouth had fallen open. Her body felt the change before her brain could register it. Humiliation morphed into sheer happiness. It was like she'd swallowed a barrel of butterflies, all fluttering and dancing inside her stomach.

"I-I'd love to," she said, her head spinning.

"Far out. But I think you're missing something."

Ruthie looked around; not sure what Ronnie meant.

"Don't worry. I think I can fix it." He said as he removed a pocketknife from his back pants pocket. He walked to the end of the gym and disappeared around the corner into the dark shadows where the glow of the streetlights couldn't reach. When he returned, one of his hands was behind his back and a silly grin on his face. Ruthie couldn't help but smile. Ronnie pulled his hand out and Ruthie gasped when she saw the fully bloomed yellow rose, he held between his finger and thumb.

"It's beautiful," she said as she leaned in to smell the sweet flower's fragrance.

"Well, my date couldn't go to the dance without a corsage. Now how do we pin it?"

Ruthie reached up and pulled a bobby pin from her hair. Using it, Ronnie helped her secure the rose onto the back of her glove. He took her hand in his and her heart soared. He led her through the gymnasium doors. The two passed Nancy, whose eyes were as big as saucers, and through the coral reef arch. Ruthie blinked her eyes to adjust to the dim lights. Blue paper hung from the walls and fake coral arrangements were scattered throughout the basketball court. The light bounced off the blue paper like bubbles on water, and lose balloons floated around their feet.

Ruthie spotted Hazel and Joel standing near the refreshment table, a small punch cup in each of their hands. Hazel was staring down at her cup, frowning. When she looked up, Ruthie waved wildly at her. Hazel's eyes brightened and a wide smile spread across her face. She reached out to touch Joel's arm. He looked up from the red liquid in his cup. She pointed, and Joel followed her finger. His eyes lit up when he saw her and Ronnie. Just then, the melodic rich tones of Roy Hamilton singing "Unchained Melody" resonated throughout the space.

"Would you like to dance," Ronnie asked softly.

Ruthie nodded, too afraid to answer, fearing she may squeal in delight. Ronnie slid his arm around her waist and moved her to the center of the floor. Her heart pitter-pattered as he pulled her close to him and took her right hand in his. His other hand tightened around her waist, drawing her in until they were practically chest to chest. He was so close, she could smell the woodsy aftershave he was wearing. She breathed in the strong, clean scent. She never wanted to forget it. Her body leaned into him. When they touched, she felt a jolt of electricity pass through her. Her head went fuzzy as they swayed in place.

Her eyes glanced around the room. Hazel and Joel joined them on the dance floor. Hazel laid her head on Joel's shoulder. Their bodies moved slowly, rocking in time with the music. Alice and David were dancing too. Ruthie couldn't hear her, but Alice's mouth was moving a mile a minute, and David nodded at her, smiling. Ruthie giggled to herself. Her giggling stopped in her throat when she saw Donald's date, Betsy Marsh, standing by herself awkwardly to the side of the dance area. Her face set in a vacant glower. Donald was nowhere to be seen. Ruthie felt sorry for her. There was no telling what kind of trouble Donald was off causing.

She looked up at Ronnie. "Are you excited about graduation?"

He smiled down at her, "Yeah, I guess."

"What are you going to do?" After the question slipped out, she could have kicked herself. She knew what he was going to do after graduation. Joel had told her.

Ronnie smiled, "I'm gonna join the army. My dad was in the army, my grandpa, my great-grandpa, practically all the men in my family join the army."

Ruthie scrunched her face. She knew it wasn't any of her business, but she had to ask. "But is it something you really want to do? Not just because your family has always done it?"

Ronnie chuckled, "Yes, I'm not just doing it because of my family. I do have my own mind you know."

She looked down at his chest and felt her cheeks heat.

"Although," he paused, waiting for her to meet his eyes. "Tradition does play a part in it. But it's what I want. I want to serve my country."

Ruthie sighed. She hated the thought of him leaving Waldron.

He smiled, "So, what are you going to do? I guess you got a few more years to decide."

Ruthie bit her lip. She'd never told anyone what she wanted to do, not even Hazel or Margarette Ann. But the night felt magical, and she felt like if she told Ronnie, maybe her impossible dream could come true. "Well, I've been thinking about it, I really have."

"And?" he prodded.

"When I was little, I took care of a baby squirrel that had dropped from its nest. I tended to him, and he grew up. And eventually he ran off to be with a girl squirrel." She sighed. The memory of the day Henry ran out the door was always tinged with sadness. She shook it off. "I realized, I really enjoyed caring for him. I think I'd like to care for people more."

Ronnie raised his eyebrows.

"I'd like to be a nurse. But I know it's impossible. The schooling is expensive, and there's no way for me to get to Fort Smith for classes. My family doesn't go to college, or even community college. They just never have. My daddy was the first to finish high school."

Ronnie made a scoffing sound. "It's not impossible. Anything's possible. Ruthie, you'd be a fine nurse."

Ruthie felt her smile widen until her cheeks ached.

"Don't give up because you think it might be hard." Ronnie gripped her waist tighter and pulled her closer to him.

She laid her head on his chest. His heart soothed her. She listened to the rhythmic sound of his heartbeat and the melody of the music. They mixed together, washing over her. She felt light as air, and her head spun with the magic of the evening. Everything around her faded away as she focused on being in Ronnie's arms. She thought maybe he was right, if this night was any indication, maybe anything could be possible.

Chapter 26

JOEL, MAY 1961

The bright afternoon sun beat down on Joel. It wasn't even full-on summer yet, and the heat was already stifling under his black gown. *I look like a dimwit in this black dress.* He shifted in the hard plastic seat. His buttocks had gone numb. He looked down at his worn dress shoes. The grass from the football field crunched under his feet. He looked from side to side. It was Saturday, and he was dressed in black and sitting in the sun with twenty other dummies. The makeshift stage sat in front of them. All Joel wanted was for the special speaker to stop talking, but instead he droned on and on about how their lives could begin now. Joel felt his life had already begun. He didn't think getting a piece of paper changed anything. Joel wanted to grab his diploma and leave. A bead of sweat tickled down the back of his neck, and he rubbed it away.

He let his eyes scan the bleachers where the audience sat. Joel thought everyone looked bored. He knew his pa wouldn't be there as he searched the faces. Since he'd moved out and into his duplex, he'd only seen his pa a handful of times. Joel made it a point to avoid wherever his pa's truck was parked like the plague. Even if that meant not getting groceries when he needed them. But mostly, his pa's truck was parked in places Joel didn't care to go, like at Quick Liquor or the Bulldog Pub. Joel shook his head, he wasn't looking for him anyway. He was looking for his real family.

Joel twisted in his seat and realized his leg had fallen asleep. He adjusted it and felt the prickly sensation run down his thigh to his foot. He wiggled his foot in his shoe. Finally, he saw them in the far corner of the bleachers. His body relaxed. Hazel sat next to Ruthie. Mr. McKay was there with Ms. Faye, even Mr. Hal and Mrs. Anne showed up. Joel swallowed the heavy lump that had formed in the back of his throat. They weren't his blood relatives, but it didn't matter. They cared for him just the same. He let his eyes fall on Hazel. Her hair was curled and held in place with a small band. Her blue dress matched the color of the sky. He breathed in deeply. Today was the day he decided. He'd propose today. He'd waited too long, searching for the perfect day, only to find out that no day was perfect. He wasn't going to wait any longer. He wanted her to be his wife. He knew they'd have to wait to marry. She'd have her turn to be the one baking in the hot sun under a long black gown, but he didn't care. Every second with her made his life better. Worth living.

The others around him began to clap and he realized the special speaker had finally stopped talking. He awkwardly joined in the clapping. The principal and his English teacher made their way to the podium. The principal congratulated the seniors and began to call their names.

"Francine Arnold."

There was a smattering of applause as she stood and made her way to the side of the stage. She climbed the stairs and walked toward the podium where the English teacher handed her a rolled-up piece of paper secured with a red ribbon. The principal shook her hand. One by one, the scenario was repeated with each senior's name that was called. Finally, Joel heard his name.

"Joel Davenport."

When he stood, he heard the whooping and hollering from his family in their small section. He could hear Mr. Hal above them all. He smiled and shook his head. He walked up the stairs and approached the podium. He couldn't explain it if he had to, but it felt good when the paper touched his hand. He held it gently, not wanting to crumple it. Joel reached out to take the smiling principal's hand. He wore a suit and sweat beaded across the principal's forehead that was red from the sun.

"Thank you," Joel said, making sure to give his hand a firm shake.

In a daze, Joel made his way back to his seat. He sat down and looked at the rolled-up paper in his hand. He touched the red bow. On his own, he had moved out, worked a job, and graduated from high school. Joel's eyes flickered up to where his family sat. He looked at their faces. *I didn't do anything on my own.* They'd helped him the entire way.

After the benediction prayer, everyone from the bleachers came down to the field to mingle with the graduates. Joel found his group quickly. Mr. Hal patted him hard on the back, sending Joel lurching forward.

"You did it, boy!"

Joel held up his diploma. The red ribbon hanging down. "I couldn't have done it without ya'll."

Mrs. Anne gave him a hug and kiss on the cheek. "We are so proud of you."

Ruthie looped her arm in his arm. "I think it's time to party."

"What?" Joel asked, confused.

Mr. McKay furrowed his eyebrows, "That was supposed to be a surprise, missy."

She shrugged, "I couldn't wait, Daddy. That speaker went on too long. Let's go get cake."

Joel glanced from face to face, not sure what was going on.

Hazel took his other arm and looped her arm through it. "We got a small surprise," she scowled at Ruthie when she said the word surprise, "party set for you at the house. With cake and everything." Her face beamed. "Ruthie and I made a yellow cake with chocolate icing, your favorite."

Joel went still. He'd never had a party thrown for him before. The gesture made it hard to speak, and his throat felt like it was constricting. "Thank ya'll. That's, uh, that's so kind," he said, stumbling over his words.

Hazel squeezed his arm, "Why don't you go change then meet us at the house. We'll have it all ready by the time you get there."

Ruthie piped up, "Hazel, you go with him and make sure he hurries. We can set everything up."

Mrs. Anne and Ms. Faye nodded their heads.

"We've got this dear, you go and make sure he doesn't dilly dally," Mrs. Anne agreed.

On the way to the duplex, Joel felt his stomach twist. He hadn't expected a party. The idea of proposing in front of everyone made his cheeks burn. He had to do it now before the party. The duplex wasn't far from the football field. Joel wished he could drive around the block a few times to shake out his nerves, but before he knew it, the truck was bouncing across the railroad tracks and pulling into the cracked, paved parking spot he shared with his neighbors, Milton and Sandra Lewis.

Their shared duplex was the same coffee brown color as all the rest. A bicycle with a missing front wheel lay on its side near the residents' shared mailboxes. Toys were scattered around the overgrown yards and the shrubs in front of the houses sprouted new growth, making them look misshapen. Joel had thought numerous times they needed a better groundskeeper.

Milton and Sandra were outside when they pulled up. Milton held a sunflower wreath in his hands, moving it up and down, right and left, across the front door of their half of the duplex. Sandra stood back to monitor Milton's work. Her pink cotton dress stretched tight across her huge, round belly. Her dark skin glistened in the sun, and her hand lay on the small of her back to provide support for her ever-growing belly.

When Joel opened his door, he heard Sandra speaking. "I told you, Mil. It was fine. I'm burnin' up out here."

Joel and Hazel walked toward the duplex and the Lewis's turned to greet them.

"She got you working, Milton?" Joel asked.

Sandra laughed, "More like he's got me working. Making a pregnant woman suffer in this heat just so he can be certain that silly thang is hung perfectly straight."

"No sense in doing it halfway," Milton said, releasing the wreath and stepping back to examine it.

"I think it looks wonderful," Hazel said.

Sandra walked up to her and gave her a hug, "Don't you go encouraging him."

"I think I might need you to hang one on your door, so they match," Milton said, looking toward Joel. "What you think?"

Joel chuckled, "I don't need a floral wreath.

Hazel swatted him. "You might. It looks nice."

Milton's dark eyes flashed brightly, and he smiled at Hazel. "It's settled then. I'm getting you a floral wreath for a graduation present."

Sandra took a lavender handkerchief and dabbed it across her forehead, "So, how was graduation?"

"Oh, it was long and boring. But we're fixin' to head to Hazel's house after I change for my party."

Milton blinked and gaped at Sandra, "I thought Mr. McKay told me that it was a surprise party?"

Hazel rolled her eyes. "It was, but Ruthie let the cat out of the bag."

Sandra and Milton laughed. "We were just about to head to your house after Mil hung that silly wreath."

Joel held up a hand. "Wait a minute, ya'll knew about this party too and never told me?"

Milton laid a hand on Joel's shoulder. "Right, that's what you commonly do when something is a surprise. Lord, help me. I've taught you nothing since you moved in here."

The laughing eased Joel's jangled nerves. He loved living next to Milton and Sandra. The long conversations with Milton were like a fresh salve, helping him to process his feelings about his pa. Joel didn't think his heart was completely healed, but when Milton prayed with him, he thought maybe one day he could forgive his pa and let go of his past. It also helped that Sandra was an excellent cook and would make extra for dinner to share with him. Joel looked at Milton and Sandra and knew, that now, in front of people who cared for him, this was the right time.

"Stay right here," he said and held up a finger. "I'll just be a minute." He ran to his front door, jerking it open. The jolt made the sunflower wreath on the Lewis's door bounce and sway. He rushed to his bedroom and threw his sock drawer open. He spilled white tube socks onto the floor. The ring box fell out. It rolled across the burnt orange shag carpet. He scooped it up and laid it on top of the dresser. He striped his sweaty clothes off, grabbed a white T-shirt, and pulled it over his head. It rolled up in the back, and he jumped around to try and straighten it. His stomach tightened. *This is it. I'm going to do it.* He slipped on his blue jeans and wiped damp palms on them before he grabbed the ring box from the dresser and hurried out the door. By the time he made it back outside, his shirt was already sticking to him.

He didn't wait for any introduction. He stood in front of Hazel, her eyes wide. He must look like a disheveled mess, he thought, as he ran a hand through his hair. "I've been wanting to do this for a while. But I couldn't find the right time or place. So, I guess now is as good as any."

He let out a long breath. Sandra gasped as he began to lower himself down to the ground. The hot pavement scorched his knee through his jeans. He opened the small box and held it out so Hazel could see inside it. Hazel covered her mouth with her hands.

"Oh my," she said in a muffled whisper.

His heart ricocheted all the way up in his throat. His body wavered on his knee, as his leg trembled underneath him. It felt like he was in a dream. He knew if he took the time and thought about it, he'd get choked up, so he just let the words pour out of him. They came straight from his heart and what he felt in the moment. "I love you, Hazel. Ever since I first saw you, I have loved you. Life just ain't worth living if you're not in it." He swallowed. "Marry me?"

Hazel looked over at Sandra. Her eyes glistened in the sun.

Sandra dabbed at the corner of her eyes with her handkerchief. She smiled, "Oh gracious, answer him. I can't stand it."

Hazel looked down at Joel. Their eyes locked together, and Joel stopped breathing.

Hazel dropped her hands from her mouth and threw herself at him, almost throwing him off balance. Her arms wrapped around his neck. "Yes, I'll marry you. I love you!"

He raised up with her in his arms and swung her around. Her feet flew in the air as they laughed. He gave her face hundreds of tiny kisses, tasting the salt from her tears. He couldn't believe it. *She said yes!* When they were both dizzy, he sat her down. She leaned into him, and he hugged her close.

Milton cleared his throat. "Aren't you gonna give her the ring?" he teased.

Joel laughed, "Shoot, yes!" He took the ring from the box. "It's engraved," he said, holding it so Hazel and Sandra could read the words written inside the tiny band.

"My forever love," Sandra read out loud.

"You are, Hazel," he said and slipped the ring on her finger.

Her cheeks blushed and she wiped at a tear that ran down her cheek. "I thought today was your special day. But it sure feels like it's really mine."

"Well, get used to that, it's called marriage—ouch!" Milton flinched and rubbed a spot on his ribs where Sandra had elbowed him. Joel and Hazel laughed.

"You know what? I think we better get going or we may miss the cake. And this pregnant woman doesn't need to miss any cake," Sandra said, laying a hand on her belly. "Mil, go grab my purse so we can head on out."

Milton raised one eyebrow and gave a pointed look at Joel, "See what you have to look forward to?"

Sandra shook her head and chuckled.

In the truck, Joel looked in his rearview mirror and watched Milton and Sandra follow behind in their car. He reached over and took Hazel's hand. He pulled her closer to his side. He interlocked his fingers in hers, feeling the ring press against his skin. He gave her hand a little squeeze. He could hardly believe it. She'd said yes. He was sitting next to his future wife.

Chapter 27

HAZEL, APRIL 1962

Hazel and Ruthie worked together to clean the house.

"Can you believe she's coming over to take us shopping for the wedding?" Ruthie said flipping the rag she was using to dust over her shoulder. "I mean, she barely has anything to do with us. I can count on one hand how many times she's come to visit us after Mama left. And now that you're getting married, and she's all about us again."

Hazel paused from cleaning the countertops. "She's our grandmother, Ruthie. She's still family. I'm sure there's not a lot of excitement in her life."

Ruthie grabbed the rag and flung it around in the air while she talked. "I know she's going to try and dominate the situation. You pick out the dress you want. Don't let her sway you."

Hazel sighed. The likelihood of her grandmother listening to anything she said was slim to none. "I won't, but she's paying you know."

"Hogwash," Ruthie sneered. "It doesn't matter. It's your wedding. Not hers. I'm just glad Mama isn't coming back from California for this. Talk about uncomfortable situations."

Hazel didn't answer, but for once, she agreed with Ruthie about Mama. She'd made peace the best she could with her mother being gone. Not only had their mother abandoned them, but she'd left them high and dry without a word or anything. No cards on birthdays or Christmas. No telephone calls to check up on them. The only word they ever heard about their mother was the information their grandmother told them, which wasn't much. Whenever her mother would come to mind, she'd shake her head and think about her father instead. She'd think about all he'd done for her and Ruthie by himself. He loved them. She did not. It still hurt, but the raw space in her heart had scabbed over, and a fresh love had flooded in, growing something new with Joel.

The sound of gravel crunching under tires made them both startle.

"Oh shoot, she's here!" Ruthie said. She jumped to hurry and finish straightening the house.

Hazel's stomach did a flip. She wondered if it was too late to jump out a window and escape, but before she could decide which window to jump from, there was a small rap on the front door. She plastered a fake smile on her face and opened the door.

The woman standing before her was older than she remembered. Her shoulders slightly hunched. Her white hair gathered in a tall beehive on top of her head. The dress she wore was dark purple, with a black belt cinched around her too-thin waist. Although it was warm outside, she wore a matching silk jacket with dark and light purple horizontal stripes. A huge metal broach in the shape of an open flower with a white pearl center hung on her right shoulder. She had not a stitch of makeup on her face. Her pasty skin looked more like a corpse's than a living human. Her eyes narrowed when she saw Hazel. Her wrinkles deepened around her mouth as it moved into a frown. Hazel sighed. She was apparently not happy with what she saw.

"Is that what you're wearing to Fort Smith?" her voice warbled as it came out.

Hazel's body stiffened. She gripped the opened door tighter and forced herself to smile. "Yes, Grandmother. Welcome. Come on in. Ruthie and I are just about ready to go." Out of the corner of her eye, she could see Ruthie scowling.

Her grandmother sniffed and came inside. Her head moved all around as she took in her surroundings. Hazel could tell, she was not impressed.

"Why don't you have a seat on the sofa. Would you like a glass of sweet tea while you wait?"

Her grandmother saw Ruthie standing to the side and her face brightened. She pointed a crooked finger at her.

"You look more and more like your mother every day. Come here and give Grannie a hug."

Ruthie tossed the rag she was holding on the side table near the sofa and walked over to the old woman. She bent down and gave their grandmother a stiff hug.

"I thought you'd be the first one to get married. You're so lovely. How old are you now? Eighteen?"

Ruthie grimaced and tried not to make eye contact with Hazel. Hazel felt her body heat with anger.

"I'm sixteen, Grandmother. Hazel is eighteen."

Their grandmother nodded, "Oh right, right. Time just gets away from me lately."

"Grandmother, would you like a glass of sweet tea?" Hazel repeated her question louder in case she didn't hear her the first time.

She glanced at Hazel. "No, thank you," she said curtly. "We had best be going if we're going to have time to find a dress for you and your sister. I can't understand why you'd choose to have a fall wedding instead of a summer wedding. There're no leaves on the trees, and everything is just so bare. Too much orange too if you ask me."

Hazel bit her lip. She didn't want to explain to her grandmother that she and Joel loved the fall. It was their favorite time of the year. The smells, the bare trees, the hint of chill in the air, the warmth inside cuddled with the ones you loved. They loved everything about it. They'd even picked November because it was a time of thankfulness, and they were so thankful they'd met each other. Plus, since the wedding was close to Thanksgiving, Ronnie, Joel's best friend, may be able to get some leave time approved by his commander. She'd love nothing more than for Joel to have his best friend standing beside him at the altar. She gave her grandmother a tight smile but said nothing. Grandmother had never understood her, and trying to explain it to her now would be as difficult as hanging clothes on the clothesline during a windy day.

"And too much brown too," her grandmother said tsking. She turned to pat Ruthie on the cheek with a wrinkled hand. "You'll have a summer wedding. Won't you?"

Ruthie flashed Hazel an evil grin before saying, "Oh, I'm planning on never marrying. I'm going to be a working woman."

It took the whole hour trip to the bridal shop in Fort Smith for Hazel to convince their grandmother that Ruthie was only joking, and she would in fact one day marry. Hazel looked in the rearview mirror, her eyes pleading for Ruthie to help her, but Ruthie wouldn't even glance in her direction. She stared out the window in the back seat of the Tempest, her arms folded and unusually silent. She was going to be no help with their grandmother today. The fury bubbled inside of Hazel, only to be replaced with a tightness in her chest. She hated the way her grandmother treated her, but she still couldn't shake the feeling that she was using her. She'd never voluntarily spend time with this woman. She was too cruel and said hurtful things, but she really needed a wedding dress. She, Ruthie, Alice, and Margarette Ann had scanned numerous catalogs. Wedding dresses were expensive, and the one she wanted was no exception. But at Antonia's Boutique, for this weekend only, the dress was on sale for a whopping six hundred dollars.

Inside the store, their grandmother found Antonia. A tall, thin woman with olive skin and jet-black hair twisted in a stylish tall bun. She wore a charcoal pencil skirt and a flowing, silk hot-pink blouse.

She had a round pin cushion ball fastened to her wrist with needles sticking out of it and a wooden pencil behind her ear.

"Welcome, come in. We are having a magnificent sale today. Please, look around," she said with a wave of her hand, inviting them to go deeper into the store.

"We're here to find my granddaughter a wedding dress and her sister a bridesmaid dress."

"And when is the wedding?" Antonia asked.

Their grandmother did an eye roll joined with a loud *tsk*. "The fall. But I thought it would be better in the summer."

Antonia's eyes flitted from their grandmother to Hazel. She smiled. "Well, summer weddings are lovely, but fall weddings can be just as lovely. Now which one is the lovely bride?" she asked, looking between Hazel and Ruthie.

Ruthie looped her arm around Hazel's shoulder. "It's her big day. And she has just the dress in mind."

Their grandmother humphed. "We need to look at many kinds of dresses. Not just one."

Ruthie's body tensed beside her, and Hazel's stomach knotted. She worried Ruthie wouldn't be able to control her words and might say something she'd regret. Although Hazel would more than likely be the one regretting it, not Ruthie.

"Right on, but after the one. I have a feeling it could be special."

Their grandmother rolled her eyes and waved her hand, dismissing Hazel and Antonia to go find the dress, her dream dress.

Antonia helped Hazel step into the dress and zipped it up from behind. Hazel's skin tingled as the fabric touched her. Antonia straightened the sleeves and patted down Hazel's hair.

"Now, what kind of veil are you thinking about? I'll go get it so you can see it all together."

Hazel explained what she had seen in the catalog and Antonia nodded. She left from under the dressing room curtain, promising to be right back. By herself, Hazel stood and stared down at the flowing, creamy white fabric that pooled on the floor around her. She twisted her head around to see as much of the back as she could. She wished she could see the whole thing, but there were no mirrors in the dressing room. All the mirrors were outside, surrounded by chairs where relatives and friends sat. When Antonia returned, she fashioned the veil on Hazel's head.

"You ready to see?"

Hazel bit her bottom lip.

"You look beautiful. I know your grandmother wants you to try on more than one dress, but you won't find one that fits you as perfectly as this one."

Hazel felt pricks form in the corner of her eyes, and she blinked them away.

"Thank you, I think I'm ready."

Antonia gathered up the loose fabric around Hazel's feet and took her hand. She helped her step out of the dressing room and onto a small circle platform in the center of the mirrors. Ruthie and their grandmother were sitting in the seats, waiting for her. Her grandmother's crinkled scowl flickered away when she caught sight of Hazel. Ruthie's mouth fell open, then formed a wide smile.

"Take a deep breath," Antonia directed.

Hazel sucked in a deep breath and Antonia helped her turn around, so that she faced the mirrors.

The sight knocked her breathless. It took a while for her mind to process what she was seeing. The cream color fabric made her eyes shine. From the boatneck collar to the long straight sleeves to the beaded waist that cinched before it flowed down to her feet, she loved every part of the dress. She raised her hand to straighten the white pillbox hat that sat on her head. The veil cascaded down from it to the train of the dress. It was perfect. It was all perfect.

Her grandmother began to stand, and Ruthie grabbed her elbow to help her. When she was upright, she walked over to Hazel and slowly circled her to take in the whole dress. Hazel's breath shortened. A silence settled over them. Her skin felt prickly and hot as she waited for her grandmother's assessment.

"Lovely, just lovely. We'll take it and the veil too."

Ruthie jumped up and down and Hazel felt her clenched muscles loosen, and her eyes blurred with tears. Her grandmother had never called her lovely before. She touched the beaded belt and ran her hands down the long draping material. The dress was hers, all hers.

"Thank you, Grandmother," she said almost breathlessly.

Her grandmother waved her hand, "Now, let's find your sister a bridesmaids dress."

They settled on a dark green dress. The color of the pine needles in the forest surrounding their little house. The dress had a boatneck collar that matched Hazel's dress. Its bow belt rounded an empire waist, and the long skirt grazed the floor. A dark green flower attached to a short, matching veil was placed on Ruthie's head. Her blonde hair was striking against the dark color.

"You look beautiful," Hazel said. "Do you like it? I want you to like it too."

Ruthie grinned at herself in the mirror. "I love it."

Their grandmother looked down at her watch. "I thought we'd be here all day. But I see you girls already had an idea of what you wanted. Efficient. I like that."

Ruthie looked at Hazel and smiled. Ever since her grandmother had spoken to her about shopping for her wedding dress, Hazel had waited for this day with fear and trepidation. But the day had been like nothing she'd ever expected or imagined.

"Let me go to the front and check out, then why don't I take you girls to lunch at Ralph's Steak House before heading back." She raised a finger and wagged it at Hazel. "But not too much for you. You have a long way to go until November. We don't want you growing too big for your dress."

Ruthie smirked and Hazel couldn't help but giggle.

Chapter 28

HAZEL, SEPTEMBER 1962

The blue sky was filled with splotches of gray clouds. The trees were bent nearly in half by the wind. The smell of impending rain was so thick, Hazel felt she could cut it with a knife. Hazel held her skirt down as she opened the Tempest door. She got in and ran her hand down her face to clear the loose tendrils of hair that haphazardly stuck to her eyelashes and mouth. The passenger door opened, and Ruthie slid inside.

"Holy moly! That wind is terrible."

Hazel nodded, pushing hair stuck to her lipstick behind her ears. "Horrible." She turned to Ruthie. "You don't have to go with me. It won't take me long. Alice's mom called last night. She bought ribbon for the small flower arrangements that will hang from the sides of the pews at the church. I've just got to pick it up and pay for it, then I'll be back. It's about to storm anyway."

Ruthie shrugged, "I'm bored. I'll go."

Hazel frowned, "You never want to run errands with me."

Ruthie flopped her arms exasperated. "I never want to run boring errands with you. I love Alice's mom."

Hazel pursed her lips and decided to drop it. If she hurried, she could get back home before it began raining cats and dogs. She started the car and backed out of the driveway.

As they drove, Ruthie adjusted the radio knob until she found a station playing rock and roll. Her head bobbed with the rhythm.

"Do you think Daddy and Ms. Faye will get married?"

"I don't know," Hazel said, not taking her eyes off the road.

"He sure left pretty early to go see her today."

"It's Saturday, Ruthie, and part of her fence fell down. He probably wanted to do it before the rain started. And if he didn't do it today, it would be another week before he could help her."

Ruthie moved her arms like she was riding a wave. Her movements matched the smooth feel of the music. "Yeah, I know. I'm just saying he left really early."

"Would that be so bad? If he did, I mean, want to marry her?"

Ruthie turned her head. She shook it to the beat, "Nah man, it'd be groovy."

Hazel started to laugh.

Hazel turned onto Peach Street. Light sprinkles began to hit the Tempest's hood and windshield. She looked into the sky. The clouds had turned a dark navy and were growing darker by the minute.

When she made it to Alice's mother's house, cars were parked along the side of the road and her driveway was full of vehicles. Hazel drove past the house to find a place to park near the neighbor's mailbox.

"What's going on?" she asked as she and Ruthie exited the Tempest.

They ran toward the house, holding hands above their hair. Ruthie yelled over the wind, "Maybe she's having a Tupperware party."

Hazel felt out of breath and damp by the time they made it to the door. The sprinkling rain had turned to a drizzle. On the other side of the door, she heard muffled conversations. She and Ruthie stood under the awning. She shivered as the wind picked up and blew her hair to the side.

"This is so strange," she said. "Why would she have us over when she's having a party?"

Ruthie rolled her eyes and raised a fist to knock hard on the wooden door. "I have no idea, but let's hurry and get in before it begins to pour."

The door swung open, and Alice was standing there.

Hazel's eyes widened, "Alice! I thought you were at college and couldn't come in this weekend."

Alice laughed and looked at Ruthie. "Even with all these cars, she still hasn't figured it out?"

"Told you," Ruthie said, pushing her way around Alice to enter the house.

Alice grabbed Hazel and hugged her before bringing her inside. "It's a party for you, silly!" As they entered the house, the rain began to fall in huge sheets. "Whoa, you made it just in time."

Hazel's eyes darted around the room filled with women. They flooded around her with huge smiles on their faces. Ms. Faye, Mrs. Anne, Sandra, her grandmother, and Margarette Ann were there along with other classmates she'd graduated with. Her eyes were drawn to a table set up in the center of the room. It had a square cake and punch bowl. One side of the table was filled with gifts.

She looked at Alice, "I don't understand. The church shower is next month. What's this all about?"

The women giggled. Mrs. Anne laid a hand on her arm. "Hazel, dear, the church shower is so people can give you gifts for your house."

Her grandmother came over and gave her a hug. She sipped from a punch cup which held red liquid. "This is a hen party. Where you receive gifts for your wedding night. Want to keep your husband interested, don't you? You want the first nights to be special."

Hazel felt her face flame. Her grandmother hiccupped, and Hazel wondered if there was more than punch in her cup.

Alice led Hazel to a comfy seat near the table. She felt entirely embarrassed being surrounded by all these women, even though many of them she'd known her whole life. She eyed the packages on the edge of the table, and her happiness about seeing beautifully wrapped gifts shriveled, and she shivered. She didn't want to know what was hidden behind those pretty bows.

The women began to sit in the chairs that lined the edges of the room.

"Open the gifts," Ruthie chanted before shoveling a huge piece of cake into her mouth.

Hazel glared at her.

Alice's mother saved her. "No, no, let's give her a chance to have some cake and punch before we thoroughly embarrass the girl. Look, her face is already redder than a tomato."

Alice's mother placed a cup with punch beside her on the table and handed her a huge slice of cake on a clear glass plate. For being small, the plate had weight to it, and Hazel laid it in her lap. Everyone watched her take a bite before sliding into different conversations. Alice talked to Ruthie about school. Sandra spoke to her grandmother about sewing. Ms. Faye and Mrs. Anne spoke about Hazel's reception and the food they would be bringing. Hazel ate in silence, enjoying the cake and the company. No matter how embarrassing this moment was, all these women were here because of her, because they loved her.

Her ears perked up when she heard Nancy Graham's voice speaking to a lady from Hazel's church. She couldn't remember the lady's name—Mrs. Bringham or Mrs. Berriname. She couldn't remember. She strained her ears to hear what Nancy was telling the poor woman.

"I'm just sayin' it makes me nervous," Nancy commented. "These issues with the Soviet Union seem to be escalating. You know, my Charles works for the government. He said our trying to land in Cuba has made such tension between us and Russia that it's liable to pop like a rubber band." Nancy laid a hand on her chest and practically wiggled her finger so that her new wedding ring would glisten in the light. The woman from church shook her head and tsked. Nancy sighed, "Then who knows what will happen."

Hazel shoved a bite of cake in her mouth. *Who invited Nancy? Her Charles works in government*, Hazel shook her head. *My foot! He works as an intern for representative Dale Alford, and he only got that job because their families were both from New Hope and knew each other.* She stuck another huge bite of cake in her mouth and shook off Nancy's worrying words, instead trying to focus on the conversation Ruthie and Alice were having across from her.

"I'd like to go to college too. I want to be a nurse."

Hazel choked on her bite of cake and coughed a bit. "You do?" she asked.

Ruthie looked startled, like she'd been caught stealing. Ruthie's teeth sunk into her bottom lip, "Yes, I do," she said quietly. Her eyes darted side to side to see if anyone else was paying attention.

"You never told me," Hazel said. She tried to keep her voice from sounding as disappointed as she felt.

Ruthie poked at her cake with the end of her fork. "I wasn't sure it was possible, but I've been looking into it. I just got a year and half left of school. I can get a job at the hospital in town and go to class in Fort Smith if I live with Daddy and he helps me pay for gas. My working money from the hospital can go to pay for the classes. It won't cover all of it, but maybe Daddy wouldn't mind helping there too."

Hazel made herself smile. She'd been thinking about asking Mr. Crutchfield for a job running the cash register at Piggly Wiggly after the wedding. She knew her and Joel would need a little extra money since he planned on taking night classes in Fort Smith like Ruthie. Everyone wanted more schooling. Everyone had dreams. She blinked, her only dream was to be Joel's wife and a good mother to their children. She wondered why that dream didn't feel as important as Ruthie's.

"I think Daddy would help you in any way you needed. Plus, you'd make an excellent nurse," she told Ruthie.

Ruthie's face brightened, "Really?"

Hazel nodded. "Of course."

Alice's mother clapped her hands to get everyone's attention. "I think it's gift time," she said.

The women in the room excitedly agreed, and Hazel felt a cold sweat break out over her body.

"I'll hand her the gifts," Ruthie said, moving her chair to sit next to Hazel. She stood and picked up a gift wrapped in shiny gold paper with a big pink bow on the outside. "Here you go, this one's from Grandmother."

As Hazel opened one gift after another, she pulled from pretty packages bras with matching slips, baby doll lingerie sets, and peignoir sets in lavender and pink. The sheerness of the fabrics and embroidered lace made her face heat like the sun. The women forced her to hold up each gift to display. They all hemmed and hawed, making comments like, "That one will be fun on your wedding night," or "Oh, Joel will love you in that." Hazel squirmed in her seat. *This is torture. Why can't someone just poke me in the eye with a pencil?*

After the last gift was displayed, Hazel thanked everyone for coming and thoroughly embarrassing her. The women giggled. Alice came and looped an arm around her shoulder. "We only do it because we love you."

Hazel shook her head, "Well, next time, could you love me with less string and lace and instead maybe with something made from actual fabric like cotton?"

Alice squeezed Hazel around the neck, "I've missed you terribly." She released Hazel and placed her hands on Hazel's arms, staring at her like she was under a microscope. "Just think, in less than two months, you will be Mrs. Hazel Davenport."

Her future name rang in her ears. Mrs. Hazel Davenport. She liked the sound of it. She liked it very much. She didn't need college or extra studies. She and Joel would make a good life together, a happy life. *Could anyone ask for more than that in this crazy world?* She didn't think so.

Chapter 29

RUTHIE, OCTOBER 1962

Ruthie held the door to the duplex open for Joel and Hazel as they made trips to and from the truck and car. Their faces beamed, and their arms were filled with gifts of new plates, a toaster, bed linens, towels, a coffee pot, and even a fancy mixer. By all accounts, Ruthie felt the church shower had been a success. They had so many new things to start their lives together. At first, she'd been worried when Hazel told her that the shower was on a Monday evening after a special prayer meeting. Hazel explained the church was occupied with a funeral and community gatherings during the weekend, leaving only Monday open. But it didn't matter, their friends and church people had flocked there in droves, bringing housewarming gifts for the couple. The kindness and love she saw extended to Joel and Hazel made her heart almost burst. During the shower, people had even curtailed discussions about the conflict between the United States and Soviet Union and just enjoyed their time together. They focused on the couple and not the politics.

Ruthie allowed her muscles to relax for the first time in a month. She'd been on edge ever since the high school began to make them practice the duck-and-cover drills daily. A high-pitched alarm would sound, shooting goose bumps down her arm. She and the other students would be forced to crawl under their desks and cover their heads. She wasn't sure how being under a wooden desk was supposed to help her if the Soviet Union decided to drop a nuclear bomb on Waldron, but she did it anyway. Everyone in the town, including her, was functioning on a high level of terror. Fear permeated every conversation she overheard. She knew as well as anyone, if nuclear war broke out, there was nothing anyone in their small town could do to stop it. Every time she passed a business with a sign that boasted of having a fallout shelter, her heart skipped a beat. Ruthie looked at Hazel and Joel's smiling faces. She felt bad for them. She wanted them to be truly happy and excited about getting married, but it was hard when the news was full of talk about the possible impending destruction of the United States. Still, the shower had been wonderful and a needed respite from the craziness of the world.

"Wasn't it wonderful that Daddy's boss gave him the day off?" Hazel asked, carrying in the last gifts from the Tempest's trunk.

"Yeah, too bad he has to go back tomorrow," Ruthie commented as she shut the door after Joel. "Ya'll sure racked up on the gifts."

Joel ran a hand through his hair, making it stand up in the back. He smiled as he surveyed the piles of gifts on the floor, the sofa, the coffee table, "We sure did."

"I can't believe it's less than a month until the wedding," Ruthie commented. She placed her hands on her hips. "What do you want to do with all this stuff until then?"

Hazel pursed her lips. "Maybe we can take it all out of the boxes and find a place for it. Then take the towels and sheets to the laundry mat and wash them before we put them away."

Joel picked up a box with a new coffee pot in it. "I'm so glad I get to use all of these things first."

Ruthie giggled, "You should call Hazel on the telephone at night and tell her how much fun you're having with ya'll's new potholders and mixer."

Hazel narrowed her eyes. "I'll be living here soon enough. She hugged the box holding the mixer to her chest. But don't you dare use this without me."

Joel laughed as he made his way around the boxes of presents to the television. He leaned down to flip it on but paused as Hazel groaned.

"Please, Joel. Don't turn it on. It's been such a good day. I can't handle it."

Ruthie agreed with Hazel. She was tired of the constant panic the news incited. She'd be happy if the television never came on ever again.

Joel looked at them both. "We have to see what's going on. How else am I going to get ya'll to safety if something happens?"

"What do you mean?" Hazel asked, plopping down on the sofa in the middle of the presents.

"I spoke to Mr. Hal, and he got us a place in Mr. Simmons's fallout shelter."

Ruthie's stomach clenched. "You and Hazel?" What would she and Daddy do? Where would they go if the unthinkable happened? Thoughts about what happens to a body if a nuclear bomb explodes nearby flooded her mind. *Does it disintegrate?* Ruthie felt her skin go clammy.

"I made sure there was plenty of room for you and Mr. McKay too," Joel smiled.

Ruthie let out the breath she'd been holding. "Maybe we should turn it on," she said, looking toward Hazel. "Just so we can know what's happening. Just in case."

Hazel reluctantly agreed as she slid a box on her lap and began to take out bed linen to set aside. Ruthie felt her heart ache for her sister. Hazel tried to act like everything was good as she prepared for her wedding, but Ruthie could tell with the pull of her mouth and the deepening creases between her brows that Hazel was worried.

Joel flipped on the television. The box popped with life. Ruthie's jaw unclenched when the picture finally focused and on the screen was an episode of *Gunsmoke,* not a news anchor delivering bad news. She watched a few seconds of Ms. Kitty in the saloon before moving near the boxes that she'd laid on the floor. She sat on her knees and began to open them. She took the items out and set the boxes to the side. Even though none of these new things were hers, she knew she'd get to use them when she stayed over from time to time. She removed a shiny toaster from a box and looked at her reflection on the side. Her blonde curls were out of place and frizzy, and she tried to smooth them down with her hand. The toaster nearly flew out of her hands when Joel rushed to the television.

"What's going on?" Hazel asked. Her face had gone as white as the fluffy towel she was holding.

"It's an alarm. See," he pointed to the television.

Ruthie lifted onto her knees. They all watched as the image on the screen flickered off for a few seconds and then back on. It repeated the sequence again.

"Maybe something is wrong with the television," Ruthie questioned, wishing it to be true, but when she heard the tone that followed, she knew it wasn't the television.

"That's some kind of alarm," Joel said, shaking his head. "Something serious is happening."

A cold sweat broke out over her body. She wanted to grab the telephone and call Daddy to warn him, but she was too afraid to move. Her body was frozen.

When the picture returned, a man behind a news desk appeared. His dark suit sat perfectly on his broad shoulders. His face was serious. She wondered if she was imagining it or of there was terror in his eyes.

"We are sorry to interrupt the regularly scheduled program," he said his voice strong. "President Kennedy will now address the country. May God be with us all."

President Kennedy sat at a table between two flags in a dark suit and tie. Hazel gasped, "It's really him."

Joel rushed to sit beside her on the sofa. They clutched hands as they waited for him to speak.

In front of the president sat a box holding two microphones pointed in his direction to catch every word. Blood rushed through Ruthie's ears as her heart pounded in her chest. She forced herself to move closer to the television. She had to hear what he would say.

Each word the president spoke made every nerve in her body stand on end. The Russians had built missile launch sites in Cuba for no other reason than a nuclear strike against the Western Hemisphere. *The Western Hemisphere.* Ruthie felt her stomach clench and bile rose in the back of her throat. *That was the United States.* Her country. Her family and loved ones. Herself. She was in danger too.

"The cost of freedom is always high. But Americans have always paid it," the president said.

The words echoed in her head, and even though her body trembled, she felt something akin to pride blossom in her belly when she thought about her father fighting in the war far away in another country for freedom. Or Ronnie wanting to do the same, just like his father and his grandfather before him.

President Kennedy looked down before raising his eyes to continue, "And one path we shall never choose, and that is the path of surrender or submission. Our goal is not the victory of might, but the vindication of right—not peace at the expense of freedom, but both peace and freedom, here in this hemisphere, and, we hope, around the world. God willing, that goal will be achieved. Thank you and good night."

And just as fast as he had appeared, the president was gone, and the news anchor was speaking again. No one in the duplex moved. Ruthie wasn't even sure she was breathing. Without any word, Joel popped up off the sofa.

"I need to go."

Hazel clung to one of his hands. Her knuckles were white as she gripped it. "Where are you going? You can't leave now."

He bent down and took her chin in his hand. "I promise I'll be right back. I have to do something. Pack a bag with some necessities and canned food. We need to be prepared in case we have to rush to Mr. Simmons's."

Tears began to stream down Hazel's face. "Please don't go. I'm scared."

Joel kissed her tears away. "I love you. I'll be right back, I swear." He looked up at Ruthie. His eyes begged her for help.

She forced her legs to move. Pins and needles flooded her muscles, and she stumbled to the sofa beside Hazel. She wrapped her arms around her. "He'll be back. Let's do what he says and get a bag ready. We need to be prepared, Hazel."

Hazel nodded and released Joel's hand. He kissed her lightly on the lips before turning to leave. She whimpered and shuddered in Ruthie's arms as he went out the door.

After a few seconds, Hazel wiped her face with her fingers. "Thank you for being here," she said to Ruthie and stood. "Will you help me choose some things from the kitchen to pack?"

"Give me one second," Ruthie said. She hurried to the television and turned down the volume before picking up the receiver of the telephone. She held it near her ear and began to dial. The rotary dial moved and returned with each number she selected.

"Who are you calling?" Hazel asked.

"Daddy. I want to make sure he's heard the news. He needs to come here, so he's closer to Mr. Simmons's shop, just in case," Ruthie paused. A fresh set of goose bumps dappled her skin. "You know. In case something happens with the missiles."

Chapter 30

JOEL

The muscles in Joel's jaw clenched and ached as he gritted his teeth. He couldn't believe he was in the truck heading to his pa's house when he should be with Hazel. For over a year since he'd asked Hazel to be his wife, he'd debated visiting his pa and inviting him to the wedding. The years since he'd lived in the house on the hill hadn't washed away the memories of everything his pa had done to him, but inside, Joel couldn't explain it, a connection with his pa still existed. He wanted him at his wedding. He was his only family, and it didn't matter how much bad he did, a connection like that didn't vanish. Blood was blood. And that's why Joel couldn't just let him die. He knew his pa wouldn't know what was going on. He wouldn't know how close to destruction and death the country was because his pa didn't have a television, and he never listened to the radio. The house was too far away from anything and everything.

Joel played in his head what he would say. If his pa wouldn't come with him, he'd grab him and knock him out, then drag him to the truck. It would be for his own good. Joel shook his head. He wouldn't hit his pa. He wouldn't resort to violence. No matter what his pa did or said, Joel wouldn't use force. He wasn't like him. Joel knew it would hurt from the inside out, but if his pa wouldn't come, then he'd leave him there. He'd left him before he moved out. He'd leave him again. Joel felt like he wanted to crawl out of his skin, and he feared nothing good was going to come of this, but he had to try.

Joel pulled into a grassy area near a pine tree. The yard was overgrown with tall weeds that scratched his ankles when he exited the truck. He noticed one of the front windows was broken. It hadn't been broken when he left. Old planks of wood had been nailed over it to keep the wind out. There were new holes where the siding was missing. Joel had thought the place was old when he lived here, but he couldn't believe how run-down it was now. It looked as if a small wind could pick it up and toss it off the hill.

He stood in front of the house, wondering if the porch boards would even hold his weight or collapse when he stepped on them. The navy sky above was black in the distance, and Joel shivered at the thought of being here in the dark. The forest around him was eerily quiet, and the house in front of him was silent. It made his blood freeze in his veins. He wondered if his pa knew he was here. Joel took in a breath. *Let's get this over with.*

Chapter 31

Hazel

The knock on the front door made her and Ruthie scream. Milton cracked the door open and peeked his head inside.

"I'm sorry. Didn't mean to scare you."

A fierce exhale left Hazel's lungs, and she ran to him and Sandra. "Oh, my goodness, my nerves are shot with all this happening. Please come in."

Sandra was holding their baby, Michael Anthony Lewis, in her arms. His chubby little arms wrapped tight around her neck. "We need a favor," she said to Hazel.

"Anything."

"Can you watch Mikey for us? In all this mess, a parishioner from church fell and needs our help. Her husband is older than she is and can't get her to the hospital. She thinks she's broken something and is in a lot of pain."

Hazel held out her arms to take Mikey. He looked at her with big brown eyes. His little mouth smiled when Hazel reached for him. Small spit bubbles escaped from his lips as he babbled. He was nearly fifteen months old and climbing on everything. He leaned toward Hazel, and she took him, positioning him on her hip. He grabbed at her hair, and she nuzzled his face near his chin, making him laugh.

"Thank you so much," Milton said, placing an arm around his wife. "The joys of being a minister."

Sandra turned her face to him and kissed his cheek, "You wouldn't have it any other way."

Ruthie stood near Hazel and played with Mikey over her shoulder. "What do you think about everything going on?" she asked.

Sandra sighed and Milton shook his head. "I guess there's really nothing we can do except trust in the Lord and pray. Well, we better get."

"Thank you again," Sandra said as they left.

Hazel closed the door, and Mikey whined briefly in her arms. She sat him on the floor and distracted him with a few of the toys she'd bought him for when he stayed with her and Joel. She couldn't explain it, but she was so glad Mikey was there with them. His bubbly laughter when she pushed a toy car from his chunky leg to his belly made her anxiety unwind. If only Joel was back, she'd be able to fully breathe. She wished he'd told her where he was going, but he'd left so quickly after the President's announcement.

Ruthie sat down next to them. She took the wooden blocks and began to build them into a straight tower, so Mikey could knock them down. "Where did Joel go, you think?"

"I don't know," Hazel admitted. "If I knew, I'd go get in the car and bring him home. Did you get ahold of Daddy?"

Ruthie shook her head. Mikey swiped his hand in the air, and blocks scattered everywhere. Ruthie began to gather them to restack. "The line rang and rang, but he never picked up. Maybe I should go over there?"

Hazel felt her throat tighten. Joel had left and disappeared somewhere. They couldn't get a hold of their father. The thought of Ruthie being out there too in all this chaos was more than Hazel could bear. She grasped Ruthie's hand tightly, forcing her to stop stacking the blocks. "Please don't leave. I don't want to have to worry about you too." She could hear the desperation and fear in her voice. Ruthie's eyes widened, but she didn't put up a fight.

"Okay, I'll stay, don't worry. I won't leave, not without you." She leaned over to hug Hazel. Her warmth soothed Hazel's frazzled nerves. Mikey whined because Ruthie had stopped stacking blocks. They both looked at him. His bottom lip stuck out in a pout. They both laughed, which made him giggle.

Ruthie picked up a block and held it out to Mikey. He took it in his chubby hand. "Look, if we don't hear from Daddy soon, and Joel isn't back by the time Milton and Sandra come to get Mikey, maybe we could go out looking for them?"

Hazel's stomach tightened at the thought of leaving the safety of the duplex, but what choice did they have? She nodded. "Yes, if Joel's not back and Daddy doesn't get here soon, we'll go look for them."

Chapter 32

JOEL

The frail door's hinges squeaked as Joel pushed it open. Even after blinking to adjust his eyes, the inside was darker than a tomb. He couldn't see anything, but he smelled everything. He felt the bile rise in the back of his throat. The smell of alcohol and stale cigarettes was overwhelming. There was also a damp, earthy smell, as if the house was rotting on its foundation. Joel stood paralyzed as memories flooded through his brain. He wanted to turn around and run out the open door, but before he could, he heard a boot scrape across the floor. The memory sent chills down his spine.

"What are you doin' here?" his pa growled.

Joel squinted, his eyes finally adjusting to the darkness. His pa sat in a boxy armchair with green cushions that Joel had never seen before.

The green material was ripped and worn in several places, and Joel wondered if his pa had appropriated it from someone who put it out for the garbage man to collect. His pa rocked in the armchair. As it swayed, it made a screech that sat Joel's teeth on edge. It was like fingernails on a chalk board, and he wished his pa would stop moving.

"I've come to get you and bring you into town."

His pa let out a loud barking laugh before he leaned over as a coughing fit racked through his body. When he stopped coughing, he leaned back in the chair and wiped the spittle off his mouth.

"I'm not going anywhere with you, boy."

"Pa, the president made an announcement tonight. The Soviet Union has missiles in Cuba, and they may strike at any time. They could launch a nuclear missile at the U.S. Don't you understand? If you're not in a fallout shelter, then you're a dead man."

His pa shook his head, "I've been a dead man since your ma died."

Joel felt his face burn as anger pulsed through his body.

"I came up here because other than Hazel McKay, you're my only family. And I didn't want you to die from some nuclear explosion."

Even in the darkness, Joel could see his pa's face change. It twisted into a snarl. "She ain't your family," he said with venom in the words.

Joel hung his head and looked at the floor. That face brought back memories he didn't want, and he shivered. He stuck his hand in his pocket, feeling for the tooth that he had thrown away years ago. Joel swallowed and tried to keep his voice steady. "She will be if we survive this thing. She and I are set to be married next month."

Joel's mind couldn't process what happened next. Everything moved in a blur. His pa leaped from his chair and charged him. He was faster than Joel would have thought. He slammed his shoulder into Joel's stomach, knocking the breath from Joel's lungs. Joel's back hit the wall, and the whole house rocked. His feet slipped out from under him, and Joel hit the floor. A sharp pain shot through his tail bone. He gasped for air, but a stabbing sensation in his abdomen kept him from being able to take a deep breath of air.

His pa reached for something on the other side of the door that Joel had not seen. The loud metal clunk echoed in his ears. His pa cocked the rifle, and Joel's blood ran cold when he felt the hard metal end jam into the side of his neck.

Chapter 33

RUTHIE

It was after ten when Milton and Sandra returned to get a sleeping Mikey. He lay snuggled in Hazel's arms on the sofa. One chubby arm extended above his head. Ruthie was glad to have Mikey with them tonight. Keeping him entertained helped soothe her frazzled nerves. She hadn't been able to get ahold of Daddy. She'd called and called, but it just rang. Hazel recommended giving Ms. Faye a call, so Ruthie had tried her too. But even Ms. Faye hadn't heard from him. *When I find him, I'm gonna give him a piece of my mind for keeping my stomach all tied up in knots*, she huffed. She'd decided to give Joel a piece of her mind too, but she knew she probably wouldn't get a chance. Because once he got home, Hazel was going to light into him. She'd said at least fifty times tonight that he shouldn't have left, and he should be back home by now. Even having Mikey as a distraction didn't stop Hazel from biting at her nails. Ruthie worried something was wrong and Joel might be in some kind of trouble, but she'd never dare say it out loud.

Sandra stared down as Mikey slept peacefully in Hazel's arms. His sweet face blissfully unaware of the state of the world. "I just can't get over him. Sometimes at night, I just watch him sleep," Sandra said.

Hazel touched his cheek lightly with a finger. "I don't blame you, he's so handsome."

"Takes after his dad," Milton said, plopping down on the other end of the sofa.

That made Ruthie and the others chuckle, which felt like a salve to Ruthie's raw nerves. "So, how was the lady ya'll went to help tonight?" she asked.

Milton's face and body seemed to deflate. A pained expression crossed his face. "I'll be honest. It's a mad house out there."

Hazel's head whipped up to look at him. "What's happening?"

Sandra sighed, "Everyone's gone crazy."

Milton nodded, agreeing. "Look, I don't want to die, same as anyone else. And I sure want Mikey to be safe, but we just got to put it all in God's hands." He paused, "But people out there are running around like chickens with their heads cut off. They are already moving to fallout shelters, either in their basements or at other people's houses. The hospital was overflowing with injured folk."

"Injured how?" Ruthie asked.

"Mostly 'cause of their own stupidity. I think someone had even been shot. I overheard that it wasn't lookin' good." Milton said.

Ruthie gasped, "Shot?"

Milton nodded, "Yeah, but I couldn't hear who, and I didn't ask because we needed to get back. But the whole town has gone mad. People are even packing up and trying to move out of town. I love our town, but I don't think the Soviet Union is going to aim one of those nuclear missiles at Waldron. It's gonna be one of those bigger cities, and we're going to have to deal with the fallout."

Ruthie felt her pulse quicken. She had to find her father and Joel. They needed to be together. They didn't need to be separated at a time like this. She needed her father, and Hazel needed her future husband.

Sandra leaned over to take Mikey from Hazel's arms, and Mikey let out a small groan. "I hate to move him when he's sleepin' so good, but we better be getting home." She laid him across her shoulder and gently patted his back to calm him, "We're going to lock our door and not leave our house. We've got extra supplies if you need anything."

Milton stood, "I advise you ladies stay in tonight too. It's not a good time to be outdoors. Lord knows what's in these crazy people's minds."

Ruthie tried to swallow the lump in her throat, but it wouldn't go down. She stood on wobbly legs and walked Milton and Sandra to the door. She closed it behind them, then leaned against its hard surface for support. She could hardly breathe. She looked at Hazel, who hadn't moved from the sofa. She sat there staring at her empty hands.

"Hazel?"

Hazel turned her head. Her eyes were watery. "They're out there in this craziness. Dad and Joel," she said.

Ruthie shook her head. She felt as helpless as a lamb being led to slaughter. She was usually so strong, but her knees felt weak, like they might give out underneath her and she'd fall to the floor. Her father was the one constant she had in her life. He always protected her, and she needed him now. Her stomach twisted and turned. "I know they're out there, but what can we do? You heard Milton. We shouldn't be going out tonight."

To Ruthie's surprise, Hazel stood up and grabbed her purse sitting on the table beside the sofa. Hazel's face took on the expression of resolve that had come to her more easily with age. She flung the strap across her shoulder. "I'll tell you what we're not going to do. We are not sitting here waiting for them like bumps on a log. We're gonna go find our men and bring them home. That's what we're going to do."

But they didn't have to go far. As Hazel opened the door and they walked outside, a police car pulled up behind the Tempest. Everything around Ruthie felt suspended in time, and her mouth went paper dry. The sight of Officer McConnell's grave face as he got out of the black and white car and walked toward them made her knees buckle. She clung to Hazel's arm. Her breath sawed in and out of her lungs with each step he took in their direction.

"I wonder if he's here because of Joel or Daddy," Hazel whispered. Her face had gone white as a sheet, and Ruthie was afraid if she passed out, she wouldn't have the strength to hold her.

Ruthie tried to calm down, but her heart hammered inside her chest. McConnell approached them. His six-foot figure towered over them. His blue uniform was crumpled from a hard night's work, and his gun hung from his hip in its black holster. The gray in his dark hair around his temples shown brighter under the streetlight. Ruthie felt Hazel stiffen.

"I'm glad you girls are here. I looked for you at the house, but Joel said you'd probably still be at his duplex putting things from the shower away."

Ruthie felt Hazel relax a little at the mention of Joel's name.

"How can we help you, sir?" Hazel asked with a waiver in her voice.

He ran a hand through his graying hair. "I'm gonna need you girls to come with me to the hospital. There's an emergency. It seems your father has been in some sort of accident." His mouth pinched into a straight line. "He's been shot, and it's not lookin' good."

Ruthie gasped and Hazel doubled over. She began to sob. Tears began to stream down Ruthie's cheeks, and it took all her strength to keep Hazel from falling onto the cement. McConnell hurried and grabbed Hazel's other arm. He helped them to the police car. Ruthie held onto Hazel's arm and let McConnell guide them, her eyes were too blurry to see.

"We don't have much time to waste," McConnell said. He opened the back door and helped them inside.

Ruthie sat on the hard seat. She felt like she was caught in a thick fog. Daddy had been shot. It didn't make sense. He was loved by everyone. He had no enemies. It had to be a mistake. The car jerked as it pulled out of the driveway. The tires squealed on the pavement.

Calm down. I have to calm down. I'll go to the hospital, and everything will be figured out when we get there.

As he drove, Hazel clung to Ruthie. Tears poured from her cheeks and dropped heavily on Ruthie's arm. Ruthie wiped her eyes. She wouldn't shed one more tear. It didn't matter if McConnell was a police officer, he was wrong. Her daddy hadn't been shot. That was preposterous.

"How bad is it?" Hazel asked, rubbing her arm under her nose.

Ruthie scowled at her in the darkness. *How could she believe this tall tale?*

"Like I said, it's not looking good," he sighed.

Hazel laid her head on Ruthie's shoulder and groaned into it. *I won't listen to this. It isn't real.* She wished Hazel would quit crying.

"How did this happen? Why would anyone shoot our daddy?" Hazel sobbed.

McConnell took a hard turn, and Ruthie and Hazel slid on the seat. "Your father told the doctor it was a hunting accident before he lost consciousness. Said some person he'd never seen before was hunting in the forest and shot him." He paused. "He said Joel and his pa found him. But I'm gonna be honest with you, I don't entirely believe his story."

Hazel's head popped up from Ruthie's shoulder, "Why would Daddy lie?"

"To protect someone. Joel and his pa were both covered in your father's blood."

"But wouldn't they be if they were helpin' him?" Ruthie asked. Her voice sounded weak to her ears.

"I guess, but Joel's pa." Mr. McConnell paused and took a breath. "Well, he's been a troublemaker and an alcoholic ever since he came back from the war. I've had my men scurry around looking at all the camping sites to find any sign of someone illegally hunting in those woods. It's only bow season right now. But we've found nothing. It got dark on us though, so we'll continue to look in the morning. And your father is a good man. He wouldn't want to cause problems. Not with you and Joel supposed to be marrying soon."

Ruthie's mind wandered to that time in the woods when she and Joel hid together in the snow. His pa yelling that he was going to kill Joel as they tried not to breathe behind a tree log. She shook from the chill of the memory.

"I'm not sure why your father was in the woods anyway, especially near nightfall," McConnell commented.

Ruthie sucked in a sharp breath. She did. She knew. Hazel looked at her.

"Do you know something, Ruthie? Tell me, please."

Ruthie looked down at her hands. She sighed. She didn't want to tell Hazel anything. If something bad happened to Daddy, Hazel might blame herself. But Hazel's eyes pleaded.

"Please, Ruthie, do you know why he was out there?"

Ruthie gulped and the spit caught in her throat becoming a large lump. She coughed. "Yes, I know why he was in the forest." She felt her throat constrict tighter, choking her. She had to spit it out.

McConnell had slowed and was looking at her in the rearview mirror, and Hazel's eyes bored into her from the side. She stared at the back of McConnell's seat and said it. "He wanted to find a nice oak branch or something to carve Hazel and Joel a wedding present. He said there was a nice huge oak near Joel's old house. He had to get the branch tonight because he had to leave early for work tomorrow. He was going to work on it while he was out of town, at night."

Hazel began to tremble. "He was out there for me? To make a wedding present for me?"

"And he was close to where Joel's pa lived," McConnell said speculatively.

"Are you gonna arrest him?" Ruthie gulped. "Joel's pa?"

McConnell blew out a long breath. He shook his head, but even from behind, she could see the skin on his knuckles tighten as he gripped the steering wheel harder. "Can't. Not right now. Not with what your father told the doctor. Can't prove anything without a cooperating witness, and apparently your father doesn't want to cooperate."

Ruthie felt Hazel twitch. "Well, maybe it was just a hunting accident, and your men aren't looking in the right places," she said with a sharp edge to her words.

McConnell pulled into the hospital parking lot. "Maybe so, maybe so, but doubtful."

Chapter 34

JOEL

He sat in the hospital waiting room, wringing his hands in front of him. Their violent shaking was gone and all that was left was a tremble. He noticed the dark crescent shape underneath his nails, right above the quick, where Mr. McKay's blood had seeped into his nailbeds and dried. He tried to pick it out. He'd washed up the best he could. Blood and water swirled together in the hospital's bathroom sink. He watched it as the red circled the drain before running to the toilet and vomiting. He gripped his hands together until the knuckles turned white. The hospital seat was hard, and his muscles ached, but he didn't care.

"Lost too much blood," the doctor said before he sent Officer McConnell to go get Hazel and Ruthie. "May not make it through the night," was the last thing he heard the doctor say to McConnell. They both glanced at him, narrowing their eyes, then moved away out of earshot. Panic flooded Joel's chest. His stomach twisted. *How could they know? Had Mr. McKay woken up and told them the truth?* All he had wanted to do was protect his pa, the only family he had, whether he deserved it or not. How could his good intentions have gone so wrong?

He sprung up from the hospital chair. "I need to get some air," he said, startling a nurse coming down the hall. She lowered her chin to her chest, not saying a word to him then rushed into the room where Mr. McKay lay dying. He wanted to follow her as he watched the doors swing closed behind her. He hadn't heard anything about Mr. McKay since McConnell left. He needed to know. He felt blood on his hands even though none was there. He pushed his hands deep inside his pockets and turned to walk out of the hospital.

The cool night air was crisp and smelled of autumn. He sucked it in, searching for the peace he'd felt on similar nights when he and Hazel sat on her front porch holding hands and staring at the full moon. He looked up at the sky. The moon and stars were hidden behind clouds. The night was eerily dark, except for the yellow glow of the streetlamps. He felt no peace. He felt numb and cold, and hidden deeper still, fear. He shuddered. Tonight, he may not only lose Mr. McKay but the love of his life. Everything they'd planned and hoped for gone in an instant with the crack of a sounding bullet.

He began to pace the length of the parking lot. Officer McConnell would find Hazel and Ruthie. They were probably on their way now.

What am I going to tell them? He had to decide. The lies they'd told already burned like acid on his tongue.

With each step, a sharp pain in his tail bone reminded him of being down on the floor. The cold hard end of the rifle pressed into his neck. Bits and pieces raced through his mind like electrical sparks, and he closed his eyes against it. *This can't be real. This can't be happening.* He shook his head side to side to erase the memories, but he could still smell the stale alcohol, the musky sweat of his pa. His pa's words rang in his head.

"You will never marry that girl. I'll kill her before I let you marry into that family."

"You don't even know her. Mr. McKay is a good man."

His pa spat. The goopy glob of spittle landed beside him on the floor.

"Not if he's friends with that traitor, Hal Sutherland, he's not."

Joel's heart began to pound, and he thought it might burst. It felt just like it had as he laid splayed on the floor of his pa's house. He'd held his hands up and pleaded with his pa all the while looking for a way to get the upper hand. If he could just distract him, maybe he could get away or get the gun. Joel knew there was no pleading with him or convincing him to do anything he didn't want to do. When his pa was drunk, there was no telling what would happen.

"Please stop, you don't know Mr. Hal like I do. He's been nothing but kind to me."

The muzzle of the rifle pressed harder into his neck and Joel winced.

"I know him better than you'll ever know him. You think I'm evil. You think I'm horrible. He's got nothing on me," his pa laughed, and it caught in his throat. As he coughed, he swayed on his feet, the gun loosened on Joel's neck.

A spark ignited in Joel's mind, and he realized this could be his only chance. As quick as lightning, he grabbed the end of the muzzle and pushed it away from his neck, then pulled it with all his strength, causing his pa to lurch forward. His pa began to stumble. He released the gun to catch himself before his face hit the floor. His knees crashed on the linoleum with a thud, and he whelped. The gun bobbled in Joel's sweaty hands before he got control of it. Blood rushed between Joel's ears. When he had the gun firmly in his grasp, he flipped it around as he leaped off the floor. His pa was still hunched over on his knees. Joel pointed the end of the muzzle and pressed it into his back. His pa stiffened under the hard metal end.

Joel tried to slow his breathing, but it came out ragged and quick. His mind spun. "You wouldn't really kill Hazel or her father or Mr. Hal, would you?"

His pa's body shook with more harsh laughter. It came out ragged and raw, igniting flames in the pit of Joel's stomach. He was transported to the forest, hiding behind the log with Ruthie. He remembered not caring what happened to himself but knowing he would give his life to protect the McKay girls.

His pa coughed. "Give me the gun back and I'll show you what I'll do. A bullet to the head is too good for Hal Sutherland, but not too good for you or your little gonna-be wife."

"Run," the word came out as hard as steel from Joel's lips. He knew what he had to do. He had to protect his new family and friends. He had to protect Hazel.

"What'd you say, boy?"

"One of us is going to die tonight and I'm the only one with the gun. I'll give you the same chance as you gave me that one winter. Run. 'Run for your life,' isn't that what you said?"

His pa looked over his shoulder. When Joel cocked the gun, his pa's eyes grew huge. He scrambled to his feet and scurried out the door.

As Joel paced the hospital parking lot, he realized it was at that moment he'd never been more like his pa. He didn't think about the consequences. Hazel never crossed his mind. All he saw was red. All he felt were flames burning him from the inside out. He wanted to hurt him. He wanted him to die. Joel looked up at the sky. One star was visible through the clouds. He could tell himself he was protecting his future family all he wanted, but deep down, Joel knew the truth. He wanted revenge. He wanted his pa to pay for the pain he'd caused him. Not only for the bruises and marks, but for never giving him one second of peace. He laid in bed and shook under the thin blanket every night, fearing what would happen when his pa got home from the bar. He wanted to punish him for the constant belittling, the repeated accusations of his mother's death. Joel wanted him to pay for it all. That was what was in his heart when he pulled the trigger. He remembered that distinctly. He hadn't even walked one hundred yards from his house when it happened. The fall leaves crunched under his work boots. Night was creeping in, but his eyes had adjusted like an animal on a prowl. When he saw something move out of the corner of his eyes, he didn't pause or call out. The rage was too great. It consumed him. Without a thought of what would happen tomorrow, he turned and shot.

It wasn't until he got closer to the fallen man that he realized it wasn't his pa at all, but Mr. McKay. Mr. McKay held up a bloody hand. His lips were moving, but Joel couldn't hear the words. His ears still rung from the report of the gun. Joel saw blood flow from a huge gaping wound in Mr. McKay's leg and Joel's body began to shake uncontrollably. He'd shot Mr. McKay. He dropped the gun on the ground like it was a viper that had just bitten him.

Joel sucked in a ragged breath and wrapped his arms around his trembling body. He stared out at the empty parking lot. He shook his head. Everything had moved so quickly. The lines of his memories were already starting to blur. He remembered reaching down and trying to apply pressure to the wound. Blood ran through his fingers. It seeped into the crevices and lines of his hands. He'd tried to clean them by wiping them on his pants, but it didn't help. The blood just smeared on his clothing. He pressed down harder on the wound. Mr. McKay groaned. His face looked so pale under the growing moonlight. The blood wouldn't stop. It kept coming, dripping, pouring from his fingers.

His pa had shoved him out of the way then. Joel fell over. He wanted to stop his pa from hurting Mr. McKay, but he watched in a daze as his pa tore off his shirt and ripped it into shreds. He began to work on Mr. McKay's wound. Mr. McKay ground his teeth as tears streamed down the sides of his face. Joel noticed a streak of blood across the man's cheek. He looked over at his pa. He didn't know his pa knew how to make a tourniquet. *Did he learn that in the war? He had to be cold with no shirt on.* Joel realized his mind wasn't working right, but he couldn't get control of it. He stared at his pa's frantically moving arms as he tightened the material around Mr. McKay's leg tighter and tighter. Mr. McKay howled, and a shiver ran down the length of Joel's back. He'd already lost so much blood. *How much blood could one person lose before they die?*

His pa motioned to him. *Is he speaking to me?* Mr. McKay's mouth was moving too, but Joel couldn't hear their voices. It was like he was on an island, and they were a million miles away. *What were they saying?* He just wanted to be left alone. He needed to lie down and go to sleep so this nightmare would go away.

"Snap out of it, Joel, or he'll die," his pa yelled.

Joel's mind clicked into place. He scurried to them on his knees.

"Pick him up on that side and I'll get this side. You need to get him to the hospital as fast as possible."

Joel and his pa grunted as they heaved Mr. McKay up into the air. His arms draped across their shoulders. They panted as they tried to keep his feet from touching the ground, each holding a leg. When his pa touched the shot leg, Mr. McKay cried out in pain, and any color that was left drained completely from his face. *We have to hurry!* Joel could barely breathe.

The trek back to the house felt like it took ages. With each step they took, Mr. McKay spoke to him between gritted teeth.

"I know this was an accident. Do not tell the police you shot me."

"What, why?"

His pa huffed, "Because they won't listen. They'll lock you up, boy."

Mr. McKay nodded. "Yes, you have to marry Hazel."

"You...you still want us to get married?" Joel's voice shook.

Mr. McKay's jaw clenched as they jostled him to walk over some brush. "This changes nothing between us. You are already family."

If they didn't need to rush so badly, Joel would have crumpled right there in the dirt and cried. Mr. McKay still thought of him as family. But he doubted Hazel would when she found out what he'd done.

As if he could read Joel's thoughts, Mr. McKay said, "You tell no one. Not even Hazel. I'll tell them it was a hunter I've never seen before. If they don't believe that—" he hissed through clenched teeth as pain overtook him. His head started to droop.

His pa shook him. "Stay with us. If they don't believe it, Joel, tell them I shot him. They'd believe that."

His pa's eyebrows knit together, and Joel wondered if he felt guilty for everything he'd done.

"But you'd go to jail," Joel said, but his words were lost under Mr. McKay's groans.

They made it to the truck and his pa had him open the passenger door as he took the majority of Mr. McKay's weight. They tried to be careful getting him inside, but Mr. McKay cried out as they slid him onto the seat. He leaned his head against the window.

Joel started to rush to the other side to get in, but his pa grabbed him by the shoulder. "Promise me. If they don't believe his story, you'll tell them I shot him."

Joel's head spun. "But why?"

"I've done nothing but make your life hell. You are my son, all I have left of Sarah, and if I could do this one thing for you, let me do it. Now hurry. He's losing too much blood."

The truck fishtailed on the dirt road, and it was all Joel could do to maintain control of it. Mr. McKay's breathing was shallow. His skin turned a grisly gray. When Joel's tires hit the paved city road, he pushed until the pedal hit the floorboard. The speed of the truck quickened with the speed of his heart.

"Stay with me," he repeated. "We're almost there." But he wasn't sure if Mr. McKay heard him. He wasn't moving except for his head, which bobbed with each pothole Joel hit. As Joel skidded to a stop near the emergency room doors, he threw the truck door open. His shoes slipped on the concrete, and it was all he could do to right himself. He crashed into the emergency room doors and the nurse sitting at the entrance desk gasped. Everything inside of him was spinning and he could feel the adrenaline shooting through his veins like bottle rocket firecrackers zipping through the air. His words came out of him like a scream as he cried and begged for someone to help. Nurses and a doctor ran towards him, but all he could do was point to his truck. They raced to it, but in the back of his mind he wondered if it was already too late.

Chapter 35

Hazel

The first thing she saw when they pulled into the hospital parking lot was Joel standing under a streetlamp. His clothes were dirty and covered in blood. *Daddy's blood*. She flung the door open and leaped out, running to him. They collided together. She wrapped her arms around his neck, and he encircled her waist, pushing his head into her shoulder. The sobs racked through his body, and he shook violently in her arms. She held him tight, smelling the woods and iron. *How could this be real?* She felt her heart ache for him and her father. She was so glad Joel had been there with him. *But why had he been there?* It didn't matter, she pushed her worries to the side. *Thank the Lord, he had been*. If not for him and his pa, her father could be dead in the woods because of some hunter's stray bullet. She didn't care what McConnell thought; they'd given Daddy a fighting chance.

Ruthie ran beside them. "Have you heard anything?"

Joel pulled his head away from her shoulder. His eyes were red and swollen, and snot dripped from his nose. He rubbed it away with his hand.

"They won't tell me anything." His voice sounded hollow.

Ruthie pulled Hazel's arm. "Come on, they'll have to tell us something."

As they approached the emergency room door, Hazel considered not going inside. She paused. She'd been so sure of herself when she and Ruthie started to leave the duplex. But that was before she saw Officer McConnell. Now her insides had turned to water, and she couldn't shake the feeling of impending doom. She couldn't lose her father. She was almost a married woman, but she still needed him. She tried to breathe. It was hard to believe that inside that building, Daddy lay dying and in pain. It was too much to face. Joel glanced at her. She looked at him with unfocused eyes. He took her hand and squeezed it. The pressure comforted her. She forced her feet to walk through the hospital door Ruthie held open.

They went to the front desk. A nurse recognized Ruthie immediately.

"Oh, sweet things, I'm so sorry. The doctor said to notify him right when you got here. Let me go tell him. Please have a seat. I'll be right back."

Hazel turned to where the nurse had motioned. The waiting room was filled with hard-backed plastic chairs. But the crowds of people

Milton and Sandra had seen earlier in the afternoon were gone. Only a man holding a blood-soaked rag to his head and a mother holding a restless toddler sat in the chairs a few seats away from each other.

Hazel looked at Ruthie. Her blonde hair was frazzled. Her eyes and face were red and splotchy. Her mouth turned down into a deep frown.

"I guess we sit and wait for the doctor?" Hazel asked.

Ruthie's frown deepened. "How long do you think that will be? I want to know something now," she said as she collapsed into a hard seat. Her body seemed to deflate against it.

Hazel swallowed as she and Joel took seats beside her. "I want to see him too. I can't wait." She swallowed the lump in her throat. *What if he only has a few minutes left and we miss them?* The words caught inside her, she didn't want to think about that, but she had to. She wanted to be with her father, holding his hand and soaking up every last moment she might have with him like a dry sponge. Hazel turned and buried her head in Joel's shoulder. Joel wrapped an arm around her, but she could feel his body go rigid. He'd been with his pa when they'd found her poor father. Hazel's heart melted. It had to have been a shock, but before she could ask him how he was holding up, the doctor approached.

"Miss McKay," the doctor said to both her and Ruthie. The formality in his tone set Hazel's teeth on edge. Hadn't he known them since they were born? He'd treated their hurts and aches all their lives, and now they weren't Hazel and Ruthie but Miss McKay.

Ruthie gripped Hazel's hand, squeezing it until she cut off the circulation, but Hazel hardly felt it. Her heart pounded, and it was all she could do to sit upright.

The doctor came and took a knee in front of them. His hair had gone completely gray, and the wrinkles in his eyes were deeper than she'd remembered. He'd need help getting up from that position, but she appreciated the gesture. He looked them each in the eye, and it was all Hazel could do to maintain eye contact.

"Your father is in serious condition." He paused to let that register. "He lost a lot of blood. If it wasn't for Joel getting him here so quickly, he'd be dead."

Ruthie whimpered. Hazel felt her head swim.

"We've cleaned out the wound and given him blood. Right now, that's all we can do."

"What does that mean?" Hazel asked, her voice barely audible.

"It means, we wait. If he can make it through the next three days and we get ahead of any infection, then he may have a fighting chance. But only God knows if it's his time or not."

Hazel began to silently beg God not to take her father, to please leave him here for a while longer.

"Can we see him?" Ruthie asked.

The doctor nodded, "Yes, I think you both can sit with him as long as you'd like. I've had three chairs put in there." His eyes looked toward Joel. "I figured you'd want to stay as well."

Joel gave a silent nod.

"The nurses will be checking on him every hour. If things get bad, you all must do as we say and leave right when we tell you. Is that agreed?"

They all three bobbed their heads in agreement.

"Good. If Joel would be so kind and help an old man up. I'll show you to your father's room."

Hazel's insides were jelly as they entered through the tan door. She felt like her heart was being ripped out of her chest when she saw Daddy in the bed. He appeared so small, and his skin was ashen. The baby-blue hospital sheet and covers were pulled to the top of his chest. A tube ran from his arm to a glass bottle that hung upside down on a skinny metal pole. It dripped liquid into the tube that ran down to her father's arm. She blinked, hoping he'd magically return to the vibrant, strong man she'd seen at her wedding shower earlier this evening. His voice deep and full of life as he laughed with Ms. Faye. She couldn't believe it was still the same day. It felt like a million years ago.

Ruthie ran to the side of the hospital bed and Hazel went to the other side. Daddy's eyes were closed, like he was sleeping.

Joel pulled a chair up for Hazel and she sat. He did the same for Ruthie. They each held one of their father's hands in their own. Joel moved his chair near Hazel. She looked over at him and when their eyes met, he looked away. She felt a pang in her heart. *He must be blaming himself for not getting him here faster.* She squeezed Daddy's hand tightly. She looked across his body at Ruthie. Huge tears rolled down her cheeks and dropped onto the bed.

Hazel felt her throat constrict. She leaned closer and whispered, "Daddy? Daddy, we're here. Your little girls are here."

Ruthie moaned and laid her forehead on Daddy's hand.

"Please be strong," Hazel said, feeling the sorrow rise in her chest until she couldn't keep it down. She began to sob.

Joel moved near her and wrapped his arm around her. "He's a fighter, and he loves ya'll something fierce. If anyone can survive this, it would be him." He stood and the chair legs made a scratching noise against the floor. "I need to get some air." He touched Hazel's shoulder, gently gripping it before he turned and walked out the door.

Hazel's eyes followed him as he left. She wished she could read his mind.

"He's having a real hard time with this," Ruthie said, sniffing.

Hazel looked back at their daddy's unmoving face. "But aren't we all?"

Chapter 36

RUTHIE

The last two days had been a blur. Ruthie laid her head on daddy's bed. She felt the rough blue cover that was spread over him scratch her forehead. *Why can't the hospital have soft sheets and covers?*

Ms. Faye sat in the corner of the room. Ruthie was so worried about Daddy, but between Ms. Faye's constant sniffing and crying, Mr. Hal's pacing, and Mrs. Anne's sighing, she was getting irritated with them all. Joel was even acting strange. He seemed stiff when Mr. Hal first came to the hospital and hugged him. She knew he was worried about Daddy too, but she couldn't help thinking it was more than that. She decided she'd ask him later if they ever got a chance to be alone. She leaned up and looked around the hospital room.

Everyone was there. She looked at Hazel who sat on the opposite side of their father. Joel sat beside her. Hazel's head was bowed, and her eyes were closed. Ruthie wondered if she was sleeping or praying.

Ms. Faye started to cry again, which made Mr. Hal stand from his seat and begin to make the same path back and forth in front of the hospital bed. Ruthie was surprised he hadn't worn a little pathway in the tile. Hazel groaned. She opened her eyes and looked at Ruthie, then rolled them.

"Ms. Faye," Hazel said in a sweet voice, but Ruthie could sense an edge to it. "Why don't you go home, get cleaned up, and have some breakfast?"

Ms. Faye took a white handkerchief and patted the smeared mascara around her eyes. "Oh, I don't want to leave him."

Hazel nodded, "I understand, but we could all use a shower and some food. You go first and when you get back, we will go. So, Daddy is never left alone. You see?"

Ms. Faye sniffed, "I guess."

"It would be such a big help," Hazel persisted.

Ms. Faye pursed her lips to the side. "Alright. Then I'll stay with him while you all go?"

"Yes," Hazel said, grinning.

After Ms. Faye agreed. Hazel turned to Mr. Hal. "Why don't you and Mrs. Anne go too? Get cleaned up, have some breakfast, and then come back."

Mr. Hal stopped pacing and looked toward Mrs. Anne. She placed her hands in her lap. "Well, I would like to bring some more fresh flowers up here."

Ruthie looked around at the bouquets of flowers scattered around the hospital room. They were on the windowsill, the nightstand by the bed, and the floor. Even though it was October, it smelled like spring had bloomed in his room. Ruthie wondered where Mrs. Anne would put the new flowers.

Mr. Hal helped Mrs. Anne up from her chair. "Then let's get going. We don't want to be gone too long." He looked at Joel. "We'll be right back. Do you need anything, boy?"

Joel shook his head. His mouth was pulled into a tight line.

Mr. Hal patted his shoulder, and Ruthie thought she saw Joel flinch before he hung his head to stare at the floor. *Something was definitely not right with him.*

When they were all gone and the room was silent, Ruthie felt a sense of peace wash over her. She loved them all so much, but extra people made it hard for her to think. They were Daddy's friends, and possibly his girl, but they weren't his daughters. They would never understand what she and Hazel were feeling and how she selfishly wanted to soak up every minute with him and share them only with Hazel and Joel.

Ruthie's stomach broke the quietness. It grumbled so loudly, she thought she felt her chair rattle. Hazel looked at her with wide eyes.

"Did you eat dinner last night?" Hazel asked.

Ruthie frowned. She couldn't remember when she ate last. "I don't know."

Hazel furrowed her eyebrows. "You need to go get something to eat."

Ruthie opened her mouth to protest, but Hazel held up her hand.

"I'm still the oldest, which means I'm still the boss."

Hazel folded her arms in front of her, and Ruthie almost chuckled. She wondered if Daddy could hear them. He'd laugh if he could see Hazel's face.

"But I'm practically a grown woman now."

Hazel's face softened, and she unfolded her arms, letting them drop on her lap. "I know, but I need you. If you get sick or too weak from not eating, I don't think I could handle it. I need you to lean on."

Ruthie felt a pang in her heart, and even though she didn't want to leave Daddy's side, she also equally wanted to be able to support her sister in case the worst thing imaginable happened. She reluctantly agreed and got up to leave.

"I won't be gone long," Ruthie promised.

Ruthie walked down the long hall to the hospital cafeteria. The nurses had graciously allowed only Ruthie, Hazel, and Joel to use their little cafeteria space. They'd been told that each day a different meal option was served. Ruthie went to the end of the line and picked up a tray. She pushed it across the metal bars. As she walked toward the selection of food items, she caught a glimpse of her reflection in the clear display glass. Her clothes looked dingy and felt damp. She'd pinned her blonde curls back, but her hair was starting to look slick and shiny at the roots.

"Ruthie, would you like a hot meal this morning?" one of the nice cafeteria women asked.

"What you makin'?"

"I've got eggs, biscuits and gravy, waffles, and bacon."

Ruthie's stomach turned. She knew she was hungry and needed to eat, but at the same time, she didn't *feel* hungry. It was such a strange sensation. She settled on having just a small plate of scrambled eggs and a piece of bacon.

The woman took her order, but instead of a small amount of food, she piled the plate high with eggs and four pieces of bacon. She also wrapped two blueberry muffins in napkins and placed them on the side of the plate. Before Ruthie could protest, she waved her spatula in the air and said, "These are for you to sneak back to your sister and Joel."

Ruthie was too tired to argue and thanked her for her kindness.

Ruthie looked at the mound of eggs on her plate as she made her way to an empty green square table with matching plastic chairs. She sat, feeling the weight of the world on her shoulders. She picked up her fork and took a bite of the eggs. The delicious warmth filled her, and she began to shovel the little yellow and white clusters into her mouth. Since she and Hazel had arrived at the hospital two days ago, neither of them had been home. They'd slept awkwardly in the hospital chairs, but after all those hours waiting and pleading to God, there'd been no change to their father. Still, he was alive. She thanked the Lord for that miracle and for all the support they'd received from their friends and the community. Alice and Margarette Ann had come to offer their sympathies and prayers. The pastor from their little church came every evening to say a quiet prayer over Daddy. Even Joel's pa showed up, which shocked Ruthie and Hazel. It was the first time Hazel had ever met Joel's pa. Although he was clean and sober with his hair combed neatly to the side, seeing him still sent shivers up Ruthie's spine.

The worst time they'd had was when their grandmother came to the hospital. Ruthie's stomach twisted at the thought, and she laid down the fork. She remembered overhearing her grandmother whispering to Hazel that Ruthie could live with her if Daddy didn't make it. Ruthie had hurried and excused herself from Daddy's hospital room. She made up a story about needing some water, but in actuality, she couldn't deal with the thought of possibly being stuck living with that pretentious old woman. The woman who raised her mother, who thought leaving her daughters and traveling to California to flitter her life away was perfectly acceptable.

Ruthie shook her head and made herself think about something else. She thought about the doctor. He was so kind. He'd said he'd known Daddy from the war. Ruthie picked her fork back up and began to eat again. She liked how he made morning and evening calls to check on his status, but still, he never told them much. She wondered if he thought they couldn't handle the truth. He'd tell them the same thing over and over when they peppered him with questions.

"Only time will tell. He needs rest."

Still, Ruthie thought it surely had to be a good sign Daddy was still alive, that he'd held on this long. She ripped half of a piece of bacon off with her teeth and crunched it. A group of nurses sat at a table next to hers. As she ate, she tried not to eavesdrop on their conversation, but she was so interested in them. She couldn't stop staring at their uniforms. The pale blue dresses with starched white aprons, and white hats. She listened to the nursing lingo they used. She wondered how you took vital signs or gave someone a shot. They were everything she dreamed of being one day.

Ruthie's ears pricked when she heard the nurses discussing their patients. Ruthie listened for any information about her father but didn't hear anything. Instead, they discussed a little boy who'd come in with a broken arm. He had to be held down so it could be set. There'd also been a woman who delivered a healthy baby girl that morning after laboring all night. Ruthie felt a twist in her heart. She desperately wanted what they had. She wanted to be a nurse. She had a little under two more years of high school. After Hazel was married, she had planned to speak to Daddy about her dreams for the future. She wanted to talk to him about getting a part-time job so she could save money to help pay for classes and expenses. Fear spoke to her heart, and she shivered as she wondered if she'd ever get the chance to talk to him about anything ever again. Her eggs felt like a walnut in her throat as she swallowed them. She took a huge gulp of orange juice to wash them down, then stared at the plate of half-eaten food in front of her. She needed to forget her silly dreams of being a nurse. They weren't important anymore. Daddy was her main concern. In the back of her mind, she heard Ronnie's voice telling her not to give up on her dreams. She remembered him twirling her around the basketball court floor during prom so long ago with a wide smile. He was living his dream now. He'd joined the army and was following in his father and grandfather's footsteps. Ruthie sighed and picked up a fork full of eggs, but before she could put it into her mouth, the cafeteria door swung open, startling her and the nurses at the table.

Joel was standing on the threshold. His face flushed as he gasped for breath.

"Come. Now," he panted.

Ruthie felt cold fingers of dread run over her body and grip her heart, "Is he?" she whispered.

Joel shook his head, and for the first time, Ruthie noticed the huge smile spread across his face. "He's awake Ruthie. He's awake!"

Chapter 37

JOEL

Joel and Ruthie raced to Mr. McKay's room. Joel gripped his side as a sharp stitch pierced him. Ruthie was right on his heels and nearly knocked him over when he stopped abruptly in front of Mr. McKay's door. Hazel stood outside. She looked too thin and frail. When she saw them, her eyes went watery, and Joel's stomach dropped. *Something bad has happened. Does she know? When Mr. McKay woke up, did he tell her the truth?* He grabbed her in his arms and pressed her body to his, knowing this may be the last chance he had to touch her. She trembled but didn't wrap her arms around him.

"What's wrong?" Ruthie huffed. She placed a hand against her side. Her chest rose and fell rapidly.

Hazel pulled away from Joel. She gave him a strange look. "The nurses and doctor are tending to him now. He's awake."

"Did he say anything?" Joel asked. He had to know.

Hazel's eyebrows furrowed, and she frowned when she looked at him. "Yes."

Her answer was short and clipped, but in that one word, all of Joel's resolve that maybe things would be okay, that maybe they could get married and be happy together, went up in smoke like a lit match dropped on a stack of newspapers. Joel thought his legs might give out under him. Ruthie grabbed his arm in excitement, not realizing that Joel's life was over.

"Oh my! What did he say?"

Hazel glanced at Joel, and he wobbled on weak knees.

Hazel's frown deepened, "He didn't say much. Just that he wanted to visit with Joel first, privately, before he saw anyone else. Even us."

Ruthie squeezed Joel's arm. "What does he want to see you about?" she asked, looking up to meet his eyes.

Joel forced a shrug, "Don't know."

Hazel took his hand and held it. "Are you sure you don't know what it's about? It seemed pretty important."

Joel looked her in the eyes and lied. "I really don't." The shame of his lies burned him from the inside out. Was this how they were supposed to start their lives together, with lies? It felt so wrong. But before he could open his mouth to blurt out the truth of what he'd done, Mr. McKay's door opened. The doctor stepped out into the hallway. Hazel tightened her grip on his hand. She was trembling.

"Oh good, you are all here now." He looked at each of their faces, pausing at Joel's.

Joel felt heat creep up his neck.

"He's doing good. He said he was mighty hungry, which is a good sign. We are going to start slowly though. A nurse is going to bring him a bowl of chicken broth. We'll see how he handles that first. He'll need to stay a few more days so we can keep an eye on his wound. Infection is what we are worried about most now. If we can keep infection at bay, then he can be released with further care instructions." The doctor paused to make sure they were all listening. "I don't need to tell you how much of a miracle this is. You all need to say some thank-you prayers. It's a wonder he's still here with us."

Ruthie hugged Joel's arm and Hazel squeezed his hand. The doctor's eyes focused on Joel. Joel swallowed hard.

"He said the first visitor he wants to see is you, Joel. So, go ahead and head on in. I'll have one of the nurses call Ms. Faye and Mr. Hal. I'm sure they'll want to see him when they get back up here."

Joel felt Hazel and Ruthie's eyes on him. His heart picked up a beat. He nodded to the doctor and looked at Hazel then Ruthie. They released his arm and hand. He could see the disappointment on their faces. They wanted to see their father so badly, and they couldn't understand why he was chosen first. If only they knew he was the one who put him in that hospital bed. If they knew the truth, he wasn't sure what they would think of him. They'd probably want nothing to do with him ever again. *I deserve to be thrown into a jail cell.*

He walked to the door. His hand was sweaty, and he could hardly breathe as he gripped the handle and pushed it open. Inside, Mr.

McKay sat propped against some pillows. His skin looked washed out, and his cheek bones jutted out sharper than they had before, but when he saw Joel, a slow smile crept across his face.

"Come here, boy. Come sit beside me." Mr. McKay motioned to him.

Joel felt a lump form in his chest. He almost turned around and rushed out of the room. It was sheer force that made him stay and walk toward Mr. McKay. Each step felt like he was walking in deep, thick mud. He sat down in the chair he'd slept in for the last two days. After he sat, a heavy silence settled between them. Joel didn't know what to say, so he gripped his hands tightly in front of him and stared at his knuckles.

Mr. McKay spoke first. "I can see you're still bent up about shooting me."

Joel's eyes darted up to see a huge broad grin on Mr. McKay's face.

"It's a joke, boy."

Joel shook his head as tears pricked his eyes. "It's not funny. You could have died and it's all my fault."

Mr. McKay didn't respond, so Joel kept going.

"I've been lying to the police, to Hazel and Ruthie. I told them what you and pa told me to say, but I can't do it anymore. It's not right. I can't marry Hazel with all these lies floating around. We can't start our life together built on lies. And if she knows the truth, she won't want to marry me anyway." Joel stopped to gulp down some air.

Mr. McKay pursed his lips to the side, and it reminded Joel of Hazel. "Well, let me see what I can do." When he yelled for the doctor, Joel almost leaped from his skin.

The door creaked open, and the doctor poked his head inside. "Ya'll need something?"

"Yeah, send in my daughter, Hazel."

Joel felt the room spin. He clung onto the bottom of the chair to keep himself from falling over. He knew this needed to happen, but his heart broke in half as he realized today was the day that he lost his true love.

Chapter 38

HAZEL

Hazel walked into Daddy's hospital room. He looked frail and small in the big bed. Her eyes glanced at Joel, sitting straight as a rod in his seat. His skin looked almost as pale as her father's, and he was shaking. Her mind raced. *What was going on?* She slowly walked to a chair and began to pull it to the opposite side of the bed. She could feel their eyes on her, watching her every move. Her cheeks heated and she desperately wished she knew what was happening, but she said nothing. The silence in the room was as heavy as the air before a rainstorm, and her stomach began to twist until she couldn't stand it any longer.

"What's wrong?" she whispered.

Joel bent over in the chair and put his face in his hands. He began to sob. Hazel started to rise, but Daddy took her hand and held it. "Stay put," he directed.

She sat back down.

"He needs to get it all out first."

Hazel wondered what Joel needed to get out. It pained her to see him so upset. Just sitting there and watching him cry felt like someone was ripping out a piece of her heart.

When he stopped crying, he didn't raise his head. He stayed hunched over, studying his hands.

"Please tell me what's going on. Ya'll are scaring me," she said.

"Joel needs to be honest with you. He needs to tell you everything from the beginning."

Joel leaned up in the chair. His face was splotchy and red. His jaw clenched, and his throat moved as he swallowed. She wanted him to look at her. If she saw his eyes, she'd know everything would be alright, but he wouldn't look at her face. He looked beyond her at the wall. A sense of dread at what he was going to say spread through every cell of her body. She decided she didn't want to hear what he was going to say. She didn't need to know. As he opened his mouth to speak, she almost covered her ears.

"The night your father was shot, well, it was—"

Daddy held up a hand to stop him and placed it on Joel's shoulder. "That's not the beginning Joel."

Joel's eyes fluttered from the wall to Daddy's face. His eyebrows knit in confusion.

"I know you've never been completely honest with Hazel."

Joel shook his head side to side, but her father continued.

"Son, she has no idea what your life was like. She knows that your pa was hard to live with, but she doesn't know really what that means. You need to tell her everything you went through, so she understands."

As realization spread across Joel's face, Hazel watched his entire body turn limp and he sagged in his chair.

"It's too hard," Joel said, laying a shaking hand over his face.

"You've got to," Daddy patted him. "It's the only way to keep her."

Two hours later, Hazel knew almost everything. She was certain there was so much more he wasn't telling her, but she couldn't stand to hear it. She never knew the little boy she'd met in the forest all those years ago would go home at night to a madman. While Joel relayed story after story, she felt like someone was taking her heart and sawing it out with a jagged knife. *How could a parent hurt a child so badly?* Her hands ached from squeezing them into tight fists, and she wished she could ram them into Joel's pa's face. He'd been here to see her father. The rage almost consumed her. Yes, he'd helped Daddy, and said he'd take the blame for the accident, but this was his fault. If he hadn't pulled that gun out on Joel and threatened to kill her and Mr. Hal, this would never have happened. Joel wouldn't have accidentally shot her father. Hazel understood why Daddy had lied and said it was a hunter he didn't know. Even if he didn't want to press charges against Joel, the law might not see it like that, and Joel could be thrown in jail. A tremor passed through her body.

"There is no doubt that the police will be back with more questions," Daddy said. "The only other person we will tell is Ruthie." He then looked toward Hazel. "This is a lie we will have to keep to our dying days. Is that agreed?" The emotion in Daddy's voice made her eyes sting.

She glanced at Joel. All those faint scars she'd seen on his arms and legs ran straight to his heart, where the wounds were still deep and raw. He sagged in the chair as if a heavy weight hung from his neck. He wouldn't look at her. A muscle worked in his jaw. What she saw before her now was a broken man. His pieces had been chipped and cracked through his whole childhood. He'd shot Daddy. *If Daddy had died, would he had ever told her the truth?* The pain Joel was in was so visceral. It was as if it stood behind him like a ghost haunting him. *He would have told me*, she decided. Even if it meant going to jail. She knew the truth of it as clearly as she knew the color of her own hair. *He'd have gone to jail before living a lie with me because that's the kind of man he is.* Maybe right now he was shattered glass, but it didn't matter to her, even glass fragments could reflect the sunlight and be beautiful. After all he'd been through with his pa, he still turned out to be a good man. Wounded, yes, but still good. More than ever, she needed him. Inside her heart, she vowed to keep his secret. She'd tell a thousand lies for him, no matter what it cost her.

A knock on the door made her jolt. They all looked toward the door as it cracked open. The doctor's head poked out from the other side.

"Sorry to bother you folks, but we need to check the miracle man's wound." He looked behind him then leaned his head back inside the room. "Also, there's a slew of people here that are threatening bodily injury on me if I don't let them in to see you soon."

Hazel's father chuckled. "Okay, just give us a few more minutes."

The doctor nodded and shut the door.

Joel stood. The chair scrapped across the floor. He looked at Daddy. "I'm sorry sir. I'll be heading out now." He hung his head and turned to walk toward the door.

Hazel leaped from her chair. "Joel?" She wanted him to look at her. To see the love she felt for him.

He stood frozen in place.

"Where are you going?"

He didn't turn. His voice sounded like he'd been to battle and lost. "I don't know."

She reached out and touched his shoulder. He flinched under her fingers. "Please don't, Hazel. I can't bear to hear it."

"Hear what?"

He turned around, catching her by surprise. He ran a hand down his red splotchy face. "I can't stand to hear that the wedding is off. That we're over." His eyes were watery.

She stood there. She could taste the words she wanted to say, but they wouldn't come out. Tears began to roll down his cheeks. Her heart lurched and she grabbed his face with both of her hands and pulled his head down to hers. She raised up on tiptoes and her lips found his mouth. His arms encircled around her waist, holding her tightly, and she kissed him frantically, pressing her mouth into his like she was starving for his kisses.

A cough behind them made them break apart. Hazel felt heat flood her body when she saw Daddy's eyebrows raised high on his forehead.

"So," he said, his voice higher pitched. "Does this mean there's still going to be a wedding?"

The wariness in Joel's eyes made her breath shorten. She took his hands in hers and squeezed. His fingers felt rough against her skin. "I understand everything now. And I don't blame you. It was a horrible accident." She worked her teeth into her bottom lip. She had to say it. "This is a secret I can keep for the rest of our lives together."

Joel's eye lashes flickered with understanding. "Are you sure?"

She nodded, "I've never been surer of anything in all my life."

Chapter 39

RUTHIE

Daddy groaned as Ruthie helped him sit up on the old sofa.

"I didn't realize how uncomfortable this thing was," he complained. "A spring was digging into my back the whole time I napped."

Ruthie couldn't help but smile. She was so happy he was home, even if he was a cranky patient. "Now take your medicine and quit your yipping."

Daddy raised one eyebrow. "I thought nurses were nice and sweet."

Ruthie grinned wider, "I'm not a nurse yet."

He shook his head and took the glass of water and pills she held out to him.

Once they'd brought him home from the hospital and he'd settled in, they'd had "confession time," or that's what he'd called it. He told her what had really happened out there in the woods. It had shocked her no doubt. But hearing the whole story and all that Joel went through made her remember that day they hid in the snow. *Would Joel's pa have actually hurt Hazel or Mr. Hal?* She had no idea. In the hospital, even though his presence gave her chills, he'd seemed a different man, normal. Maybe he was trying to change. To be a different man than the one that chased Joel in the snow with a gun all those years ago. But she didn't care to find out.

Still, Daddy felt the need to swear her to secrecy. He didn't have to do that though, because she'd die on any hill Joel stood on, and she'd never do anything that would potentially ruin him or hurt Hazel. Her mouth was sealed shut. Except when it was her confession time. She finally told him about her dream to be a nurse. She had talked herself out of saying anything about it a million times. She told herself it wasn't important, and that Daddy needed to heal. She also worried her wanting to go to college would stress him out because, like everything, it cost money, and he didn't have a job anymore. Hospital bills would soon be pouring in. The thought of how his boss had called the day Daddy was released from the hospital to tell him he'd been "relieved" of his duties still burned her up inside.

"He can't do that!" she'd yelled. "Isn't there something we can do?"

Daddy shook his head. "No, peanut. I've missed too many days and now I'm injured. There's no way they will make concessions for me, an old man without a high school diploma."

She remembered how even though she didn't want to say anything, he'd coaxed her confession from her.

"I know you want to tell me something, peanut. Don't be afraid. If I've learned anything from this experience, it's that life's too short to keep things bottled up. Spit it out. You'll feel better."

And he was right, she had felt better. She'd spilled out her hopes and dreams as she sat beside him on the couch. Her leg jiggled and she had to press her hands down on it to keep it still. She didn't realize until the words were out, how desperately she wanted—needed—him to encourage her to chase after her dreams. Even if that meant traipsing back and forth to Fort Smith for classes. She knew if Daddy said one negative word about it, her insides would fold, and she'd give up on her dream entirely.

But when she'd finished, he didn't even flinch at her words. She'd blushed like a silly girl when he told her she'd be a wonderful nurse. He'd taken her hand and promised that they'd make a plan. They'd find a way to pay for the classes and get her a car.

Now she watched as his throat moved while he swallowed each of his pills. He stared at her with a side eye glance, his brows furrowed.

"What?" she questioned. "What's wrong? Are you hiding your pills in your mouth? Open your mouth."

"No," he said, opening his mouth wide and sticking out his tongue. "You are a mean nurse. I'd never do that."

She took the glass from him and set it on the coffee table. "Then why are you looking at me like that. Like you're hiding something." Her head spun, trying to figure out what was wrong. She remembered the day Officer McConnell had come to the house to question

Daddy about the "incident." Joel and Hazel had been there too. Her insides had squirmed so hard, she thought she'd be sick. When she handed Officer McConnell a cup of coffee, her hand shook so badly, she thought she might spill it on him, and then he'd know the truth of what happened for sure. Hazel had stayed in the kitchen the whole time, acting like she was making dinner, and Joel sat in the chair opposite McConnell. His face was the color of ash. Ruthie hoped McConnell didn't notice. *They were horrible at this—inexperienced liars.*

"Look Jim, I've told you what happened," Daddy had said without a waver in his voice. "And if you don't leave me and my family alone, I'll have to speak to the Sheriff about this harassment." Although he'd smiled when he said it, there was an edge to his words. "Come on, Jim, how long have we been friends. If it had been Davenport, I'd tell you. It was a hunting accident. Plain and simple. Nothing more."

Ruthie had been amazed at the ease Daddy spun the lie. If Officer McConnell had looked in Joel's face, he'd have known there was so much more to it, but instead, he sighed and handed Ruthie the coffee cup. "Well then, if you're gonna stick to this story, I guess I better be going. Arvel, I'll come to see you soon. I'll bring you some of that oak we talked about for your whittling." With that, McConnell stuck out his hand and Daddy shook it. She'd hoped that would be the end of it. But in a small town, does the suspicion ever end?

"Is it something with Joel?" she asked, her chest beginning to tighten. "Is that why you're staring at me so funny-like?"

Daddy furrowed his eyebrows. "No, no, it's nothing with that." He grabbed her hand and pulled her down on the sofa beside him. "Don't you worry about that."

"Then what are you hiding from me."

He'd been stuck at the house, and she'd watched him like a hawk. The only time she wasn't watching him was when she was at school, but Ms. Faye was here with him the whole time. Of course, he'd had other visitors since being home, but nothing out of the ordinary that she'd heard of. She was pretty certain she'd been able to keep her cantankerous patient out of trouble.

"I'm not hiding anything," he protested.

"I know you too well. You've done something, and I'm not going to bring your lunch until you tell me."

She started to get up to take the glass back to the kitchen, but he reached out and grabbed her arm, stopping her. "You know, if you decide not to be a nurse, you could always be one of those female detectives."

Ruthie rolled her eyes and wrapped her hands around the smooth surface of the glass. He scooted over a little more on the sofa, wincing only slightly as he made more room for her.

"Are Hazel and Joel coming over today?" he asked.

She pointed a finger at him. "I know, you're trying to change the subject, but yes. Are you sure you're still going to be able to walk her down the aisle? The wedding is just three weeks away."

"I'll make it. I'll have Hazel and my cane for support," he pointed to a wooden cane laying against the side of the sofa. He'd made it himself.

Instead of being bored at home, he'd made Joel find him a long branch in the forest near her and Hazel's magical spot. He'd worked on the branch, whittling away day and night. Every morning, she'd clean wood shavings off the floor and sofa, but she didn't mind. She was glad to see him occupying his time with something he could do while lying down. When it was finished, the cane was smooth and gleamed from the wood polish he'd worked into it. He'd formed the handle to look like the head of a mallard duck. The carving was exquisite. All his visitors admired it, and Hazel even said she thought if he'd make more, she might be able to get her new boss, Mr. Crutchfield, to display and sell some at the Piggly Wiggly.

When Daddy removed the glass from her hands to place it on the coffee table, Ruthie's nerves pricked. "Let's put that there," he said before taking her hands in his. "You're right. I do need to confess something."

She frowned, which made him smile.

"Now I know you might be upset with me, but I think in the end, you'll see it's for the best."

She scrunched up her face.

"Don't make that face until you hear me out, peanut."

She tried to make her face expressionless, but it was difficult. Daddy's face was a blank wall, and she couldn't tell if what he was going to say would be serious or not. Her heartbeat raced, making it harder to focus. She took a deep breath in, but it did little to calm her.

He gripped her hands firmly and she met his eyes. His smile was soft but when his mouth moved to say the words, "I sold the house," it was like electricity shot through her body. She bolted up from the sofa, hitting the coffee table. The glass wobbled, and her father quickly leaned over to catch it before it could fall. He groaned at the sharp movement.

Ruthie immediately felt bad that her reaction had caused him pain. She helped him get situated, then forced herself to sit down beside him. She tried to make her voice calm, but her mind popped in one direction after another. *He sold the house. Where will we live? Who bought the house?* What about her and Hazel's magical spot? She'd just found her and Hazel's old bird book near a dusty set of binoculars stuffed in the back of one of the drawers. She'd even snuck out a few times to birdwatch. Without warning, tears began to leak from her eyes. Daddy's eyes went wide, and his eyebrows shot up to the top of his forehead.

"Are you crying?"

She sniffed, rubbing at her face. "Well, yeah. I love this house. I've been here my whole life." She touched her chest as panic began to set in. *Do we even have a home anymore?* Ruthie twisted around in place, surveying the little living room and old kitchen. "This is our home. My home. You sold it without even tellin' me?" *How could he have done this?* Then realization set in, "Does Hazel know?"

He nodded his head. "Yes, I told her yesterday when they came to visit, and you were out with Ms. Faye getting groceries."

Ruthie sucked in a sharp breath as the shock settled in. Hazel knew and said nothing to her. In the pit of her stomach, it felt like a match had been struck. "She knew and didn't tell me!"

Daddy placed a hand on her knee. She felt his warmth through her jeans. "I asked her not to tell you. I wanted to be the one to give you the news. I promise, it's not as bad as it seems."

Ruthie's body slumped forward. "When did this happen?" she asked.

"While you were at school. But I'd been thinking about things after we talked. I want you to be able to follow your dreams, and this house is a burden, especially now that I don't have a job. And with my injury, it would be harder for me to get around to take care of it."

Ruthie's face burned. She should have known not to trust Daddy's care to Ms. Faye. She was a softy and would let him get away with anything.

"Where do we live now?" Ruthie asked, unsure she wanted to hear the answer.

"A duplex close to Joel and Hazel opened, and I filled out the paperwork to rent it. We move in next week."

"Next week!"

He shook his head, a smile crept across his face. "Yes, we gotta get out of here. It's almost hunting season, and the doctor that purchased the property wants to get in here so he can use it all season long. Everyone will be here this weekend to help get us moved. We'll leave some of the big things and sell the things we don't need or want." He cocked his head to the side. "Ironic that it sold so someone can hunt in it."

Ruthie noticed the gleam in his eyes. She sighed. "So, it's not going to be his home?"

He patted her knee. "No, but he said if you and Hazel ever feel any nostalgia, you could come back any time and sit under your magical spot. He just recommended not during hunting season."

Daddy gave a little chuckle and Ruthie couldn't help but grin. She couldn't believe they were going to be neighbors to Joel and Hazel. She'd get to visit more with Sandra and Milton and little Mikey too. She bit her lip. It wasn't a bad place to live. It was closer to the school and closer to practically everything in town. Hope began to sprout inside her like newly bloomed flowers in spring. *Maybe this isn't a bad thing.* They'd be closer to everyone they loved.

Daddy cleared his throat, "There's one more thing."

She met his eyes, immediately worried about what it could be.

"We had a little extra money from the sale of the house. I'm going to put it in a savings account for your nursing classes. I think by the time you graduate, we can put away enough money to pay for your first year and maybe part of your second. Especially since I got a new job as a janitor at the elementary school. I start after Christmas."

Ruthie threw her arms around his neck. He tensed then relaxed in her embrace. "Oh, Daddy! I can't believe you've already found a new job! That's far out! Thank you so much for everything! I don't know what to say."

"You at a loss for words? Did you see a pig fly by?"

She released his neck and lightly slugged him in the arm. He chuckled then placed his hands on her shoulders. "I may joke with you, but I do think you will make an excellent nurse one day. And I promise that I will try until my last day to help you and your sister's dreams come true."

Chapter 40

HAZEL, NOVEMBER 1962

In the Sunday school room window, the afternoon sunlight reflected off the thin, full-length mirror her grandmother had brought for her. The light bounced off it and onto the ceiling, where a huge white spot danced. Hazel collapsed down in a tiny red chair beside a small table meant for children. The skirt of her cream-colored dress ballooned, and she pressed it down on her lap. Broken crayons and leftover coloring sheets depicting David with his slingshot reared back were scattered across the table. She ran her hands along the beads around her waist. Her grandmother stood near the Sunday school teacher's desk, straightening the long sheer veil attached to the back of the pillbox hat.

Her grandmother hadn't stopped fussing since she'd arrived at the church. Although Hazel appreciated all she had done for her, her grandmother's constant nit-picking was making her stomach unsettled. Everything had to be in a certain place or look a specific way to meet her grandmother's high standards. Hazel didn't say anything in protest but followed her grandmother's every wish. She knew her grandmother wanted everything to be perfect for her on her wedding day, or at least she hoped it was for her, and not to satisfy some delusion of self-importance her grandmother possessed. How many times had she already heard her grandmother cluck and say how terrible it was that Daddy had been shot under such suspicious circumstances. Maybe she thought perfection would wash all the unsavory stains away.

Hazel looked around the room. Alice and Ruthie had silently escaped and left her to fend for herself. *Traitors.*

"Although, I still don't like the idea of a fall wedding, I am glad you didn't get married right after your graduation," her grandmother said, holding up the hat to inspect it. The long veil fell across her lap. "People would have thought you were trying to hide something because you'd gotten caught up in a bad way. You know how people like to talk, and after your father was shot," she paused. "Well, I'm afraid your reputation couldn't take the hit."

Hazel's face warmed, but she bit her lip and sighed. "Yes, I know how people talk."

Her grandmother narrowed her eyes, "Sometimes I think you and your sister are still so naive."

Hazel bit down harder on her lip. She looked at her hands and began to tear at one of her fingernails.

"Don't pick at your nails. It's not ladylike." Her grandmother stood up and walked toward Hazel. The material of her dark navy dress swooshed as she walked. "Let's see how this looks." She carefully placed the hat on Hazel's head. She moved behind Hazel and straightened the veil. It cascaded down Hazel's back like a sheer waterfall tickling her shoulders. Her grandmother moved to face Hazel and bent over. Her lips pulled to the side as she adjusted it. She stepped back and put her chin in her hand. "Hmm, it looks better now," her grandmother moved over, so when Hazel turned, she could see herself in the long mirror.

"Yes, it does look much better," Hazel agreed. "Thank you."

Her grandmother picked up some bobby pins and put a few in her mouth. She used them one at a time to secure the hat to Hazel's hair. "Just one more little adjustment," she said, touching the back of the veil. "Good, now that's done."

Her grandmother looked down at the little table where Hazel's bouquet lay near the broken crayons. She picked it up to admire it, Hazel hoped. It wasn't made with real flowers. They were too expensive, but Hazel had made the bouquet herself using a combination of white plastic carnations and baby breath. She'd tied the stems of the flowers with a thick cream ribbon that matched her dress. Her grandmother turned the bouquet side to side. She clucked her tongue. "You should have used white roses instead of carnations. They are classier. Like I was telling your mother yesterday, the flowers in her front yard need to be elegant, her neighborhood has standards."

At first, Hazel wasn't sure she'd heard her grandmother correctly. She blinked her eyes. Her head grew fuzzy with emotion. How did grandmother know what kind of flowers were in her mother's yard? She's never traveled to California. If she did, Hazel was certain she'd have filled her and Ruthie's ears with stories about her trip. The blood in Hazel's veins went cold. Her heart pumped so hard, she was afraid it would tear through the bodice of her wedding dress. Not thinking, Hazel's hand shot up to catch her grandmother's wrist as she laid the bouquet back down on the table.

"My goodness, what is your problem, child?"

Hazel sucked in a long breath through her nose. She let go of her grandmother's wrist and stood facing her. Her pulse raced.

"You spoke to my mother yesterday? You've been to her house?"

Her grandmother's face twisted in anguish, and her complexion went gray behind her thick makeup, as if she hadn't realized what she had said. But Hazel would never forget it. The lines around her grandmother's lips pulled tight, emphasizing the wrinkles around her mouth.

Hazel pointed a finger in her face. "She's not in California. Is she?"

The sound of her raising voice made her grandmother flinch. She silently shook her head no. Hazel began to pace around the room. Her grandmother's eyes went wide, like she was a cornered animal, waiting to be pounced on.

Hazel flung out her hands, "Was she ever in California?"

Her grandmother's body seemed to slump forward, and she sat in the seat Hazel had occupied. "I thought it would be easier if ya'll thought she was gone. Somewhere far away."

"Easier for who?" Hazel screamed the sound echoed in her ears.

"Now don't get dramatic."

Hazel roared, "Dramatic? You knew this whole time where our mother was, and you lied about it. We grew up without a mother!" Hot tears flowed down her face. Her wedding makeup was ruined.

"I don't expect you to understand," her grandmother attempted to explain. "I love you and your sister because you're my granddaughters, but your mother is my daughter. And she wanted more than what your father could give her. Apparently, you're perfectly happy living like, well, like you do."

The rush of blood that passed through Hazel made her dizzy. It took all her strength to keep from rushing toward her grandmother and ripping off her netted navy-blue hat. "Where is she?"

Her grandmother's mouth fell open, then she shook her head. Her gray bobbed hair swayed with each shake. She stammered, "I-I don't think seeing her would be appropriate."

Hazel looked up at the ceiling, willing herself not to resort to violence. "Appropriate? Shes my mother! If you don't tell me where she is, then I'll make sure this whole church knows you're a liar!"

Her grandmother rapidly blinked her eyes.

"Tell me where she is now, or you can leave," Hazel said, pointing to the door.

Hazel ran from the Sunday school room, clutching her skirt in her hands so she wouldn't trip on it. She'd torn off her pill box hat and left it in the room with her grandmother. She found Ruthie in the church's kitchen, sampling the homemade ice cream punch. The sleeves of her dark green maid of honor dress pushed up above her elbows.

She smiled. "It's November, why is it so hot in this church?" she said as she fanned herself. Her smile faded when her eyes took in Hazel's appearance.

"What's wrong?" she asked. She set down the small glass cup she'd been holding.

Hazel slumped, feeling like all her energy had seeped from her. Ruthie wrapped an arm around her shoulders and led her into the women's bathroom at the back of the fellowship hall where the reception would take place. The back of the church seemed to be deserted, and Hazel was glad they didn't run into anyone.

In the bathroom, Hazel gripped the sink so hard, her hands hurt. She stared at her face in the mirror. Her eyes were red, and black streaks stained her cheeks. Her lipstick was smeared across her mouth. Ruthie grabbed a paper towel and wet it. Without saying a word, she began to gently wipe Hazel's face. The paper felt rough against her skin. A whimper escaped from her lips, and she was glad it was just her and Ruthie in the bathroom. She stood there and let Ruthie continue to scrub her wedding makeup away. She felt the anger at her mother and grandmother begin to dissipate and be replaced with old feelings of self-doubt. Daddy was a good man, but he wasn't enough for her mother. *What if in a few years Joel felt the same about her? What if he wanted more than she could give? What if he left her?*

She looked at Ruthie's face, which was pinched in concentration as she tried to rub gently with the harsh paper towels. When Ruthie was finished, Hazel turned toward the mirror. Her face was clean and red. She saw Ruthie reach into her purse and pull out something silver. Ruthie unscrewed the cap and threw her head back, taking a quick sip from it.

"Is that a flask?" Hazel asked.

Ruthie raised an eyebrow and, with a half-smile, took another quick sip. She pushed the flask toward Hazel.

"Take a sip. It'll calm your nerves."

Hazel took the flask from Ruthie's hands. She held it out to examine it. She sniffed it. She flinched away, scrunching her nose. Even the smell of the liquid inside felt like it burned the insides of her nostrils. She couldn't believe Ruthie was drinking it so expertly.

"What is it? Where'd you get it?"

"Margarette Ann. She said it's the only thing that kept her sane during her cousin's wedding. You know her cousin, Janice."

Hazel shook her head. She did know Janice, and she wasn't sure even this potent liquid could keep anyone sane around her. Hazel looked at the flask then shrugged. She lifted it to her lips and tilted it up to take a sip. Although the flask was cool to the touch, what was inside felt like fire going down her throat. She began to cough, and Ruthie patted her back. Hazel wiped her mouth with the back of her hand and pushed the flask back toward Ruthie. Ruthie took another sip and hid the flask back in her purse.

"So, you ready to tell me what's going on? Is it Joel? Do I need to punch his lights out?"

Hazel closed her eyes and blew a long breath out through her nose. She opened her eyes and looked at Ruthie. "It's mom."

"Mom?" Ruthie scrunched up her face. "What about her? She dead?"

Hazel swatted her, "Don't say things like that."

Ruthie rolled her eyes. Hazel bit the inside of her cheek. She hated how her sister could forget they had a mother so easily and toss her and any feelings she had for her to the side. The hot liquid settled in the pit of Hazel's stomach and a queasy feeling came over her.

"She's not dead. And she's not in California. She lives in Mansfield. She's been living thirty minutes from here the whole time."

Ruthie's hand flew to her mouth. Saying the words out loud made Hazel feel like she'd been transported into some horrible horror movie she couldn't escape.

"I want to see her."

Ruthie dropped her hand and crossed her arms in front of her, "What? Why?"

"I want to see her now."

Ruthie rubbed her forehead. She grabbed Hazel's shoulders and spun her to face the mirror. Hazel looked at her face. It was red and splotchy. Her hair was sticking out erratically, and her eyes looked wild, like she'd been transformed into a savage animal. She and Ruthie locked eyes in the mirror. Ruthie spoke to her in slow, overly pronounced words.

"Your wedding is in three hours. That's ridiculous!"

Hazel shook her head side to side. She wasn't going to listen, not today. It was her wedding day. She was calling the shots.

"Mansfield isn't that far from here. We can go and be back in plenty of time."

"But-but look at yourself," Ruthie said. "Your hair is a mess. Your makeup is gone."

Hazel met Ruthie's eyes in the mirror again.

"I have to do this," and she felt with every fiber of her being that it was true.

Ruthie's head dropped forward. She released Hazel's shoulders and reached inside her purse. She pulled out the flask and threw her head back, taking a long drag from it. When she was finished, she screwed the cap back on, then dropped it inside her purse. She looked back into the mirror, meeting Hazel's eyes.

"Well, let's get this over with. But you better drive."

Chapter 41

RUTHIE

Ruthie's brain swam, and she wondered how much she'd drunk. She stared at Hazel trying to focus, but there seemed to be a hazy filter in front of her eyes. *At least there's only one Hazel.* Still, she didn't like the way Hazel gripped the steering wheel so tightly. The skin on her knuckles turned white. The color almost matched her wedding dress. It had taken both of them to push and tug the skirt of her dress into the car without getting it caught in the door. Ruthie couldn't believe no one had seen them. She half wished someone would have stopped them. This whole idea of Hazel's was ludicrous, and it worried her that Hazel hadn't said a word since they'd left the church. Her face was pinched into a somber stare out the car window.

Ruthie coughed to clear her throat. "So, what are we gonna do when we get there?"

"I don't know," Hazel's voice sounded clipped.

Ruthie decided not to ask any more questions. She had never seen Hazel like this before, and it made her stomach feel queasier than it already did. Hazel had always felt the loss of their mother more severely than she did. In Ruthie's memories, their mother was a cruel woman. It was like she loathed them for being born. They were inconveniences. Feelings of hate for the woman who'd birthed her began to worm their way back into her heart. She sucked in a sharp breath. She thought she'd dealt with all of this and was over it, but now it felt like their mama was hurting them all over again. *How dare she live thirty minutes from us this whole time. And how dare she cause Hazel so much pain on her wedding day.* Ruthie despised her all over again.

Ruthie felt bile burn the back of her throat when they passed the rusted metal city sign that read MANSFIELD POPULATION 881.

"Do you know where you're goin'?"

"Yeah, we're close."

In a few moments, Hazel turned the steering wheel, slowing only slightly to make the turn into the Magnolia Chase subdivision. Ruthie looked in awe at the red brick houses with manicured lawns. Some houses were tall with two stories, and a few even had garage doors. There were white picket fences with lush green lawns that barely showed hints of yellow and brown. Prickly bushes decorated the sides of large wooden doors, and perfect cement sidewalks stretched in front of each house. *This is where Mama had been living all this time?* If she wanted to find more than what Daddy had, she'd succeeded. Ruthie wanted to kick down those nice fences. She wanted to get Joel's truck and run his tires all through these immaculate lawns.

The car jerked as Hazel put it in park near a shiny silver mailbox. She pointed toward a two-story brick house across the street that looked like all the other brick houses in the neighborhood, except this one had no garage attached to the house.

"That's it."

Ruthie took it in. The house was triple the size of their house. There was no rotting front porch or chipped paint on the shutters. But it was dark inside, and no car was parked on the driveway.

"No one's home," she told Hazel.

Hazel didn't respond. Instead, she twisted a strand of her brown hair, now past her shoulders, with her fingers and stared at the empty house.

They stayed there for too long, just watching the house, like it might move if they took their eyes off it. The minutes ticked away. Finally, Ruthie couldn't stand it any longer. *This is silly. Our mama doesn't want to see us. Why are we even here?*

She reached over and lightly touched her sister's arm. "We need to get back. You don't want to miss your wedding."

Hazel's bottom lip began to quiver. "I just gotta see her. Just a few more minutes. We can wait a few more minutes."

Ruthie nodded. She couldn't understand why seeing their mother was so important to Hazel, but she could give her a few more minutes.

Time passed, and there was no change. Finally, Hazel's shoulders slumped forward as if in defeat. She reached for the key in the ignition and twisted it to start the car. The car roared back to life, and Ruthie felt her heartbeat start to return to its normal pace. They were going back, and relief flooded through her. For a moment, she felt like they were going to leave this nightmare behind them, but as Hazel began to shift into drive, a glossy tan Cadillac Coupe pulled into the driveway. Hazel's hand froze on the gearshift. Ruthie sucked in a breath and held it.

The car door opened and a man in khaki pants and a dress shirt exited the driver's side. His head was bald except for gray hair around his temples that encircled the bottom of his head. He had a small moustache and wore glasses. When their mother exited the passenger door, Ruthie felt like someone kicked her in the stomach. Her heart ricocheted inside her chest. Her mother was wearing red heels and a tight knee-length red dress that matched. The dress clung to her hips, and a small white belt was cinched around her waist. Her blonde hair was shorter now. An animal print hat sat sideways on her head. Together, she and the man walked to the back of the car and began to remove bags of groceries from the trunk.

Ruthie looked at Hazel. Tears streamed down her face as she watched their mother. Hazel audibly groaned, and Ruthie glanced back up in time to see a young girl with blonde ringlets exit the back of the car. The girl looked to be around eight years old. She skipped to the back of the car and their mother handed her a small bag of groceries. The smile on their mother's face spread from ear to ear. They were all smiling—the man, their mother, and the little girl. Ruthie's eyes stung, and she blinked the tears away. She wouldn't cry. She wouldn't shed one more tear for that woman, and she wanted to leave before she got sick.

Ruthie's heart leaped into her throat when the car wrenched forward as Hazel put in drive and spun out. The tires squealed as they searched for traction on the too-smooth pavement. Ruthie reached to grip the side of the door, bracing herself.

When they were back on the highway past the Magnolia Chase sign, Hazel slowed down and pulled into the parking lot of a run-down supply store. She threw the car into park, and it rocked back and forth. Hazel began to beat the steering wheel with her fists. She screamed, a loud, high-pitched scream that filled the entire car and made Ruthie's ears ring.

"Why? Why weren't we good enough for her?" Hazel sobbed. "She gave us up for a fancier house, a skinnier husband, and a better daughter." She screamed again, "I hate her!"

Ruthie felt warm tears begin to leak from her eyes, and she couldn't stop it. She wiped them away, tasting the saltiness on her lips. She looked at the black smears across the side of her hand where she'd wiped away her eye makeup. She felt like a crazy person. She started to laugh. *Maybe I am crazy.* The thought made the laughter roll out of her uncontrollably.

Hazel cocked her head sideways and stared at her. A little crease had formed between her eyebrows, which made Ruthie laugh even harder. Ruthie held her side and began to hiccup between laughing fits.

"What are you laughing at?"

Ruthie could hear the frustration in her voice. She turned in her seat toward Hazel and placed her hand on her stomach. She sucked in a breath, "What exactly did you have to do to grandmother to get this information about Mama out of her? I keep picturing something involving force, like you squeezing her into something orange and making her wear it. Or threatening to have someone play the fiddle during the ceremony as they dance a jig. She'd flip her lid."

The corner of Hazel's mouth began to lift, and she snorted, which sent her and Ruthie over the edge, laughing uncontrollably. Ruthie held her stomach.

"Did you threaten to pick your teeth during the wedding or dance a hoe-down during the reception?"

Hazel shook her head, "I just yelled at her."

Ruthie raised her eyebrows, "That's it?"

"Well, yeah, but it was a lot. I don't know what came over me."

Ruthie smiled, "Sounds like you found something you lost."

"What's that?"

"Your backbone." Ruthie pulled the rearview mirror down so Hazel could see her face. "You look terrible." Hazel's face was red and splotchy. Her eyes were practically swollen shut from all the crying.

Hazel touched her face, "I do look terrible."

Ruthie reached over and took Hazel's hand. "We need to get back. You're getting married today."

Hazel's eyebrows pinched together. "What if Joel leaves me one day like Mama left us and Daddy?"

Ruthie shook her head, "Something was broken inside Mama. But Joel's whole heart is yours. You are all he wants. He's your prince. Ya'll are meant for each other and always have been. He's family now."

Hazel squeezed her hand. She sniffed, "Well, let's go get me a husband and make it official."

When they made it back to the church, Alice ran out to meet them in the parking lot. She looked frazzled.

"Where have ya'll been? The preacher has been asking questions, and I was running out of things to tell him."

"How much time we got?" Ruthie asked, helping Hazel out of the car.

"Um, I think we got about fifteen minutes until the wedding starts." Alice took in Hazel's face and gasped. "Oh my! We need more time."

Hazel touched her cheek, "Is it that bad?"

Ruthie grabbed Hazel's hand, "It'll be fine. We'll use some ice to hopefully decrease the swelling. You are beautiful. Let's go."

She pulled Hazel into the back of the church, with Alice following close on their heels. They entered the Sunday school room they used to dress in, and Ruthie pushed Hazel down into a small chair.

"Where's Grandmother?" Ruthie asked.

"When I couldn't find ya'll, I asked her if she knew where you went, but she just shook her head. I asked her to go sit in the sanctuary with the other guests. I thought she'd protest, but she didn't say anything, which was surprising and not like her at all."

Ruthie hugged Alice, "That's wonderful! You ready to get down to business?"

She and Alice looked down at Hazel.

"Yes, I love a challenge," Alice said, grinning.

Hazel rolled her eyes and sighed.

They went to work on Hazel. Alice tackled her hair and veil. Ruthie worked on her makeup, holding ice near her eyes to help relieve some of the swelling. They finished and stood in front of the full-length mirror with only a few minutes to spare.

"You look stunning," Alice said. "I'm so happy for you, Hazel."

Hazel lightly touched her cheeks. Her watery eyes gleamed under the florescent lights.

"Don't make her cry again," Ruthie joked. "I'm out of rouge!"

Chapter 42

JOEL

Joel and his groomsmen had been isolated in the nursery for hours, but he wasn't upset. It was his wedding day, and he was enjoying the time visiting with Ronnie and David. Ronnie told them about basic training. Some of his stories were unbelievable, and although going into the army was Ronnie's dream, the stories solidified Joel's decision to stay in Waldron and work with Mr. Hal while he took classes in Fort Smith. He still didn't understand why his pa hated Mr. Hal, and he couldn't find the courage to ask Mr. Hal about it. But since the incident with Mr. McKay and the forgiveness he'd shown him, he'd decided to put whatever this was involving Mr. Hal behind him. Mr. Hal had been nothing but good to him. And whatever the history was between Mr. Hal and his pa, it didn't involve him.

The door of the nursery opened, and the preacher poked his head inside. Joel could hear the notes of Pachelbel's "Canon in D" being played on the piano. His palms became wet, and he wiped them on his black suit pants. He and all the groomsmen wore black suits with white collared shirts and dark green ties. On their left breast pockets, Alice had pinned white carnation flowers.

"It's time," the preacher said.

Ronnie clapped him on the back. "You're about to be a married man."

Joel swallowed the lump that grew in his throat with the swell of the music. He couldn't explain the nerves he was feeling. He wanted to marry Hazel. He'd wanted to be with her since the first time he'd seen her. Maybe it was the anticipation that their whole lives were leading up to this time, this day, when they would be together until death tore them apart. It almost made him sick thinking about how it nearly didn't happen. There'd been so many downs in his life, she was his brightest up, and he'd try to be that for her as well.

Joel stood on shaky knees. It made him smile remembering how his knees wobbled the same way all those years ago when he came out from behind the tree to meet her. Her face had turned beet red when she saw it was him. She didn't blush anymore when she saw him, only when he was joshing with her.

The preacher cleared his throat, "Follow me, please."

Joel turned to face Ronnie and David. "Ya'll ready?"

They nodded, so Joel stepped out of the nursey and followed the preacher. They walked down the aisle. Family and friends turned to watch them, and Joel felt the heat creep up the back of his neck. The church was nearly full. He walked up the three carpeted steps to the front of the sanctuary where the wooden pulpit had once stood. The creases in the carpet still marked the place it would be returned to after the ceremony. He positioned himself beside the preacher and turned to face the aisle to wait for his bride.

His chest rose and lowered rapidly, and he tried to calm himself by looking at the faces of the people in the audience. Milton and Sandra were there sitting toward the back. He smiled as Mikey bobbed up and down on Milton's lap. His little hand waved, and Joel gave him a quick wave back. Mr. Hal and Mrs. Anne were there in the second row on the groom's side, wide smiles shining brightly across their faces. Ms. Faye and Hazel's grandmother sat in the front row of the bride's side. Although Hazel's grandmother wasn't smiling and her mouth was pulled into a tight line, he was glad she was there. He made a mental note to thank her again at the reception for helping with the wedding and paying for the dresses. His eyes scanned the whole sanctuary. So many people from school and the little church had come. Joel stopped breathing. At the back of the church, standing in a corner with his head down, was his pa. He was wearing old blue jeans and a button-up shirt. His arms crossed tightly in front of him. As if he could feel Joel's eyes on him, his head raised, and his eyes locked on Joel. Joel felt his stomach clench, but his pa nodded and smiled.

Joel couldn't remember one time in his whole life that his pa had ever smiled at him. A lump formed in the back of his throat again, but before he could think about it, the doors at the back of the church opened and "Wedding March" began to play.

Chapter 43

Hazel

Although her wedding party was small, the church's vestibule still felt cramped and stuffy with the doors closed. Hazel felt a drop of sweat roll down her back to her slip, but she didn't care. Her father stood beside her, and she grabbed his arm, squeezing it close to her. In his other hand, he grasped the handle of the cane he'd made himself.

"When it's time, you set the pace," she whispered to him. "I don't want to rush you."

"Don't worry about me, girl. This is your day."

She smiled but dropped her eyes. She wanted to tell him everything, but she and Ruthie agreed today wasn't the day to tell him about what they'd discovered. That only thirty minutes away from this church, their mother was living with another man and daughter. She wondered if he'd even care, they were divorced and had been for years. Maybe he'd brush the information off like someone brushes loose dirt off their shirt. But she couldn't chance it. Today was supposed to be a happy day, and she wanted everyone to enjoy it, especially Daddy.

In front of her, Ruthie and Alice stood talking and giggling. Their bouquets wiggled in their hands. Their dark green dresses complemented both of their skin tones, making them look radiant. Hazel felt so grateful for her close-knit family and friends, and even in spite of her mother, she felt happy. Behind the wooden doors, the muffled "Canon in D" played on the piano. An overwhelming feeling of lightness spread over her. She was going to marry the love of her life today. It was really going to happen. She was going to be Mrs. Joel Davenport. She'd written that name in her curly-q handwriting on the back of her notebooks for years now. And when she could find alone time to write her stories, she'd noticed the knights and heroes she wrote about always seemed to resemble Joel. Ruthie was right, she'd found her prince, and she was never letting him go.

The doors to the sanctuary swung open, and the notes from "Wedding March" hit Hazel in the face like a fresh breeze. The notes landed on her skin. She closed her eyes and took a deep breath. It was time. She was going to be Joel's wife.

Chapter 44

Ruthie

The wooden doors opened wide, and Ruthie could hear music being loudly played on the piano. She waited until Alice reached the eighth pew before she started to slowly follow behind her, just like they'd practiced at rehearsal. She tried to time her steps with the music, but who could really get the timing right when the song wasn't rock and roll. She gripped the small bouquet of white carnations she held tighter in front of her body. Her fingers fumbled with the thick gold wedding band she'd tied to the stems with ribbon. It was her responsibility to hand it to Hazel at the right time. Her hands felt slick, and she hoped she didn't bobble it. She tried to focus her eyes on the preacher, but she was weak. She couldn't stop herself from sneaking a peak at Ronnie, who stood beside Joel. He looked handsome in his black suit and green tie. She liked how his tie matched her dress. His eyes met hers and he winked. It sent tingles down her spine, and her heart fluttered. She felt her cheeks flush, and she wanted to kick herself for being so much like Hazel. She made herself give him her best and brightest smile.

Ruthie noticed that Joel and David looked handsome as well, but Joel's face was expressionless, and she wondered if he was nervous. As she took her place on the platform across from Ronnie, he smiled at her, his grin big, showing all his perfectly straight teeth. A jolt of electricity zipped through her, and she quickly looked down at her bouquet. She knew he wouldn't be in town long. He'd have to leave to go back to wherever he was stationed. At one time, that would have made her sad, and if she was being honest with herself, it still kind of did, but he was following his dreams, and soon she'd be following hers.

The music stopped, and Ruthie looked up. The preacher motioned for everyone to rise. Everyone rose to their feet and turned toward the back of the sanctuary. Ruthie looked toward Joel and watched as his face changed in front of her. His eyes came alive, and his mouth spread open into a huge, beaming smile. She followed his gaze down the aisle and saw Hazel, walking arm and arm with their father. His body leaned slightly toward the cane, but Hazel kept a slow, steady pace as they walked down the aisle. Hazel's eyes gleamed with moisture under the church lights. Her cheeks flushed pink. *She looks radiant.* No one would ever guess that fifteen minutes ago, she'd been a disheveled mess. Her pillbox hat sat neatly on her brown hair that Alice had pulled back in a loose bun. The veil cascaded down her back like a sheer waterfall. Ruthie remembered when her hair used to hang long past her waist and how she'd cut it to her jawline just for her.

The afternoon light from the glass windows sent beams of white rays gleaming across the sanctuary walls, filling the church with a heavenly glow. When Hazel and Daddy approached the front, the preacher asked, "Who gives this woman away?" The hitch in Daddy's voice as he said, "I give this woman to be wed today," made Ruthie's eyes blur, and she had to blink the tears away.

"You alright?" Hazel whispered as she handed Ruthie her larger bouquet. She touched Ruthie's hand and held it. Her fingers cool against Ruthie's warm skin.

"Yes, I'm just so happy for you."

When Hazel leaned over to embrace Ruthie, she couldn't hold the tears inside anymore. They ran down her cheeks and off the tip of her nose onto the back of Hazel's wedding dress. She wasn't sure how long they stayed like that, but no one rushed them.

When they pulled apart, they both looked at each other's tearstained cheeks and laughed. Alice held a tissue box out to them while she dotted her own eyes with a tissue. Ruthie glanced at the faces of their friends and family in the audience and saw that all the women, including their grandmother, were crying. Ruthie let Hazel take a tissue first, then grabbed one for herself. Hazel smiled at her before turning to face her future husband.

While the preacher read scriptures about love from the Bible, Ruthie's mind wandered to memories of her, Hazel, and Joel playing in the forest around the old house, drinking Coca-Cola on hot summer days and roasting marshmallows over the open flames. She shook her head, her memories interrupted when the preacher said, "Joel and Hazel have decided to recite their own vows for the ring ceremony."

Joel turned to Ronnie, who handed him a small gold wedding band. It looked so tiny in his huge hand. Joel held out his hand palm up and Hazel slipped her left hand in his. Joel grinned as he gently slid the ring onto her ring finger. He didn't release it when it found its place on Hazel's hand but held it and looked into Hazel's eyes. He took a deep breath before speaking.

"Hazel, from the first moment we met, I was in love with you, and practically everyone knew but you." Some giggles came from the audience and Joel paused to take in another breath. "The happiest days of my life have all been spent with you. And I will cherish every day we have together. Thank you for loving me. I promise for the rest of my life to always keep your heart safe. To keep your heart close. To never wander away. And to never take your love for granted." His eyes became watery, and his voice thick, "I will love you forever."

He released Hazel's hand, and she turned to Ruthie. Ruthie jolted. *Is it my turn?* She placed Hazel's bouquet in the crook of her arm and held her bouquet up while trying to untie the ribbon with one hand. Her fingers fumbled with the ribbon. Hazel raised her eyebrows, trying to stifle a laugh. Alice hurried beside Ruthie and took her bouquet from her shaking hands. Ruthie could feel everyone's eyes on her. Her body temperature rose a hundred degrees, and her dress began to feel damp. Alice held the bouquet up while Ruthie's trembling fingers worked to untie the ribbon. Once freed, the wedding band plopped in her palm. She gripped it so it wouldn't fall to the floor. She held her whole hand out to Hazel, too scared to pick the wedding band up with her fingers. Hazel grinned, then took the ring. When she turned back around to face Joel, Ruthie blew out a large breath. Alice patted her on the shoulder.

Hazel took Joel's hand in hers and slowly slid the ring on his left ring finger. When his wedding band had found its place on his hand, Hazel kept hold of his hand and looked into his eyes. Ruthie couldn't see her face, but she heard her voice break and knew she was crying.

"Joel, I wasn't like you. I didn't fall into love so quickly, but when I did, I fell hard and strong." She sniffed. "You have filled my days with so much more than I could ever imagine. You are strong when I am weak. You give me joy when I am sad. You are calm when I am unsettled. You complete me in every way. I also promise, for the rest of my life, to always keep your heart safe. To keep your heart close. To never wander away. And to never take your love for granted. I will love you forever."

Ruthie wiped tears away with her forearm. For the first time, she realized she wasn't bothered by the thought that she had no one special in her life, like Joel and Hazel had each other. She'd keep her own heart for the time being. She'd follow her dreams and see where they led her. She smiled as she watched Joel grab a giggling Hazel around the waist after the preacher gave him permission to kiss his bride. He leaned her back with one strong, smooth movement and heat radiated through Ruthie's chest when he pressed his lips firmly on his wife's. Hazel's face flushed as they came back upright.

"It is my pleasure to present to you for the first time, Mr. and Mrs. Joel Davenport."

The church erupted in cheers and applause. Ronnie let out a loud holler, making everyone laugh. Ruthie followed behind the newly married couple as they made their way out of the sanctuary, but instead of turning to the right toward the fellowship hall where the reception would be, she made a left out the side door.

The crisp fall air filled her chest, and she sucked it in, letting her lungs expand like balloons. She lifted her face to the sun, feeling its warmth kiss her skin. She closed her eyes and stood there, just existing in the space around her. She thought about her mother. How so very long ago, she'd said Ruthie was just like her. Ruthie shook her head with her eyes closed. It wasn't true though. She was nothing like her mother. Her mother didn't want more, she wanted replacements for what she had. She replaced the people in her life for something she thought was better. She didn't know what she already had, but Ruthie did. She'd rather die than live without her father and sister and her new brother-in-law. Her desire to explore the world wasn't hindered because they were in her life, it was enhanced because of them. Her dreams were able to grow and expand because they gave her the self-confidence and love to succeed. The squeak of the door startled her.

"You okay, peanut?" her father asked.

She turned and threw her arms around his neck. He groaned under her weight.

"I'm so good, Daddy, so very good."

She pulled back and looked into his loving eyes. The crinkles around them were more pronounced than she remembered.

He chuckled, "Well, if you want a chance at getting a piece of that good wedding cake Ms. Faye made, you better get your keister inside."

She laughed. "Okay, I'll be there in just a moment."

When she was alone again, she looked toward the old pine trees that stood near the church. Their trunks thick with years. The green and yellow pine needles swayed in the breeze. She hated to leave and go back inside, but she knew everyone would be looking for her soon if she didn't. They'd expect her to be in the crowd of single girls vying for the chance to catch Hazel's bouquet. She breathed in the woodsy smell, and in the pit of her heart, she desperately missed her time in the forest with Hazel and Joel. As she turned toward the door, something caught her eye and made her pause. She studied the branches of the swaying trees, wishing she had the old set of binoculars she and Hazel used. Then she spotted him. The flash of brilliant red on the branch. His wings were outstretched and fluttering. A cardinal. The branch beneath his claws shook as he took flight. He soared through the pale sky. She stood there frozen, watching him until he was only a tiny speck on the horizon. She longed to chase after him, but she willed herself to stay. It wouldn't be long until she'd be out there in the big world too, and she couldn't even imagine the adventures awaiting her.

Acknowledgments

Thank you, Lord for allowing me to complete a dream that I have had hidden deep in my heart since I was a little girl. Every day, pecking away at my computer, I tossed around feelings of self-doubt and inadequacy. But you, Lord, gave me a wonderful support system and without them this book would not have been possible.

On that note, I want to thank my dear husband, Todd. You listened to me when I was delirious with excitement and then in the next moment, crying over whether I could actually do this thing. Thank you for being there through all my ups and downs and loving me. You have always been my biggest champion.

Thank you to my wonderful boys, Wyatt, Michael, and Joseph. You boys always keep me grounded and help me to remember the most important thing in life is the ones you love.

I want to say thank you to my dad, Eddie, and mom, Jannet. Dad, the love you give to me, and my sisters, and all your grand babies is an inspiration. Mom, I miss you every day. I hope you're proud of us.

To my sisters, Tiffany and Tasha, thank you for always being there for me when I need you most.

Thank you to my father-in-law, Gil, and mother-in-law, Pat Pat for loving me like a daughter.

To my stepmother, Becky, and the rest of my lovely family. Thank you for your love and support in all I do.

Thank you to my magnificent editor, Julia Hilton. Your expertise made this book beautiful!

Thank you to my cover designer, Mary Ann Smith/Book Design. Your cover brought the story to life!

Last but not least, I want to thank my beta readers, Jessica Cassidy and Andrea Thrash. Thank you both for being willing to read my book, with all the rough spots, and give me your wise help. This book wouldn't be what it is today, without your advice and insight.

About Author

Born and raised in Arkansas, Tennille Marie, now calls Louisiana her home. Her favorite things include walking on sunny days, exploring new places with her family, coffee, and her cats.

Tennille is also obsessed with books, no matter the genre. She finds her heart and writing are inspired by her southern roots, her close family connections, and the kindness of others.

If you'd like to follow Tennille Marie on her author journey or get more information about upcoming books, come be a part of her heart-to-heart community! As a special gift, for joining her mailing list, you will receive a complimentary copy of *A Blackberry Kind of Love* and other country stories. https://tennillemarie.com

Or follow her on Instagram and Goodreads to see what she's reading now.

instagram.com/tennillemariewrites

goodreads.com/tennillemaire

Also by

Want more

Tonnille Marie?

Look for the next book of the

Waldron Hearts series…

OUR SCORCHED HEARTS

Coming November 2024!

Made in the USA
Columbia, SC
31 March 2024